ANOTHER NOTCH IN THE BELTWAY

L.A. LONG

AVN
PUBLICATIONS

Another Notch in the Beltway
AVN Publications

This book is a work of fiction. The characters, names, places, and incidents are the products of the author's imagination or are used fictitiously. Any resemblance to actual events, locales, business establishments, or persons, living or dead, is entirely coincidental.

ISBN: 978-09977273-0-2

Cover Design: Ashley Victoria Nugent
Cover photos used under license from Shutterstock.com:
DC beltway, copyright © 2016 Sean Pavone/Shutterstock.com
Couple, copyright © 2016 conrado/Shutterstock.com

❈ ❈ ❈

To new beginnings, second chances and those who recognize what a gift they are.

ANOTHER NOTCH IN THE BELTWAY

CHAPTER ONE

"Addy, I am sick to death of this Victorian romance stuff. I feel like turning Duke Thunderballs into Lord Blueballs. All the heaving bosoms and throbbing members are getting to me."

LaSandra Lacy, yes, a pen name, was ranting at her personal assistant, Addison Connelly.

"But, La, you're so good at it. You're always on the bestseller list, people flock to your book signings, and preorder your works by the thousands. What's not to like? You have critical mass."

"Don't placate me. I'm bored to tears with deflowering vestal virgins in the dark of the night or while fleeing on horseback to avoid some loveless marriage to a well-placed peer destined to cement the family's place in society or shore up its financial position."

"You write escapism, La, that's what people want. They need a few hours of heated passion and romance. It helps to get them through their dull, harried lives. You should feel good about that.

"I've been watching the numbers and even with the economy in the toilet and half the publishing houses laying off thousands of staff, sales for romance books are up three percent and yours are up five. People can't afford a lot of things but they'll still spring for a romance paperback."

"Who would have thought?"

"Hey, La, you're in a place where you can coast. They want to re-release some of your backlist, kind of like a retrospective."

"Great, maybe we can unveil a boxed set at the next Bodice Ripper Convention," she quipped.

Addy, seemingly oblivious to the dark sarcasm, said, "That's a great idea. I'll mention it to Nikko the next time I talk to her."

Nikko Martenstein of Martenstein, Martenstein and Hubble, the leading romance literary agency for over thirty years, was LaSandra's agent.

"I was joking, Addy."

"It's still a wonderful idea. I think we'd need to go with three or five in a box; for some reason the box sets are never an even number, have you noticed that?"

"Toss in a vibrator, too, like a Cracker Jack surprise, a little pink one. That ought to increase sales."

"I don't think they can do that, La."

"Of course not. The Victorians were supposed to be repressed prudes; that's why they were screwing every bush in the garden! What would Victorian romance devotees want with a vibrator? They're looking for that pulsing manhood to pop out between the buttons of Duke Thunderballs's waistcoat and make them swoon! Addy, are you even listening to me?"

"La, I'm listening, but what are you planning on doing? Why ruin a good thing?"

"You're still not hearing me. I need to do something different, something fresh, contemporary. I've had it with corsets and pantaloons. I want people to screw themselves silly and not have to worry about their virtue or social position. I want the female character to put her parents in assisted living so she can get her groove back. Her parents can take a bus trip to Las Vegas or Atlantic City and play keno while the little miss goes off and screws some Harley-riding entrepreneur who invented a better iPhone and wants not only to fuck her blind, but give her mind-blowing oral sex, too.

"I don't want muffled cries of ecstasy because Lady Windsor might hear Lord Hardrocks and Lady Tightbud in the conservatory. I want Stone Mason and Marsha Moistcakes to come in a frenzy of loud grunts, groans and, okay, shrieking, in the neighbor's backyard hot tub while they're asleep upstairs. I need a change, Addy!"

"Then change, write a contemporary romance, better yet an erotic romance, maybe even under a new pen name. Anne Rice had Anne Rampling. I'm sure you remember the guilty pleasures of the *Sleeping Beauty* trilogy."

"Yes, but Anne stopped at three, went on to vampires and witches, very hot vampires and witches, I might add."

CHAPTER TWO

Lenore Held, a.k.a. LaSandra Lacy, was driving home from spin class, forty-two years old and looking for a change. Despite her success as a romance writer, she felt there had to be more. At least Lady Tightbud was getting it in the bushes. Her own love life was lackluster on a great night.

John Irving, the name should have been the tip-off, was more boring than . . . she'd say watching paint dry, but that was actually more exciting, because at least you got to see what the color truly looked like when it dried. Irving's color was always nondescript gray, like once-snowy-white underwear washed one too many times. Lenore continued to plunder her vast store of words, both old world and this world, and could not find a word to describe him adequately.

Barbra Streisand and Bryan Adams were crooning on XM. What she wouldn't give to have a man with a voice like that, whispering his urgent need for her into her ear.

What she'd get, if she got anything, from JI was straight missionary sex, by which she never achieved orgasm, he'd finish her off manually and be all pleased with himself. Foreplay consisted of his rubbing up against her, like a half-dead Saint Bernard and maybe, just maybe, running his hand down her leg.

He needs to go. I'd be better off with my fantasies and a large cucumber, she thought as she pulled into the garage. These pleasant musings brought me all the way home. "Ugh."

She noted her son's car was in the garage and wondered what he was doing home. Lenore didn't think he had a break from college. She hoped this wasn't going to be a twenty-question night.

Nathan Held was twenty-one, a senior at Georgetown, majoring in International Relations. He was accepted to Yale Law and would start there in the fall. Nate was a brilliant, handsome, funny young man who until recently had never given his mother a moment's grief. Even now, it wasn't grief. He wanted something from her, something she couldn't give him.

Two years ago, Nate began making noises about wanting to know who his father was. She was lucky the drumbeat hadn't started earlier. But Lenore had sworn her silence on that front. Nate's father was a major politician, a very wealthy, very married, very conservative politician who couldn't keep it in his pants. It made her laugh now. It was the age old story, young intern, gentrified senator, late nights, stolen moments, intern gets knocked up, senator wants her to have an abortion, she refuses, so he buys her silence.

Money can't buy a lot of things. But his money gave her the freedom to be a doting mother and get her writing career off the ground. By the time Nate was five, she didn't need the senator's money and invested it for her son. Nate didn't even know how much money there was. He didn't need to know now, but it would give him a good solid start in life.

Lenore's career took off, but the senator kept his end of the bargain, and she kept her silence. Nate didn't care about financial arrangements and promises of silence. He wanted to know who his father was.

She sighed. "Nate," she called, walking in the door.

"Over here, Mom," he hollered back.

She went to join him in the great room of their Yardley, Pennsylvania, home.

They met halfway and embraced.

"What are you doing here?" she asked, holding him at arm's length.

"Not happy to see me?" he teased.

"I'm always happy to see you," she replied with a warm smile that lit her vibrant hazel eyes. He looked happy. No sign of his being there to fish for information on his father.

"The admissions counselor at Georgetown asked if I wanted to help with the booth at the George School college fair, and I said sure. It should be fun."

Nate was a graduate of GS, and he always liked to go back when he had time.

"That's great. I don't recall GS having a college fair when you were there."

"No, we didn't. The college reps would come and talk to anyone who was interested in the school. I think the fair makes sense so students can see a number of prospective schools. They might find they're interested in one they never considered before."

"I agree. Maybe you should go into college admissions instead of law."

"Law is a good springboard for anything, Mom. I don't even know that I'll ever practice law."

She nodded, ruffling his deep brown hair. "Whatever you do, you'll be great."

"You're my mom; you have to say that."

"No, I don't, but I mean it. Do you have time for dinner?"

"I'll grab something at the Hoagie Shack on the way over, but I'll let you make me waffles tomorrow morning."

"Chocolate, chocolate chip?"

"You're the best, Mom."

"You're my son; you have to say that."

CHAPTER THREE

Nikko Martenstein was lunching at Lenore's house the following Wednesday. It was their habit to trade lunch spots; the next one would be in New York City. It got each of them out of their respective habitats. The women were eating in Lenore's sunroom; despite the cool day, the room was warm and bright. The sunny appearance was enhanced by vibrant yellow, overstuffed cushions that graced Victorian-style wicker.

"Lenore, it's great to be here; maybe I'll move." Nikko always called her Lenore unless they were at an industry function, book signing, or other professional endeavor. She once told Lenore that LaSandra Lacy sounded like an aged whore who dressed in fuchsia spandex, crotchless panties, and feathered stiletto mules. They'd both gotten a good laugh out of the visual.

"You'd be bored after a while, Nik. I've known you long enough to know you need the excitement of the city."

"Maybe, but since Howard's death, it's not been the same." Howard was the first Martenstein of Martenstein, Martenstein and Hubble. They had been married for twenty years, and Howard was twenty years her senior. Even so, he was only sixty when he dropped dead of a heart attack a little over a year ago. They met when Nikko was his college intern and fell in love.

Lenore had always thought that Nikko's internship romance had a much better outcome than hers, but as the years went by, she wasn't so sure. At least she had Nate. Nikko and Howard never had children and now Nik was all alone.

"Come down and spend a few days; in fact, stay now if you want. The guest room is always ready. It has its own bath so you'd have privacy."

"Can't. I've got meetings, my clients, and Howard's that don't want Hubble."

"When things calm down then. How is Hubble working out?"

Hubble was Nolan Hubble; he had joined M&M as a partner shortly before Howard died. He came from a large agency and had his own clients to bring to M&M. Lenore had met him several times and had found him friendly, witty, and attractive.

"Great, it's the writers; they're the temperamental ones," Nikko teased.

"Speaking as a writer, if, God forbid, something happened to you and I needed a new agent, I'd be a bit shell-shocked myself."

Nikko nodded. "I know that's why Nolan and I decided that once we hire another agent, we'll have a meet and greet and then do it at least annually so that, should anything ever happen to one of us, our clients have at least a passing relationship with the other agents."

"That's a great idea, but I still want you for my agent," Lenore said in a mock whine of a temperamental author.

Her friend laughed.

"Lunch, as always, is wonderful. This sorbet is to die for."

Lenore had made poached salmon salad for lunch and raspberry sorbet for dessert. The two friends were sipping Paul Hobbs Chardonnay. It was cool and crisp, making a great pairing to the salad. Lenore liked to cook and didn't often get the chance, especially since Nate had gone off to college.

"Thanks."

After lunch, they got down to business.

"Addy tells me you're bored with Victorian romance and need a change," Nikko said.

Lenore nodded.

"Do you want to abandon Victorian romance altogether or merely throw something new into the mix?"

"I don't think I could ever abandon it. Contrary to the way I carried on to Addy the other day, I realize I have a following, and they've been loyal to me, so I will continue to write VR for the foreseeable future. I want to do something else along with it."

"That's a relief. The way Addy sounded the other day, I thought I'd need to talk you off a ledge."

"I did lay it on pretty thick. Addy is so literal I sometimes go out of my way to antagonize her."

"Like suggesting a pink vibrator tucked into your retrospective gift pack?" Nikko smiled, merriment dancing in her eyes.

"Exactly, although I do think I may do a series of books about widows: young, old, in-between, and the many uses of a widow's comforter, as they used to call it, to stave off loneliness or the desire to feel the engorged organ of a new suitor between her creamy thighs."

Nikki was laughing unrestrainedly now. "God, Lenore, stop."

"What? They were used by Victorian women to pleasure themselves, a precursor of the vibrator, if you will, but the term dildo, believe it or not, was a euphemism used at the time."

Her friend kept laughing and shaking her head. "Enough," Nikko said. "What do you want to write?"

"A witty, sexy romance with a strong independent female and an equally matched male."

"Chick lit?'

"I'm not sure I'm quite there, but I suppose."

"Would you consider working with another writer?"

Lenore cocked her head. "I never have, and I guess I never thought about it."

"How about a male co-author?"

"Tell me more. I'm interested in hearing what you have to say."

"You know MP Finnegan?"

"Michael Patrick, right?"

"Did you already know?"

"Wild guess with a name like Finnegan."

"I suppose." Nikko eyed her dubiously.

"Really, I haven't even read any of the man's work."

"That's surprising, too, but he wants to come out as a man and thinks it would help if he were paired with a well-recognized female author."

"He wants to come out as a man? What was he before, a really big ferret?"

Her agent was laughing again. "Lenore, please be serious for a minute. You know a lot of male romance writers only use their initials or gender-neutral names. Heck, some even take on a totally female persona for their pseudonym."

"You mean Lisa Marie Rice is a man, not a woman?" Lenore asked. "That's why all the guys hate oral sex until they meet that special chick."

"I don't know if Lisa Marie Rice is a he, she, or it. I'm trying to talk about MP."

"Got it. Michael Patrick wants to come out as a man and co-author a book with a known female romance writer. In this case, me. How does he feel about that? From what little I know of him, he writes contemporary romance."

"I haven't asked him yet; I figured I'd talk to you before I say anything to him. Plus, I need to see if your publisher would even consider it."

Lenore was silent, then said, "Do your thing. Talk to Finnegan and the publisher. In the meantime, I'll read a few of his books over the next couple of days and get back to you, but yes, I'm interested."

"Good."

That settled, they went on to talk about other industry happenings.

CHAPTER FOUR

Lenore purchased three of MP Finnegan's books. They were edgy and fast paced both in and out of bed. Even without knowing MP was Michael Patrick, she would have guessed the writer was male by the heavy usage of cock, pussy, cunt, and fuck. Not that female writers didn't use those words as well, but male writers tended to use them literally and almost exclusively. Plus, there were lines like, "She took his cock deeply in her throat and sucked him with the proficiency of a well-practiced whore. Marisa didn't even flinch when he came full throttle, hot and thick in her mouth. When he finished, she looked at him vapidly and licked him clean, savoring every drop of his cum."

LaSandra Lacy would have written something more like, "Genevieve took his swollen, pulsing manhood in her bee-stung lips and suckled him hungrily. Before he came, he pulled her to him and whispered huskily, 'Evie, I want to be inside you, make love to you.'"

But was it male versus female or contemporary versus historic? She'd have to think about that some more.

MP stopped before what she called the squirm factor. Meaning the point where one might start to feel oneself flushed, wet, and overtly sexually aroused to the point of needing release. Some of the good erotic writers had left her feeling that way. Yeah, she thought wistfully, recalling some of those scenes were about the only way she'd come with John Irving.

Maybe that could be the plot line of a new book, getting rid of Mr. Gray and meeting Mr. Makes Me Squirm. She laughed. It would be great fun to write something truly visceral. Lenore liked the idea. It had potential.

She'd told Nikko that she'd have an answer for her today. Throwing caution to the wind, she decided to do it. "La Sandra Lacy and MP Finnegan team up to write . . . Write what? I guess that is to be determined," she answered herself, picking up the phone.

CHAPTER FIVE

Between Lenore's schedule, MP's, and Nikko's, it was three weeks before they could finally meet. In that time, she'd read all eight of Finnegan's books and a number of other contemporary and erotic romances.

When she was done, she had decided two things: MP's writing was decidedly male, and there was a fine line between the squirm factor and the yuck factor.

Lenore also thought she'd prefer to do a contemporary romance that bordered on erotic but wasn't quite there. Of course, she would need to collaborate with MP on that. She was looking forward to meeting him. She wondered what he looked like. In her experience, Irish men came in two molds. The first was short, round, and full of blarney, and the second was tall, ruggedly handsome, and full of intensity, with or without the blarney thrown in. She didn't need any blarney in her life.

They were having lunch at Michael's, a well-known New York City restaurant for agents and writers. Lenore was the first to arrive and sat so she could see the incoming patrons. Nikko joined her a few minutes later.

"What's MP like?" Lenore asked, shifting in her seat to look at Nikko.

"I'm not going to tell you. I want you to form your own impression. I will tell you he's very handsome: tall, dark wavy hair, blue eyes, easy to look at."

"You have a thing for him or with him?"

"Heavens, no," Nik snorted a laugh. "First of all, he's my client; second, he's not my type; and third, without sounding too un-PC, he's not Jewish."

"I didn't think you even practiced your faith."

"I don't, it's an ingrained cultural thing. Plus, Jews tolerate one another's idiosyncrasies better than non-Jews."

"Okay," Lenore said, raising her eyebrows, still amused.

"We are a strange lot, Lenore."

"No stranger than Catholics."

"Well, both religions are seemingly founded on guilt," Nikko mused.

The women laughed.

With that, Lenore saw an extremely attractive man approaching the table. He smiled and kissed Nikko on the cheek.

"Michael Patrick Finnegan," he said extending his hand.

"Lenore Held." She took his proffered hand.

"Sure and I'm delighted to meet you." He continued looking her directly in the eyes, smiling like he meant it and holding her hand a beat too long in a warm, strong embrace.

A charmer. Lenore had met several over the years, recalling one more clearly than all the others, her son's father. She'd need to guard her heart and her chastity, VR speak, from this man. Nonetheless, he was intriguing.

MP sat, still beaming a high-wattage smile at the women. He spoke with a lyrical accent to boot. "I'm the luckiest man here today, having lunch with two lovely lasses such as yourselves."

"Cut the crap, Michael Patrick," Nikko said. Then she turned to Lenore. "This guy is full of Irish bullshit; watch him."

"Count on it."

They ordered lunch and got down to business.

Nikko started, "MP wants to write a book with a well-known female romance writer to come out of the closet –"

"I don't think you need to put it quite that way," Finnegan interrupted.

"Of course I do; it makes it seem more sordid and noteworthy," she cut back in. "And Lenore wants to do a contemporary romance, hot and steamy bordering on erotica or, as she calls it, the squirm factor."

Michael Patrick looked directly at Lenore with expressively raised eyebrows. "Is that so?"

Lenore maintained eye contact, managed not to blush, and nodded.

"And might I ask, lass, what the squirm factor is?" He asked a touch of amusement playing on his full mouth.

"If you have to ask –" Lenore started.

"She'll tell you in a more appropriate setting," Nikki said, cutting her off. Which was fine because she didn't want to explain anyway.

Finnegan continued to smile. "I think I'd enjoy working with you, lass."

Dimples, too, Lenore thought. Quite a package.

Their agent continued, "I've talked to the publisher and they'd consider looking at a collaborative work, only because you two are so well known and have popular appeal. But they want to see several sample chapters before they make any commitments. Do you think such a collaboration could work?"

"Sure, don't you agree, Lenore?" MP asked.

"I'm willing to give it a try," she answered.

"Good, now to financial arrangements should the project get picked up. It might be a bit premature but I'd like all the issues addressed up front." Nikko began.

"I thought we'd split the profits 50/50 with you taking your usual percentage, Nik," Lenore offered.

"But, lass, I know you make a fair bit more than I do," MP said without ego.

"It doesn't matter; it's a neat clean transaction that way. Plus, I don't know a thing about contemporary romance. Presumably you, on the other hand, MP, know a thing or two about being a man."

"Yes, a thing or two," he agreed, amused. "Perhaps one day I'll even show you." His brogue was heavier now and mischief danced in his cloudless blue eyes.

Lenore smiled back but thought, yes, I'll have to watch this one.

CHAPTER SIX

Several weeks later, MP and Lenore/LaSandra met at her Yardley home. She had a large office and they had decided it was as good a place as any to brainstorm and plan what they were going to do and how. He was staying at the Hampton Suites, only a couple miles from her house.

Addy was fluttering like a butterfly on speed in a purple silky batik top.

"Stop already," Lenore told her.

Addy looked at her questioningly.

"You're flitting around for no reason. Go and read some fan letters, update the web site, do something before I shoot you."

"Sorry, La, I'm excited to meet Michael Patrick Finnegan. I've read all his books, and they are so yum."

Lenore rolled her eyes and shuddered. You'd never believe that Addy had a brain in her head if all you did was listen to her speak, but she was very bright and competent, so as much as she annoyed her, Lenore tolerated her eccentricities.

"Save your yum for him, and get some work done. Have you made the changes to the first three chapters of *Moon Over the Garden*?" She had a little secret that she shared with no one. All of her titles had the word moon in them somewhere. It was her little joke, moon was for the bare butts that were often exposed in the moonlight, thus the titles of her books *Moon Over the Garden*, *Under the Full Moon*, *Midnight Moon*, *Cloudy Moon*, *Moon Over Westcliff Castle*, and so on. If anyone ever discovered her secret, they'd probably excommunicate her from the Romance Writers Association. She smiled.

Addy had been speaking, and she had heard not a word, "I'm sorry, Addison, what did you say?"

"Yes, the chapters are edited, and they should be on your computer."

"Thanks." She turned back to her computer and went to work.

Twenty minutes later, the doorbell rang, and Addy all but skipped to get it.

She could hear her admin's excited voice talking to MP. Lenore smiled, sure that the woman would be swooning over him at any moment.

"I've been with Ms. Lacy for five years now, and it's been wonderful," Addy gushed as she entered the office.

"Ms. Lacy, Mr. Finnegan is here."

"Please call me MP," he said to her.

Addison giggled and blushed. "Would you like some coffee?"

Lenore couldn't remember the last time Addy offered to bring her coffee.

"I'm fine, lass, but thank you all the same."

Yup, the swoon was coming any second now.

"Addison, I'd like a cup, thanks," Lenore said, more for spite than anything.

"Grand place you have here, Ms. Lacy," MP said, smiling.

"Please, it's Lenore. For some reason, Addy insists on keeping in character."

"Hmm." He smiled.

"Here's your coffee, Ms. Lacy; is there anything else?"

"We'll be fine thanks, Addy."

She left closing the door behind her.

One wall of the office was comprised totally of French doors that led to a deck with a stairway going down, overlooking her backyard and pool. MP was taking in the view.

"I love the pool and often work outside. I'm always dismayed when summer ends and the pool has to be closed for the winter," Lenore said, noticing his gaze.

"Summer girl, are you?"

"Yes, there's something about being able to be outside in the light until nine o'clock. I hate the cold and dark of late fall and winter."

"I'm distracted by the sun myself. It's rainy and misty a lot in Dublin. When the sun is out, I like to go into the country and feel the warmth of its rays on my face." Then turning back to the room, he added, "I like your office, too."

The space was well appointed with heavy, rich walnut furniture and comfortable, overstuffed, distressed leather chairs and couches. There were bookcases filled to overflowing and books, stacked artfully, topped with glass that served as coffee and end tables.

"It gives me sanctuary from the rest of the crazy world."

"Everyone needs a private hideaway now and again. Mine, too, is my office."

"Come sit," she said motioning with a slim graceful hand.

They each sat on a chair that flanked the flagstone fireplace.

He steepled his chin on his two index fingers and looked at her. She returned his gaze, his eyes intent on hers.

"Your eyes are beautiful, lass. They change like rare opals when the light hits them, sometimes blue, sometimes green, and sometimes an intoxicating mix of the two."

She looked at him for a moment, said nothing, then offered, "Thank you."

"I didn't mean to embarrass you," he said as the pink blush tinted her cheeks.

"Have you given any thought as to how you want to tackle this project?" she asked, totally ignoring his comment.

"Yes, many, in fact. I'm sure you have as well." He winked at her.

She simply continued. "You're right. But this is your genre so, at least for now, I'm going to defer to your expertise."

"At least for now? At some point do you intend to become the alpha on the project?"

She actually thought about her choice of words. "I should warn you I sometimes have a tendency to take over. I'm fairly independent and do what I want to do."

"And the consequences be damned?"

She paused and remembered how she had thought she knew best when it came to her son's father, then spoke, "Yes, but I take responsibility for the consequences."

"I'm sure you do." he replied evenly, watching her shift in her seat and changed the subject. "Why don't we switch off? I'll give an idea, and then you'll give one. More of a give-and-take."

"Sure, let me get a notepad. I'll write the ideas down. Kind of like a brainstorming session. You first," she said as she sat down again, pad and pen in hand.

She crossed her long legs out of habit. They were clad in black leggings and on top she wore a black ruched tunic that showed a hint of cleavage. Lenore watched his eyes start at her bare feet with their pink painted toes and travel unashamedly up her body.

"No laptop or tablet?" he asked when his eyes finally settled on her face again.

"Not for this. If you want a copy, I'll make you one, or if you can't read my handwriting, I'm sure Addy would willingly put it in Word for you." She gave him a placid smile, hoping her face was not bright red, inflamed as the rest of her was starting to feel.

"She's a fan. She told me," he commented, his eyes not leaving her face.

"Yes, but I'm sure that's the reaction you'll get a lot once you come out of the closet. Are you sure you and the women in your life are ready for that?"

"I'm kind of a homebody, so a few adoring fans at a book signing shouldn't be too hard to handle. There are no women in my life, at present. I think coming out as a man will help sales. People, I'm guessing mostly women, will want to get a man's take on romance.

"Money." It was a statement.

"Yes, money, lass, it makes the world go round."

"It does at that, laddie."

He laughed, and then grew serious. "I have medical bills that are threatening to bankrupt me. My nephew had a brain tumor, and my sister didn't have the funds for private doctors and hospitals. You know, we have socialized medicine in Ireland, and my nephew was ruled a hopeless case, so getting him anything but hospice care was out of the question. I paid for his surgery and treatment. He beat the cancer only to be killed in an automobile accident along with my sister. He was ten."

She gasped. "I'm so sorry."

"Thanks, but I'd do it all over again. I don't have children of my own, but I can't imagine loving a child more than if he was mine."

His eyes welled up and held hers; he was not embarrassed to let her see the raw emotion that dwelled there. Most men would have looked away and quickly changed the subject, most women, too, for that matter.

Lenore, her own eyes filling but still locked on his, said again gently, "MP, I'm sorry. I had no idea. If anything happened to my son, I don't know what I'd do."

"I didn't know you had a son."

"Yes, he's a senior at Georgetown, going to Yale Law next year. I'm very proud of him. He's the light of my life."

MP smiled warmly, a real smile and not the high-voltage stage smile. "It seems like you have good reason to be proud."

She gave a Mona Lisa smile and thought, there's more to this man than the package reveals. He's warm, compassionate, and has a sense of family. *Can't judge a book by its cover* flitted through her mind.

"Okay, you were going to tell me what you were thinking about relative to our book collaboration." She wanted to get back on track; she had no intention of getting personal this quickly. When working closely with another individual, it's natural that personal stories and secrets come out but not in the first twenty minutes.

MP began, "I was thinking that whatever story we decide to tell, it would be fun for you to write the female parts and for me to write the male parts. Like a back-and-forth and together kind of thing."

Lenore began. "Something like: When he dropped her off, he kissed her breathless and stupid on the porch. Then simply disengaged and loped back to his car on those long, strong, sexy legs, leaving her panting and aroused. And you'd write: He kissed her hard and left her wanting more. He knew it. He would have taken more. Jesus, he needed more as his cock painfully reminded him in the tight jeans, but he knew he had to make her want it, want him. So he'd left her stupefied, hot, and wet."

"Yes, exactly, very good, Ms. Lacy. Now it's your turn."

"I thought it might be fun to write about a couple who is doing exactly what we're doing, collaborating on a book or some other project. One thing leads to another, and you know the rest. I think that would have potential in the marketplace, especially once you come out."

A slow smile crossed his face and he said, "Life imitating art."

"I guess."

"Almost sounds dangerous."

"How so?"

"It'll be a love story, yes?"

"A romance, you can have romance without love."

"Can you?"

Lenore shrugged; she never thought you needed love for romance. It might be nice but was it essential? You could certainly have love without romance. She was thinking that this plot line would have worked better if she had kept her mouth shut and wrote it herself.

"I guess we'll write the book and see. Let the story tell itself."

"To a point, but it still needs to be shaped."

"Agreed, but don't you find your characters take on a life of their own? Don't you find yourself thinking that's not what Lady Westcott would say or do?"

"Yes."

"And on occasion doesn't something happen or evolve that you didn't plan or think about? A new twist or turn that often adds to the story? A murder? An assignation? An illegitimate heir?"

"Of course."

"Then we start writing and let nature take its course, so to speak." He raised his eyebrows at her and his eyes glimmered with what? Amusement, excitement, creativity?

"Will that work with the two of us, do you think?" She pretended she didn't get his double entendre.

"It will be better, especially if we take different paths to get to the same ends."

"And if we don't reach the same ends?"

"We're writing a romance; there has to be a happily-ever-after."

"No romantic tragedy?"

"No, we need an HEA. People buy romance, because they want the happy ending. So often in life, there isn't one," MP said with conviction.

She thought about Addy saying the exact same thing not too long ago.

"Escapism," she commented simply.

"Yes, or wishful thinking. The human spirit looks for love to triumph regardless of the hurdles that might be thrust in its way."

She laughed. "Are you a psychologist by training?"

He shook his head. "Merely a person who studies people."

"Hmm."

"You're thinking I'm full of blarney?"

"Hmm," she said again with a small smirk and then, "So, you like the idea?"

"Very much."

CHAPTER SEVEN

Amanda Loring saw him all smug, arrogant, and pure male, leaning against the bar. His look was lingering and appreciative. She held his gaze a moment longer than necessary and then continued into the room. Amanda was looking for her agent, Jake Bishop. He should be here somewhere. There he was. She smiled, waved and went to meet him.

Oh baby, Casper Grossman thought as she entered the room. The woman, not three feet from him, was of medium height, buxom, and very real, all of her: blond hair, couldn't see the eyes, but he'd bet green or blue, a smattering of freckles on her bare creamy shoulders. He'd bet there were more on her face, probably sprinkled around her nose. She was smokin'. Who was she? Casper wondered. He'd have to find out; a sly smile crossed his face as he set off across the room to follow her.

"What kind of name is Casper Grossman for our hero?" Lenore asked, not even attempting to conceal a smile. They'd begun working on the book and wanted to get the sample chapters to Nikko as soon as possible. It seemed there was more interest in their potential book than their agent had anticipated.

"I thought it was unusual. You don't like it?" MP asked, surprised. They were seated across from each other at Lenore's long desk, computers back to back.

"I'm picturing this urban cowboy kind of guy, and Casper Grossman is kind of anticlimactic, stuffy, like some nerdy little computer guy or stultified elder statesman. I'd be looking for someone named Chase or Chas if you want to make him a pseudo player from a wealthy, old-money family. Chase/Chas Sinclair or something similar."

"Ahh, historical romance meets the twenty-first century," he smiled.

She felt herself flush. "I guess." He was right, she was overlaying her VR on the modern. "You're right. We can go with Casper Grossman. Tell me how YOU picture him.

"I actually like your urban cowboy idea. I had thought of him as a self-made man after his father left his family in financial ruin, old man being an unscrupulous politician or industry scion. Casper's trying to regain the cachet and financial standing they once had."

"Now who sounds VR? Politics, money, social standing?"

"You're right, lass, I hadn't thought of it in that light. Some things never change do they?"

"I suppose not."

She sat thinking for a moment.

There was a message from Senator Byron Maxwell's senior aide, Gerald Morris, wanting her to call. So far she'd not done so. What could Maxwell want after all these years?

Michael Patrick's voice caused her to focus back in. "Have you thought of something else?"

"I was thinking of unscrupulous, amoral politicians and how they might play into the story."

"Like one of daddy's old cronies coming after the son for some indiscretion of the father?"

"Yes, but it could be anyone coming after Casper, let's call him Cass, maybe even an unacknowledged half brother or sister."

"I like it."

"Great."

He was still talking. "But I think it was more than that, lass. Care to share?"

"No."

"Okay, then. Where were we?"

"Sorry, I didn't mean to snap. You didn't do anything to deserve that."

"And I didn't mean to pry."

But of course he did, Lenore thought. They had been working together over a month. He was an open book and she was a diary with a padlock and a deadbolt, both securely locked. She knew he was interested in her as a woman, not merely a writer. If she was honest with herself, she was interested in MP the man.

"I would, however, like to get to know you better, lass. I find you interesting, and my curiosity is piqued," he continued.

She laughed. "I'm a curiosity."

"Indeed."

"What do you want to know?"

"What makes you tick, what makes you happy, what makes you sad—everything, I guess."

"I'm not that interesting, MP, sorry. Only daughter of two teachers, both died recently of natural causes; they were in their eighties, had me later in life. I think that's why there's only one of me."

He laughed.

"Lived most of my life right here in Bucks County. Went to American University for undergrad, University of Michigan for grad school, started writing while I was in grad school, had a modicum of success along the way, and here I am."

"And here you are. I think there's a lot missing from that bio."

"Read my jacket cover."

"I have, not much there either. What or who makes you so self-contained?"

"I'm a private person," she replied primly, a quick flash of annoyance flushing her cheeks.

"I see that."

"So we call Casper *Cass* most of the time?" she asked, wanting to get back on task.

"Sure." She saw him eye her, a grin crossing his face.

They continued on with their collaboration, her private life on hold for the moment.

Jake Bishop watched her approach and noted, not for the first time or the hundredth, that Amanda Loring was one stunning woman, not any one particular thing but the neat little package in total. The sexy sway of her hips as she moved, her full mouth, and beautiful teeth when she smiled . . . Stop it, Bishop told himself, also not for the first time. She's a client.

"Jake! I had a devil of a time finding you." Amanda gave him an affectionate peck on the lips.

At the same moment, Mr. Smug Arrogance from the bar joined them. She gave him the same appraising look he had given her when she entered the room. He seemed to revel in her attention. She wasn't surprised.

"Cass, allow me to introduce Amanda Loring. Amanda, Casper Grossman."

"A pleasure, Mr. Grossman."

"Please call me Cass, and the pleasure is all mine, Ms. Loring."

She didn't tell him to call her Amanda. Her agent eyed her suspiciously.

Cass gave her a smirk and asked, "Can I get you a drink, Ms. Loring?"

Bishop rounded on her when Grossman departed to get her a glass of white wine. "Why are you being a bitch? You said you thought you'd like to work with him."

"It's a woman's prerogative to be a bitch, and I want to explore the possibility of working with him—working with him, not sleeping with him."

"Jesus, Mandy, be nice. He's my client, too."

"Oh, I'll be nice to him, don't worry, Jake."

CHAPTER EIGHT

Corrine Kennedy Maxwell sat in front of her vanity mirror. She was a few years over fifty, but to her aquamarine eyes, she appeared twenty years older. Sadness, disillusionment, anger, bitterness had all taken their toll. When did the acceptance come? That acceptance she'd heard others talk about and write about. Perhaps she was not one to accept.

At least her body was still slim and shapely. She had the rigorous demands of her personal trainer to thank for that. One man who hadn't let her down.

As she ran a silver brush through shoulder-length hair, she noted the strawberry blonde was now more of a strawberry ice. She needed to give up the ghost and start coloring it. Peering more closely into the glass, Corrine now inspected her skin. Might as well critique every inch and get it out of the way. Her complexion, once glowing, pale pink, smooth, and vibrant, was now sallow, age-spotted, and dryly wrinkled. The skin would call for more drastic action than a trip to the salon. She doubted she'd do anything about it.

Pulling up her once-firm chin, Corrine thought maybe she could duct tape it behind her ears and into her hairline. No one ever touched her, no one would know. She laughed at herself. It was either that or sob.

She allowed her shoulders to slump. This was a private moment of reflection. Corrine had been doing that a lot lately. Wondering where her youth had gone. Wondering where that hopeful, vivacious, twenty-five-year-old bride had disappeared. Her eyes glanced involuntarily to an eight-by-ten wedding picture that was on the antique maple highboy and shook her head wistfully.

Corrine Kennedy had not been a stupid young woman. She held bachelors and masters degrees in education from the University of Virginia and had a Phi Beta Kappa key in the back of her jewelry box. She'd guarded her virtue for her wedding night, thinking that the man who married her would value her all the more for being a virgin. She was every bit the high society debutante. But Miss Kennedy's strategy in picking a husband had been less than sound. In choosing her husband, she had been, quite simply, dumb as a rock.

Her father had introduced her to Byron Maxwell, the son of one of his business associates. He came from a long line of bankers. Byron's father's family owned Virginia Bank and Trust. She'd been immediately attracted to his handsome features and almost pretty face. He had seemed taken with her, too. Byron told her he was ready to settle down. He was ten years her senior, and she had believed him.

Corrine reasoned that he'd had plenty of time to sow his wild oats and would be a faithful, companionable husband, if not a loving one. In her social circle, it wasn't about love but about perpetuating power and money. Looking back, she should have gotten a purebred dog.

Footsteps. Sitting up straight and squaring her shoulders, she let go of her thoughts.

Byron Maxwell caught her eye in the mirror. They still shared a bedroom and a bed—perception is reality. But she was certain the household staff knew the truth.

As was his habit, Byron approached her, giving her a chaste peck on the cheek. She leaned away from contact.

"That St John knit looks lovely, dear," Maxwell simpered.

"Can we cut the pretense, Byron? There's no one to see or hear us. We hate the sight of one another," she spat bitterly.

"If you'd tried a little kindness, Rin, it might get you further in the long run. You know the old saying, you catch more flies with honey than vinegar."

"But I don't want to catch any flies. They're dirty, disease-carrying creatures. Much like yourself, Byron."

He had no retort. Corrine thought he was too stupid for one. If Morris wasn't around to tell him what to say, he said nothing.

She continued. "Anyway, I tried kindness for the first ten years of our marriage, and all it got me was misery and pain, two miscarriages, two difficult pregnancies, and two dysfunctional children. Progeny who take after their father. In Carter's case, *took* after his father is more appropriate."

Despite the harsh words, sadness crossed her face, but just as quickly the mask was back.

"You wanted children as I recall, Rin."

"Yes, I foolishly thought they would bring us closer, bind

you to me in some way. I was obviously wrong. And as you may recall, I had no input on the second one," she said darkly.

"I'm sorry you feel that way, but living with the Ice Princess for the last thirty years has been tough."

"Living with a philandering hypocrite of a husband has been no picnic either. You think I wanted to make love with you after you slept with every slut on the Beltway?"

Her voice was loud, bordering on angry hysteria. They were both standing and facing one another now.

"Make love? I don't think we ever made love. Had sex is even a questionable statement. You're the most frigid woman I've ever seen."

Wham! A crystal perfume atomizer narrowly missed his head, crashing into the wall. The smell of Chanel No. 5 began to overpower the room.

He was lucky he'd ducked or he'd have been knocked out, maybe killed, based on the crater in the wall.

"Get out! Get out!"

"I'll be more than happy to, you insane bitch," Senator Maxwell said quietly, in stark contrast to her high-pitched scream. He then turned and closed the double doors softly behind him.

Corrine sat at her vanity table and sobbed, face in hands, until all her make-up needed to be replaced. She gazed at herself in the mirror again. She was nothing but a dried-up has-been or maybe, even more pathetically, a never-was.

****

Senator Byron Maxwell retreated to his office. As he sat in his leather chair, he swiftly turned over all the obligatory family photos that were in his line of sight. He wasn't in the mood to stare at the fucked-up lot of them.

His father's photo was last. Byron placed it upside down in the darkest drawer of his desk. He no longer wanted to see the man's arrogant face. The son of a bitch was long dead, and if Jacob Maxwell hadn't nearly bankrupted the family business, VB&T, with gambling debts and other vices, he wouldn't be here today.

His father had needed money to save the bank, and Corrine Kennedy had been the answer. Not only did her father have money, she was wealthy in her own right through a trust set up by her maternal grandmother. Furthermore, she was an only child, so when her parents died she would be even wealthier.

Corrine had been young and beautiful. Byron believed that even if he didn't love her, he'd enjoy her as a companion and a lover.

While he had been surprised to discover she was a virgin, he had found it equally intriguing. They'd had a wedding fit for royalty. He remembered how his loins stirred as his virgin bride walked down the aisle on their wedding day. Corrine had taken his breath away. Her gown was designed to make the most of her alluring shape and her breasts swelled over the top of her bodice . . .

"Jesus," he said aloud, looking down at the bulge in his pants. He was getting a hard-on thinking about his young wife, who was now a worn-out woman. If he was honest with himself, part of that was his fault or his father's.

Corrine had been an eager student of carnal knowledge and had gotten pregnant on their honeymoon. He remembered how beautiful and ripe she looked when she told him, her face glowing and eyes bright . . . he shook his head and closed his eyes.

Then came the closed-door meeting between his father and father-in-law. Jacob Maxwell was in big trouble and needed Andrew Kennedy to bail him out.

Needless to say his papa-in-law was less than happy. Andrew had seen the match not as a marriage but as a merger to amass more power and money. If word got out that Jacob Maxwell was on the verge of bankruptcy, he and his daughter would be a laughingstock. Kennedy made the decision to purchase Maxwell's bank and take it over.

Andrew accused Byron of marrying Corrine for her money and getting her with child to lock her into the union. The first part of the statement was true, but the second was only chance. The older Kennedy made it clear that Byron would never get a penny of his money and took legal steps to make sure that he was totally dependent on Corrine for every penny he had. Andrew told Byron he was to enter into politics—run for the senate—one day the presidency, but only if it didn't get out as to how hopelessly stupid he was.

When Corrine confronted Byron herself, needing to know that it wasn't the money he married her for, he denied knowing of VB&T's financial position. Maxwell wooed her with the empty platitudes she needed to hear.

They ended up in bed. Later that night, his wife awoke in God-awful pain, blood flowing from her body. She was raced to the hospital.

Corrine had an ectopic pregnancy that caused her right fallopian tube to burst. Not only did she lose a child but her right ovary and fallopian tube as well.

It was the beginning of the end. Corrine was afraid to have sex, even protected sex. When her second pregnancy the following year ended in a miscarriage, she all but sewed her legs shut.

He turned to other women to give him what his wife wouldn't. Byron made every effort to keep his dalliances private. But one was not as easily discarded as most and wanted Byron to marry her. Somehow the other woman got to Corrine, and all hell broke loose. He remembered the scene.

"I don't want a divorce, Corrine, but I won't be celibate because my wife won't participate in the act. I'd much prefer my wife, but she keeps her legs crossed and denies me access."

"Your wife is the one with money. You're paid well to keep your pants zipped," Corrine raged.

From her tone, she made it clear that she'd cut him off if he weren't careful. But he played her; she was still young and innocent.

"Let me love you," he pleaded. "We don't need to have children. I won't allow you to get pregnant unless it's what you want. You're a beautiful, compelling woman. I ache with need for you." He'd taken her face in his hands and kissed her until she gave in.

Things settled down, and Corrine decided she wanted to get pregnant again. Once she did, she cut him off totally, even though the doctor told them having sex had nothing to do with her other miscarriages.

Maxwell found solace with other women. He told himself it was only until Corrine delivered and she let him back into her bed. The pregnancy was difficult and when Carter was born, he tore her from her vagina to rectum, even with an episiotomy. Looking back, he should have intervened and insisted she have a caesarean section. Corrine was a tiny woman with the hips of a twelve-year-old.

As he got up to go to the wet bar, his phone rang, ending his thoughts.

CHAPTER NINE

Several days later, Lenore sat at her butcher-block kitchen table drinking coffee and reading the Philadelphia Inquirer. She was enjoying the warmth of the sun streaming through her sliding doors when a national news blip caught her eye.

"Four-term Senator Byron Maxwell of Virginia confirmed rumors that his twenty-year-old son, Jack, was diagnosed with stage four multiple myeloma. Maxwell's older son, Carter, was killed in 2009 when the car he was driving skidded off the road and crashed head-on into a tree. Carter was not wearing a seat belt, and drugs and alcohol were found in his blood."

She let out a long sigh and continued to read the rest of the paper with only half her usual focus and a second cup of coffee. A while later, she decided toast would keep the caffeine from eating a hole through her already churning stomach. But she knew the coffee had nothing to do with the storm that was not only brewing in her stomach but in her mind.

Pacing in front of the counter while her bread toasted, she looked out the window and said a silent prayer for Jack, the boy who was her son's half-brother and also said a prayer of thanks that her own son was happy and healthy. While she was at it, she tossed in a job that she loved and friends she could count on. She also added a prayer for MP and his lost loved ones. The anxiety did not leave her, prayers or not.

Lenore took her dry toast with her to the office, started her computer and brought up the partial manuscript of *Moon Over the Garden*. Addy was off today, and Michael Patrick wouldn't be there for an hour, so she thought she'd get some work done on her own book.

She sat for a moment reading the last ten pages she'd completed. But she was distracted. Lenore had a strong feeling she knew why Gerald Morris was calling her after all these years. She Googled Jack Maxwell, multiple myeloma, and hit Enter.

There were ten articles about Jack and literally thousands about Byron. Over the years, she'd made an effort to block his existence out as much as possible. He'd made the decision to shut Nathan and her out without a thought, so she felt it was only fair that she do the same. At first it was painful, but over the years her feelings toward him had moved to ambivalence. She had never wished him or his family any ill will. He'd given her a precious gift. Though he chose not to share Nate with her, Byron had lived up to his end of the bargain. They both had, very civilized, actually, and very unusual.

The article said Jack had been fighting the cancer since shortly before his brother's death. He'd been undergoing chemotherapy and radiation. He would need a bone marrow transplant from a donor as his own bone marrow was too badly damaged by the treatments to be effective in an autologous one. All the articles said that the closest match was a sibling or parent, but siblings of the same parents were usually the best.

"Maxwell wants Nate to be tested to see if he's a match for his half brother," she said to herself in an almost inaudible voice. After never wanting to acknowledge Nate, Byron needed something from him. She didn't know what to think about the situation. Lenore didn't know what Nate would make of it either. He wanted to know who his father was, but like this? Using one child to save another. One acknowledged and loved, the other a financial obligation and shunned. Would he publicly acknowledge Nate? She didn't think so, and if he did, after all these years, the media would be all over her and her son.

Lenore felt nauseous at the thought. She continued to scroll though the articles. "My God," she gasped, when she came across a picture of Jack. He looked almost identical to her Nate. The similarities were unmistakable. Both boys had their father's classic handsome features. Nate did have her hazel eyes, however, and for that she was grateful. She believed that eyes were the windows to the soul, and Lenore had always been secretly pleased that every time she looked into her son's, they were not those of her former lover. In fact, she'd even forgotten how much he looked like Byron, because in every other way she saw little in Nate that brought to mind his father.

She got up and hit the iTunes on her computer. Lenore put on some music to keep her and her thoughts company for a few minutes. She cranked the music so it was loud. The speakers on her computer were high quality, and she liked the fact that when random fancy overtook her, she could make the room vibrate. Queen's "We Will Rock You" did precisely that, followed by a guilty pleasure, Barry Manilow's "Copa Cabana." Her taste in music was eclectic and that's what she got as the shuffle mode continued.

****

MP watched Lenore from the doorway. He'd never seen her dancing and singing like no one was watching. It took his breath away. He'd rung the bell but she hadn't answered.

Today was Addy's day off, and he was looking forward to spending the time alone with Lenore, getting to know her better, mentally and physically. She had up walls so thick he didn't think anything could penetrate them. He was attracted to her. Yes, she was physically appealing, but she was also smart, witty, and willing to listen to him about his craft, how he wrote. She wanted to know how he constructed his books. While she would generously share her writing experiences with him, she shared little else.

Lenore turned, looking wide eyed and embarrassed.

"Sorry. I didn't mean to startle you," MP said, moving toward her and taking her hand. "I rang the bell, but with the music, you didn't hear me. I tried the door and let myself in. You should lock it, you know," he finished, pulling her closer.

MP had never touched her before, not really. He felt some type of current pass through them. Barbra Streisand's and Bryan Adams's "I Finally Found Someone" filled the air.

Lenore started to move away, but he drew her back to him easily. "Dance with me. I enjoyed watching you before, *mo chuisle*." He nuzzled her neck and sang the lyrics to her. His lips found hers. They were warm and yielding. MP traced the seam of her mouth with his tongue as if asking for admittance; she granted it. He ran his hands through her hair, he deepened the kiss, swaying with the music, cupping her bottom, and pulling her toward him.

"I should have known," a voice boomed from the doorway.

Lenore and MP jerked back from one another.

Before them was a nondescript man. He was about five ten, one hundred and sixty pounds with mousy brown hair and dull gray eyes. He was dressed casually in a bluish gray sweater and jeans.

"You're right. I should lock the door," she said, looking at MP. "Can you give me a minute?"

MP nodded and left but only into the room next door. The man was obviously angry, and he wanted to be close in case she needed him.

****

Lenore turned her attention to the intruder. "John, I'm sorry," she began, seeing the furious passion on his face. She'd never seen any type of emotion from the man before.

"You're sorry? You're only sorry you got caught. How many other guys are you stringing along?" His hands were on the back of the couch, gripping it until his fingers were white-knuckled.

She moved slowly, farther away from him, noting that his face was an unpleasant shade of muted red.

"Love Stinks" began to play. Lenore started reaching for the computer to turn it off.

"No leave it," John Irving spat, then turned and stormed out of the house, slamming the door behind him so hard it rattled the glass sidelights.

Lenore took a shaky breath and let it out.

Michael Patrick came to her. "Are you all right, lass? I'm sorry. I didn't know you were dating anyone."

"It's all right. I stopped dating him weeks ago. I never got around to telling him," she said almost sheepishly.

A small smile crossed MP's face. "Glad to be of service then."

She laughed a full-bodied sound that he'd heard only a few times before. "Yes, thank you for your help, Michael Patrick. I'm not good with ending relationships. I thought maybe if I kept putting him off, he'd get the hint." Lenore sobered. "I should have told him. It wasn't nice, and I wouldn't like to be treated that way. He isn't a bad guy, just gray."

"Gray? You rate your men with colors, do you, lass?"

"No, only John Irving for some reason."

"If you were to give me a color, what would it be?"

"Scarlet," she said without any hesitation.

"Why?" he asked, amused interest in his voice.

"You're dangerous."

He laughed. "How so?" He was moving closer to her.

"As if you didn't know." She avoided giving him a direct answer.

"No, tell me, *mo chuisle*." He was inches from her now. Survivor's "The Search is Over" morphed on.

He closed the distance between them. "We didn't finish our last dance if I recall correctly," he said, pulling her into his arms.

She smiled, grateful for a reprieve in answering the question.

MP sang to her, holding her closer, running his hand down her back.

She looked into his face, lips parted as if in invitation. He took it.

This time the kiss was hungrier and carried a sizzle of desire. They had all but stopped dancing, lost in the sensation of discovering one another.

Survivor was now replaced with Journey's "Open Arms." Music forgotten now, he slid his hands up the back of her long-sleeved black T. She arched into him. His arms pulled her tighter.

"Excuse me," a deep, raging voice all but commanded.

They jolted apart as if the words were bullets.

Lenore shrieked, and MP muttered, "Jesus."

"Wha . . . what are you doing here, Byron?" Lenore asked, stunned, yet not, that he was standing in her office.

Byron Maxwell was a big man. Attractive, almost too pretty, but at sixty-two his hair was now more gray than sable, and his eyes were not the vivid, ice blue they once were. He was beginning to look like a faded rose.

"I did ring the bell, but with the music and all . . ." He smirked and let his sentence trail off.

"Again, Byron, what are you doing here?" she demanded, angry that he had invaded her personal space.

"Gerald called you and you didn't return his call."

"Sorry, but I'm not in the habit of making campaign contributions to any political party these days. I didn't know the RNC was going door to door now, or are you a member of the Tea Party, grass roots, and all that?" she asked hotly, anger spilling into her tone.

"Don't be a bitch, Lenore."

"You haven't seen bitch."

"The lady deserves more respect than that, Byron, and if you can't behave with a modicum of decorum, I think you should leave," MP said hotly.

Maxwell looked MP up and down, as if noticing him for the first time, and then nodding his acknowledgment of MP's statement, he held out a hand and said, "Byron."

"Michael Patrick Finnegan." MP gave Byron an appraising looking as well.

"Lenore, I'm sorry. My intrusion was poorly timed, and my behavior thus far uncalled for," Byron said, shifting his attention back to her.

About seven snippy comments flashed through her mind, but MP's hand gliding down her back somehow kept them at bay. So she simply nodded and waved him to the couch. She did not, however, offer refreshments. When they had been seeing one another, he liked to come to her apartment and watch her cook. He loved her food. Mrs. Maxwell didn't cook.

"*Mo chuisle*, I won't be far if you need me."

"Okay." She looked into his blue eyes; they were filled with concern. "I'll be all right, Michael Patrick," she said softly.

She watched him go, then turned back to Maxwell, her own eyes stormy and her voice cold. "All right, for the fourth time, what do you want?"

"Jack is sick, he has multiple myeloma and needs a bone marrow transplant."

"I'm sorry to hear that," she said, meaning it and not breaking eye contact.

"The best chance of a donor is a sibling. Carter most likely would have been a match, but I'm sure you heard he died several years ago."

She sat impassive, gaze never wavering.

"Nate may be a match, even though he and Jack do not share the same mother."

Lenore waited him out with barely suppressed anger. Jack was only a month younger than Nate. Maxwell had told her when they first got involved that his marriage was over and he'd not had "intimate relations" with his wife since she became pregnant with his first son. When he told her his wife was pregnant again, she remembered asking him exactly what his definition of intimate relations was. She never did get a sufficient answer from him. It was the last time she'd ever seen him.

All of their communications after that went through Morris and her attorney. Thank goodness she was not so besotted with him that she didn't take precautions to protect herself and unborn child. At the time, Lenore told her attorney, "He fucked me once, and he won't do it again." She certainly wouldn't let him fuck her son.

"Lenore, would you ask Nate to be tested to see if he's a match?"

"No."

"No?"

"I said no. I don't believe I stuttered. You want him to be tested—you ask him. I'll be more than happy to be present at the meeting, in fact, I insist on it. You have no idea how many times he's asked me who his father was. I told him I didn't know, but he didn't buy that."

"Really, if you carried on the way I found you –"

Byron Maxwell was suddenly reeling backwards. The full force of her open palm had slammed into the side of his still too pretty, too smug face.

She was on her feet pointing to the door.

"Get out of here, you bastard. Yes, that would be you and not my unacknowledged son."

Maxwell stared at her, a hand absently stroking the cheek she had so ruthlessly slapped.

"I said get out of here. Now!"

MP entered the room. "The lady asked you to leave. I will remove you by force if I need to."

"I'm sorry," Byron said under his breath, turned, and left.

CHAPTER TEN

Michael Patrick followed Byron out and made sure the door was locked this time. When he returned to the office he found Lenore, arms wrapped protectively around her waist, staring out the window.

He wasn't sure if he should go to her but figured if she didn't want or need him, she'd tell him to go.

MP enveloped her from behind and kissed the side of her face. "You okay?"

"I think so."

"Guy was jealous, that's why he acted that way," MP said.

"I haven't seen or spoken to him in almost twenty-one years."

"He was still jealous. I know. I'm a man. Maybe he liked to think that you'd never get over him."

"It's not that I haven't gotten over him, but his treatment of me when I got pregnant pretty much colored my life and my relationships."

"Yet you write beautiful romance."

"Set in another century, on another continent, with people real or imagined, long dead."

He let that be and instead asked, "I take it that was Nate's father?"

"Yes."

"Want to talk about it? I'm a good listener."

"Maybe in a little while. I've never talked about it with anyone, so I don't take it lightly."

"Nor do I, *mo chuisle*, nor do I."

"What does it mean? The word you called me; it sounds lovely and Gaelic."

He smiled gently at her, "That's because it is. It means my love or my darling." Its literal meaning was *my breath*, but he wasn't ready to share that yet. It had already been a crazy enough day for her.

She turned to smile at him, "That's nice. I like it."

He ran his thumb across her bottom lip, "I'm glad. So you're not expecting any more crazy men, are you? You told me I was scarlet; what color are you?"

She couldn't help but laugh. "Usually a shade above pale yellow."

"I find that hard to believe. I see you as teal green, I think, rich, warm, and intricate."

"See, you are a charmer, Mr. Finnegan, a definite scarlet."

"How about we get out of here for a bit? I'll take you to lunch at that charming inn by the Delaware River."

"Maybe another day. How about I cook for us?"

"Sure, I don't think I knew you cooked."

"Hmm, where do you think all those cookies you devour come from?"

"You make them, homemade? I always thought they came from the bakery in town. That Addy picked them up."

"Nope, it was I."

"You make them for me?" he inquired hopefully.

"I like to cook for anyone who enjoys my food, so I suppose the answer is yes."

He beamed at her.

"Let's go; I'll make lunch."

****

The kitchen was bright with the early afternoon sun and made Lenore feel better. Not so chilled to the bone. MP seated himself at the counter and watched her move about the kitchen.

"Any foods you're allergic to or absolutely despise?"

"Calves' liver, hate it." He wrinkled his nose in disgust to make the point.

"Me too, so you're safe on that account. How about some Parmesan-encrusted tilapia and wild mushroom risotto?"

"I think I'm in love."

"The way to a man's heart is through his stomach."

"I don't think we're quite that simple," he mused. "I know it's early, but do you have some wine?"

"It's after twelve; wine would be good. There's a wine cooler behind the bar in the lower level; choose whatever you like. One side has white and the other has red."

"Any preference?"

"None."

What was happening to her? Lenore silently questioned herself. She was letting this man, a man she didn't know well get close to her. Closer than anyone had ever been, except maybe Byron Maxwell. Was she ready to do that? Was that why she wanted to write a contemporary romance? Was she ready to move into this century, on to this continent, with live people, maybe even herself?

"How about a Chardonnay?" he asked, bounding up the stairs.

Momentarily startled, she regrouped. "Sounds great."

Oven going with the fish, pots and pans simmering with risotto ingredients, she took her glass of wine and sat on the counter stool next to him.

"Cheers." She tapped her glass to his.

He leaned in and kissed her lightly.

Her eyes shimmered as she looked at the man facing her. She would tell him. Tell him what she'd told no one, not even her parents. Maybe it was time and, hopefully, she could trust him. Trust, risk, passion, lust, hope . . . love, wasn't that what she filled her books with? The road to get there was never easy in fiction or reality, but maybe it was time to give her heart another try.

He cocked his head to get her attention.

A slow grin crossed her lips. "Sorry, wool-gathering, I guess."

"Back in the Victorian Era, are you?"

"People still use the term today. I've heard them."

"Yes, people in your circle who write VR like you."

"You're right. I never thought of that."

"It's okay; I like it."

She took his hand and laced her fingers through his. MP's hand was warm, strong, and confident; it made her feel the same when he squeezed hers.

"Byron Maxwell . . . " she started.

"Ahh, he does have a last name. I thought he was one of those famous people that only used one name."

"Like Prince," she laughed as a visual image of Byron singing "Little Red Corvette" flashed through her mind. "No, he's a legend in his own mind."

He nodded.

"Maxwell is a four-term senator from Virginia. He was beginning his first reelection campaign when I met him. I was an intern in his Washington, D.C. office. Young, idealistic, with stars in my eyes, ripe for infatuation, hero worship, and lies."

"You're being too hard on yourself."

"I'm not, Michael Patrick. People, even his closest staff members, tried to warn me about him, but I knew better or thought I did."

He ran his thumb over top of her knuckles. "If this is painful for you to recall, please don't put yourself though it on my account."

"It's okay, the classic story of the older male and younger female. Byron is a conservative, prolife, anti-gay politician. But he is the biggest hypocrite who ever walked. Do you know what the first thing he said to me was when he found out I was pregnant?" She didn't wait for his response. "He told me to get rid of it. He didn't want it. He'd pay for the abortion, even have his senior staffer, Gerald Morris, drive me. On the campaign trail, he still preaches prolife. Prolife as long as an unwanted pregnancy doesn't affect his life."

She got up to stir the risotto and check on the fish.

"I'm sorry, Lenore."

"Please don't be sorry; it was my own fault and my own vanity that did me in. I wanted to think I was different, that I mattered. I knew the consequences of unprotected sex; I'm lucky I only got pregnant and not some sexually transmitted disease. I was smart enough to know how not to get myself into the predicament to begin with, so it is my fault."

He looked at her across the counter top. Her face was set in a hard grimace. "You should cut yourself some slack for your youthful behavior. As far as I'm concerned, Maxwell took advantage of you and should be shot."

"I let him take advantage of me."

A sigh escaped his lips. "I'll set the table if you like."

"That's nice, thanks."

They agreed, at MP's suggestion, to suspend talk of her son's father until after lunch.

"No need to cause acid reflux."

CHAPTER ELEVEN

After lunch, Lenore and MP adjourned to her sunroom with the remainder of the wine.

Lenore stretched like a cat before sitting down on the couch. Her companion watched, wanting to run his hands over the slim band of creamy skin that appeared when she lifted her arms and her shirt rose above her waist. However, he decided to keep his hands to himself for the moment.

Had it not been for Maxwell showing up, he was hoping to make love with her or at least get off first base. But that would have to wait. He wanted making love to be about them, himself and herself, not Mr. Gray or Byron Maxwell. Although he'd been prepared to overlook John Irving, Maxwell could not be overlooked. He'd played too important a part in her life, in how she formed relationships with men. MP wanted to be the only man on her mind when they made love. He didn't want to share with memories of Maxwell. She'd obviously thought she loved him at one point.

He topped off their wine glasses and joined her on the couch.

Lenore spoke first. "I can't work up the energy to finish the sordid story of my relationship with Byron Maxwell at the moment. I haven't seen him in two decades, and the way he scared the shit out of us just walking in, I think I'm coming down from the adrenalin rush. All righteous anger has gone for the moment. Now I'm worried about my son and how all this may affect him."

"Are you going to tell Nate about his father then?"

"I don't know. If Maxwell pursues the subject, he has the right to know. While we didn't get that far in the conversation, I could tell Byron expected me to talk Nate into getting tested."

"The man is despicable, Lenore."

"Yes, he is."

Despite his deciding not to touch her, he took her hand and gave it a reassuring squeeze.

She looked down at their joined hands.

"Michael Patrick," she said disengaging her hand from his.

"What is it, *mo chuisle*?" he asked gently, lifting her chin so that they looked into one another's eyes, sapphires to opals.

Her face was sad and cloudy as she replied, "I can't start something with you now, MP −"

He cut her off, "We started something the moment we met. You can't go back now."

She shook her head. "I can't, MP. This, whatever this is, will be ugly."

"All the more reason not to face it alone."

"I can't −"

"You can and you will. I'm not faint of heart."

She gave him a weak smile and ran a hand down the side of his face. "But I am."

"No, you're not," he said, taking her hand and kissing the center. "You've never had the right man in your life before."

"You're that man, Michael Patrick?"

"I think I am, lass. Give me a chance. Give us a chance," he said, a simple plea in his voice. He looked into her brimming eyes.

"See what you get? You came here today hoping to seduce me, Mr. Finnegan, and instead you walked into a soap opera."

"No, *mo chuisle*. I walked into your life. Life is messy. I know that as well as anyone, better than some."

"I suppose you do. But if this gets ugly −"

"I'll still be there. This isn't your doing, Lenore. It's Maxwell's."

"I don't care about Maxwell or myself for that matter. I care about my son."

"All the more reason for me to stick around and make sure you're safe. You see, I care about you."

"I feel something for you, too, MP but the timing is all wrong."

"You can always make excuses."

"I wasn't going to. I was going to give you—us—my best shot. Maxwell isn't an excuse; he's a problem."

"If two people can outmaneuver a problem in a love affair, it's us. Remember the formula, lass: hero, heroine, plot, obstacle, happily ever after."

"You forgot marriage, babies, extended family. But seriously, this isn't a book plot."

"Can be."

"It's bad reality TV in the making."

"Ye of little faith." He leaned in and kissed the tip of her nose. "I'm not backing away; plus, we have work to do, a book to write. I'll be in your face day in and day out. Why not enjoy my face?"

CHAPTER TWELVE

"Maxwell, you're a flaming asshole," Gerald Morris spat at his boss and longtime friend.

They were in Morris's home office. Maxwell didn't want to discuss the matter at hand in his office on The Hill and couldn't discuss it in his own home, because he was convinced Mrs. Maxwell had his office bugged.

"I know I handled it poorly." Maxwell had spilled the scene at Lenore Held's house to his senior staffer.

"Poorly is an understatement. You fucked the woman over, literally, years ago, but she's kept her mouth shut and never caused a moment's grief, and you go to her house and verbally attack her?"

Maxwell sat in the wingback chair that flanked the fireplace, staring into his scotch.

Morris continued. "She wasn't like all the others or all the others after. She was a decent girl. A GD virgin that you bragged about deflowering. Then you tell her to get an abortion—you prolife hypocrite. She could have sunk you, your political career, and your equally political marriage if she had chosen to, but she didn't."

"I know."

"By your own admission, you let yourself into her house, find her with a man, and as much as call her a whore. You are a piece of work."

"I saw her with that guy, and I snapped. I don't know what came over me."

"Jealousy, lust, want – take your pick. You're a pig."

Morris could get away with saying these things to his boss, because he didn't need to work. He came from a very prosperous, well-to-do family who had closets, trunks, and attics full of skeletons. He could never run for office himself but was able to impact many things by working behind the scenes and manipulating Maxwell. Maxwell was too stupid to know he was being manipulated.

They had been fraternity brothers in college. Morris had helped get Maxwell elected as frat president on a platform of better beer at parties and a condom dispenser in the common area restroom. Things were so simple back then.

"I should have left Corrine for Lenore all those years ago."

"While you might have had the balls to fuck her, Byron, you never had the balls or the backbone to leave her. But that's neither here nor there. Why did you go to Lenore's house? She could have called the cops. Her companion could identify you. She could tell him her tale of the former intern done wrong, and he could go to the press. You're a dumb fuck."

"He's a foreigner. I don't think he knows who I am. Only introduced myself as Byron. His name is Michael Patrick Finnegan."

"Foreigner?"

"British, Scottish, Irish, Australian—something with that kind of accent."

"Are you as stupid as you appear to be?"

"Look, Morris, are you going to help me or not? I know I fucked up. Seems to be my life's work. But Jack needs that bone marrow transplant, damn it! While I don't even like the kid, he's my kid and I won't let him die."

Morris didn't point out that he'd be a sympathetic figure on the upcoming campaign trail if he were the father of two dead sons. In fact, he tried to soften his approach. "Okay. Do you want Corrine and Jack to know of the donor's origin, if indeed Nathan Held is even a match?"

"God no! I wanted Lenore to convince him to get tested."

"You are ignorant. While Cater and Jack were/are wastrels, Nathan Held is, by all appearances, a brilliant, decent young man. He takes after his mother."

"That's why I thought Lenore could convince him." Byron commented, oblivious to the disgust in Morris's voice.

"You're the bastard, not your unacknowledged son."

Maxwell gave a wary laugh. "That's exactly what Lenore said before she threw me out."

"Imagine that," Gerald offered with scathing sarcasm. "The point is you're attempting to prey on his goodness as you did on Lenore's all those years ago."

"She's been paid well to keep her silence."

"If she'd gone public, written a book, she'd have made millions, and it would have launched her own writing career into the stratosphere a lot sooner. But no, she was honorable, worked and established her own success, raised a decent son, and you're looking to suck blood, or should I say bone marrow, from them?"

"Enough insults and bad clichés. I need help." Maxwell ran a hand over his face.

"You're the epitome of a bad cliché, any number of them," his friend taunted.

"You seem to be her champion here, Gerald. Are you sure you weren't doing her, too? Maybe I should have demanded a paternity test all those years ago."

"Poor kid looks exactly like you and, unlike you, Lenore didn't hop from bed to bed, but yeah, I liked her. If things had been different, I might have made a move on her myself, but unlike you, I wasn't married with a child."

Maxwell looked at Morris for a moment but said nothing.

Finally, Morris said, "I'm sure the kid will ask questions and I'm sure that Lenore will tell him about it being his half brother needing a bone marrow transplant. I bet he's had plenty of questions over the years about who his father is."

"Lenore said as much. She told him she didn't know. He didn't believe her."

"Like I said, smart kid. Knows the measure of his mother and, short of rape, she wouldn't have sex with a man she didn't know."

Maxwell winced at the comment.

"A little too close to home for you, Byron?" A sardonic laugh resonated from deep in Gerald's chest.

"You son of a bitch. You know I cared for Lenore."

"Not enough to do the right thing by her all those years ago."

"I would have ruined her life—the media circus, the loss of my career. Like you said, I didn't have the balls to leave Corrine and even if I had, there would have been nothing left. I would have been a bleached carcass on the side of the road."

"I hate to admit it, but you're right. You would have ruined her life. I for one am thankful that she didn't let that happen."

Both men were quiet for a while.

"Are you going to help out here?"

"You shouldn't have gone to her house in the first place."

"We've established the fact that I'm a stupid, pussy-whipped, fucking prick bastard, but my kid still needs a bone marrow transplant. I've already lost one son —"

"You lost Carter before he died, Byron."

Morris knew that while the words stung his boss, they were true. Carter Maxwell had been strung out on drugs and alcohol when he smashed head-on into the tree. No one knew if it was an accident or a suicide, but there was never a note found, so the death was ruled an accident.

Morris shamelessly orchestrated Carter's death into Maxwell's public appearances, garnering him sympathy and votes. Carter's legacy was to be a warning to others that there are consequences to one's irresponsible behavior. He'd even gotten Maxwell to do public service announcements about the tragic effect Carter's death had on his family.

The truth was Morris was secretly glad Carter Maxwell was dead. His addictions and conduct were an embarrassment to the senator. Morris thought that's why Maxwell's kid did the outrageous things he did, to embarrass and damage his father's reputation. Well, it came back to haunt the little SOB. And, oh yes, Carter Maxwell was a son of a bitch, Jack, too, for that matter.

Byron refilled his empty glass with a trembling hand.

"I'm not sure why I keep you around, Gerald."

"Sure you are," he said. Fact was Maxwell couldn't form a comprehensive thought without Morris.

"I should have him kidnapped," Maxwell said, tossing back his scotch and going back for more.

"Jesus, have you lost your mind? I'll pretend I didn't hear that," Morris said and took the bottle of scotch from Maxwell's hand before he could refill his glass.

Maxwell looked up, surprised.

"I'll take care of it. Are you willing to meet with Nathan Held? I don't think you'll have much choice."

"I don't want to, no. But if that's the only way, I will. It all needs to be under wraps."

Morris raised an eyebrow. "That goes without saying. I'll give her a few days and contact her again. But you are to stay away from her and her son."

"He's my son, too."

"No, he's not. Genetic material does not a father make. Plus, your name isn't on the birth certificate; it's blank."

"Come on, he even looks like me, except for the eyes; he has his mother's eyes. Lenore's eyes."

"How do you know that?"

"There were several pictures of him online for the things he did in high school and college."

"Don't Google him again, Maxwell. If it ever becomes an issue, the media vultures will comb through your computer files, and won't everyone wonder why you were looking at Nathan Held? Same goes for LaSandra Lacey," Morris added.

Neither man said anything for a long while. Finally, Morris got up from his chair, signaling the meeting was over.

CHAPTER THIRTEEN

Lenore received another call from Gerald Morris, as she knew she would, early the following week. In order to save herself another scene, she called him back.

But she wasn't dealing with this on her own. Lenore wanted her attorney involved, and the meeting would take place in his office two days from now. Morris stressed that time was of the essence.

Lenore paced her office talking on a hand held phone. She absently straightened books as she walked.

"I don't know why he doesn't try for a match in the national data base," Lenore commented.

"He has, and there are no matches. Some people offered to be tested after the news went public, but nothing so far. Plus, Maxwell doesn't want to take the chance of the blood not being tested properly and Jack getting AIDS or hepatitis or something equally as gruesome," Morris offered.

"I didn't know he was smart enough to realize the potential pitfalls of an unknown donor. I'm sorry there were no matches in the database."

"Thanks, we all are too," Morris lied smoothly. "Corrine might have been the one to put the tainted blood idea in his mind."

When she made no comment, he said, "So we'll meet in your attorney's office at 10:30 on Wednesday?"

"Yes, but I don't want Maxwell involved. If he's there, I'll walk out, and there will be no further discussions. If he doesn't want to send you, have him send his own counsel."

"Not sure he trusts them. He's paranoid they'll tell his wife anything he says."

"Just because you're paranoid doesn't mean someone isn't out to get you." Lenore mumbled the overused adage in an inaudible tone.

"I'm sorry, Lenore, I didn't hear you."

"Still afraid of Corrine, is he?"

Morris's response to the question/comment was a sarcastic laugh that told her what she already knew.

Lenore hung up the phone and let out a sigh as MP and Nikko entered the room.

She pushed back her dark thoughts and went to embrace her agent.

"You look fabulous," Nikko trilled, holding Lenore at arms' length.

Lenore was wearing a gray cashmere sweater dress that skimmed her curves; her hair was loose and wavy, and she wore a bit of make-up that looked natural but somehow accentuated her eyes and lips, making her look sexy and kissable.

"She does, doesn't she," MP said, looking into her eyes from behind Nik. A smile formed, causing small, appealing crinkles to appear in the corners of his eye.

Lenore turned her gaze to Nikko who simply raised a well-tended eyebrow at her.

"Let's go into the great room, shall we?" Lenore asked but continued out her office door, forcing the other two to follow.

"I thought we'd do lunch at the Lambertville Station Inn in New Jersey for a change," Lenore continued. "Are you game?"

"Fine with me, although your food is better than any restaurant I've ever had," Nikko complimented.

"I thank you, but I'm sure you've had better."

"Don't count on it," MP said, taking her hand and kissing it as they sat on the couch.

"Life imitating art?" Nikko asked, unabashed.

"Life, Nik," MP said.

"A word to the both of you: take care of one another's hearts because if either of you hurts the other, there'll be hell to pay."

"Hear that, Lenore? Be nice to me," MP teased.

The two women laughed.

Nikko got down to business. "I've read what you've sent me, and I like the story line, the plot is solid. But, Lenore, where is the squirm factor? Your vestal virgins are more creative in the carnal knowledge area than your smart-mouthed, take-no-prisoners Amanda. And, Michael Patrick, what in the hell kind of name is Casper Grossman?"

Lenore smiled at MP, her eyes dancing. "I thought the same thing at first, Nik, but it kind of grows on you after a while, and we call him Cass most of the time."

Their agent waved her hand dismissively. "It's of no consequence at the moment; a name is easy enough to change. But this is supposed to be a romance, and all I see this couple doing is snarking at one another.

"There needs to be a thaw between them. I get why Cass continues to call her Ms. Loring after she was a bitch to him the first night, but you're 120 pages in, and Amanda has asked him repeatedly to call her by her name or Mandy. But does he? No, Casper tells her Mandy makes her sound like an under-aged hooker—nice, MP. Then Amanda tells him Casper sounds like a ghost, a very little, very wispy ghost, as she looks at his crotch, I might add."

She chuckled a little, then continued, "Either you guys are repressed or very boring in bed." She stopped, looking from one to the other, then started talking quickly. "Oh my God, you haven't had sex yet, have you? Well, I mean you've had sex, at least, Lenore, as she has a child. But you haven't had sex together, have you?"

When neither one confirmed or denied, their agent said, "Then hop into the sack and get to it. That's why your characters are bitching at one another all the time. You're taking your own sexual frustrations out on your characters." She let go an exasperated sigh. "You are two best-selling romance authors. Don't make me say you write about it because you don't do it, can't do it, or you don't get any."

"Low blow there, Ms. Martenstein," Lenore said.

Nikko laughed. "Want to weigh in, Finnegan?"

"Yeah. I was saving this—but I'd already decided that Cass would utter Ms. Loring's given name the first time he climaxed with her."

"I like it," Lenore said.

"I do, too," their agent agreed. "But maybe he can do more than utter."

"I suppose Amanda will have to concede that Casper is neither little nor wispy," Lenore said.

"I'm sure Cass would appreciate the reassessment of his manhood, lass."

Nikko rolled her eyes and made a gagging motion with her finger. "Do me a favor, and start screwing each other or even someone else, but you both need to get some."

"And what about you, Dr. Ruth, are you getting any?" Lenore asked to get even.

"As a matter of fact, I am," Nikko said with a smug smile.

"Really?" Lenore and MP said at the same time and immediately looked at one another and laughed.

"Oh, brother. Yes, really."

"Do tell," Lenore teased.

"A lady does not kiss and tell."

"Yeah, but we're talking about you, Nik," her clients said in unison.

"Okay, now you two are starting to scare me."

CHAPTER FOURTEEN

"Soft, sexy," he murmured in her ear as he ran his hands down her cashmere sweater dress. After dropping Nikko at the train station, they had returned to her house and were currently in the great room.

Somehow the skimming lines of the dress were more alluring to him than if the garment were form fitting. As he ran his hands back up the dress, he saw her nipples through the soft fabric. He ran his fingers over them, and she arched into him. He murmured, "I want you."

"I want you, too," she breathed.

His kiss was fiercely possessive; it proclaimed *mine.*

She couldn't help but smile under his plundering mouth.

"What?" He pulled back. "What's so damn amusing?"

Lenore looked into his eyes, which were already dilated and dark with desire. "Nothing, I'm happy. I never imagined you'd want me as much as I want you."

"Are you daft, woman? Have you not heard a word I've said to you over the last ten weeks? I wanted you the moment I walked into your life." He didn't give her time to respond or react, rather he moved in and kissed her with primitive, carnal need.

He slid his hand up her dress and gasped when he came to a garter. "I want to see all of you, *mo chuisle.* Come with me."

"I hope to."

He laughed, taking her hand and leading her to her bedroom as if he'd been there before.

At the edge of the bed, he stopped. "Are you sure?" he asked, eyes searching hers.

"Yes," she breathed. "Are you?"

"I've never been more certain of anything in my life."

He lifted the dress over her head. Lenore shimmered in the dove-gray silk of her teddy, sexy garter, and silky stockings.

"Hmm, where to start," he mused, taking her all in. "*Ta tu go h-alainn*, you're beautiful."

She flushed under his smoldering gaze.

He continued to whisper Gaelic endearments to her as he touched her lightly.

Drawing the thin straps of her teddy down, he let the garment flow from her body and pool at her feet.

Her breath hitched as he caught her nipples between each of his thumbs and forefingers. Kissing her, he gently nudged her backwards onto the bed, coming to rest on top of her when she landed. Lightly pinning her arms above her head, he took her left breast into his mouth.

She arched up to meet him, heat flooding her body, wanton lust threatening to take over. He relinquished his hold on her arms and skimmed her breasts.

Lenore unfastened the buttons of his shirt, tugged it from his waistband and pushed it off his shoulders, finally able to feel and see him for the first time. Dark, soft curls covered the muscles of his chest, which was hard and unyielding.

He kissed her and she pulled him to her, his hard body against her much softer one. Michael Patrick groaned into her mouth.

"I want you. Oh, how I want you," she panted.

He quickly removed his remaining clothes and rejoined her on the bed. Slowly rolling down the silk stockings after disengaging them from the garter, he skimmed his hands down her legs, causing already heightened nerve endings to explode. He glanced up and saw the pulse point in her neck beating frantically.

His own pulse was hammering as erratically. Sliding up her form, he stopped to kiss the throbbing vein and take a little nip. She writhed beneath him.

His hand wandered to the intimate folds between her legs and stroked her. She was hot and wet and ready. He slid his middle finger into her moist heat and felt the muscles contract around it.

"I want you," she said again, reaching to grasp the object of her desire as if to put an exclamation point on the statement.

"I'm getting the point," he said, rolling on a condom as she watched.

He stopped short of entering her. His eyes locked on hers. "Watch, *mo chuisle*, watch."

She did, and he watched her, saw her eyes widen as he entered her for the first time. He groaned as her muscles gripped him tightly, drawing him deeper.

MP held still for a moment waiting for her body to become

accustomed to him. She lifted her hips to encourage his participation.

"Impatient are we, wee one?"

"Yes."

He chuckled and thrust into her fully, deeply.

"Now, now," she chanted.

"No, not yet, savor the moment," he breathed, deliberately slowing his pace.

He was surprised, but she followed his lead. But soon there was no slowing down or holding back, as they both raced toward climax.

After, he gathered her in his arms and breathed in her essence.

"Marvelous."

"It was, wasn't it?" He smiled at her, his voice still thick with desire.

She ran a hand through the springy hair on his chest as she rested her head there. He kissed the top of that head, and eventually they drifted into a doze, sated and relaxed.

They stirred several hours later.

"Are you hungry?" Lenore asked him as he leaned in to kiss her.

"Starving," MP replied with a provocative smile and rolled on top of her.

She laughed, letting him have his fill of her and enjoying every minute.

"I fear I may be obsessed with you, Ms. Held."

"Hmm, so it's Ms. Held, is it now?"

"I thought I'd try the opposite of what we're doing in the book and see how it worked."

"Truth be told, I have a soft spot for endearments you murmur in your native tongue."

"I could be cussing you out, and you'd never know it."

"Even if you are, it never sounded so good. So keep it up."

"I plan to, *mo chuisle*. I can't help it. Love and anger flow from one's first language. Both such strong emotions, I think."

She looked deeply into his eyes, "What are you trying to tell me?"

"Ah, the lass is very perceptive. I'm obviously not angry with you, so I guess that leaves love. I'm falling in love with you, Lenore, hard and fast." He continued to look into her fascinating eyes, facets of rich blues and greens coming together, then floating apart again, almost like a kaleidoscope. "I've scared you, haven't I?"

Deflecting the question, she said, "*A chuisle* means love and *mo chuisle* means my love."

"Yes, you catch on quickly. I'll have to watch my cussing; you'll be giving it back to me in no time."

They both laughed to defuse the tension, sexual and otherwise.

CHAPTER FIFTEEN

Wednesday morning, Lenore looked at herself in the bathroom mirror and frowned. She didn't know what look she was going for, but she was thinking severe and serious. Somehow she wasn't getting there. No, her lips were full and bee-stung and her face was flushed an innocent pink. The activity that gave her the rosy glow was anything but innocent.

She turned sideways; even her breasts looked larger and firmer. She'd read in a health magazine that when a woman's breasts were stroked or kissed, blood flow dilated the arteries and caused them to increase in size by up to 25 percent, at least temporarily. Until this instant, she never had reason to think about whether it was true.

Lenore glanced up and saw Michael Patrick leaning casually on the doorframe.

"Yes?"

"You look sexy, *mo chuisle*, even a brown burlap sack wouldn't take the glow away and the sparkle out of your eyes. Why would you want it to? Haven't you ever heard the best revenge is looking good?"

He was grinning at her, merriment dancing in those clear eyes. Eyes sky blue, unlike those of her son's sperm donor, which were ice blue and cold as his heart. Lenore mentally shook those thoughts from her mind; MP didn't deserve the comparison. Instead she quipped, "So I should go looking like a well-satisfied woman?"

"Indeed."

She laughed as she slid into a conservative, navy-blue pinstripe suit and two-inch-heeled navy pumps. Glancing up, she observed MP donning a gray wool blazer. "Are you going somewhere?"

"With you, lass."

"Michael Patrick, I don't think that's a good idea."

"I do. I won't go into your meeting, but I will be waiting for you when you leave."

She was about to argue but stopped. Why shouldn't he be there? He'd distract her from her disturbing thoughts on her way to the meeting and maybe save her from whatever emotional state she'd be in after.

****

An hour later, Lenore and MP were in Attorney Connor Walker's office. Lenore had arranged to arrive a half-hour early to discuss the situation, as she'd taken to calling it, with him. There had never been reason to before. Her attorney in Michigan had set up the financial arrangements with Maxwell's camp, and she had invested the funds over the years, sometimes with the advice of a financial advisor but usually on her own. She trusted financial advisors about as much as she trusted politicians. Connor took care of all her business dealings, and another member of his firm dealt with her estate planning.

"You're nervous, *a chuisle*," MP said, taking her hand.

"I suppose the cold, clammy, dead fish-like feel of my flesh was the giveaway."

"That sounds like something Amanda might say."

"Maybe, but I said it and wasn't thinking about Amanda. What would Cass say to her in response?"

That response would have to wait because Walker's admin came to escort her back.

They exchanged pleasantries and got down to business.

"Tell me why you're meeting Byron Maxwell's aide and why you're doing it here," Connor Walker said.

She took a deep breath. "Byron Maxwell is my son's father. I was an intern for him during my final year of college, and we had an affair."

"I see," Walker replied. "Is he making trouble now? I'm guessing whatever arrangements were made after your son was conceived have worked satisfactorily until this point." He then asked, "Maxwell's son has cancer and needs a bone marrow transplant. Is that what this is about?"

Grateful that her attorney kept up with the news, she nodded her head and explained the deal they'd struck all those years ago. Then she described the scene Maxwell had caused at her house the week prior and Gerald Morris's subsequent phone call.

"Is Maxwell violent, Lenore?" her attorney asked with concern.

"I remember he enjoyed yelling a lot but was never physically violent with anyone. Never even yelled at me, until

I had the poor taste to get pregnant." Remembering the day she had told him could still cause acid to churn to the surface.

"I'm sorry, Lenore. I didn't mean to upset you," Connor said when he saw her pale face. "Do you want some water or something else to drink?"

"No, I'm fine. I hadn't thought about how painful that time was for me in years."

"Man was a jackass, if you don't mind me saying so."

"Those are much kinder words than I have for him."

They shared the expected chuckle.

"What is it you want to accomplish here today?" Connor asked.

"I'm certain Morris will want to talk about the bone marrow transplant Jack needs. He'll try to convince me to get Nathan to be tested to see if he's a match without disclosing who it's for or why I want him to do it, but he's not a child anymore, and I wouldn't insult him.

"That being said, he's asked about his father a number of times over the last few years, and if he's going to do this, I think he has a right to know who his father is. I also want Nate to be able to meet with Maxwell if he chooses to do so. If he does, I want the meeting facilitated here on a weekend so Nate does not have to miss classes and, more importantly, so it's less likely someone will see them meeting."

Her attorney listened intently, taking down the occasional note.

"I could be wrong, and Nate might not want any part of any of this, his father, or his half brother, but I know my son fairly well, and if donating bone marrow will help save Jack's life, I'm sure he'll do it, half brother or not."

"You've raised a great kid, Lenore, and you should be proud of that."

Nate had done an internship with one of Connor's partners who specialized in patent law over the summer and had received a great deal of praise for his work.

"I am very proud of him. He's my best work." She looked up, giving her attorney a genuine smile. "I want to spare him as much pain and grief as possible. If word that Maxwell has an illegitimate child gets out, it will be a media feeding frenzy, especially when the mother is none other than LaSandra Lacy." She said that last bit with some dramatic flair to lessen the tension.

"You're right. But I can't imagine Maxwell would want it to become public knowledge."

"I wouldn't think so either, but the more people who are involved, the more problematic it becomes."

Before Connor could say anything else, his admin buzzed to let him know that Gerald Morris had arrived.

"Is it okay for him to come back?"

"I wish I never had to see him again in my life, but, yeah, let him join us."

"I can deal with him alone if you want."

"I want, but I won't. Not when Nate is involved."

Gerald Morris joined them. He was about six feet tall, balding but in a distinguished sort of way that did not detract from his appearance; his eyes, deep brown, seemed to take in everything around him.

"Lenore," he said, extending his hand and looking her over from head to toe then settled on her face.

"Mr. Morris," she said, giving his hand a quick, firm shake.

"You used to call me Gerald."

"In another life. Connor Walker," she said, not missing a beat, "this is Gerald Morris, Byron Maxwell's chief of staff and oldest friend."

"Mr. Morris," Connor said by way of greeting and took the man's outstretched hand.

"Please call me Gerald."

Connor waved to a seat while saying, "Connor."

"It is my understanding that you wished to meet with Ms. Held," Walker said, moving right to business.

"Yes, you see, Jack Maxwell . . ." Morris took the next several minutes to rehash what Lenore had told him. Connor did not interrupt him.

"Lenore," Morris turned to her and said, "Byron asked me to extend his apology for his intrusion into your home and his behavior in general."

She acknowledged the statement with a barely perceptible nod. Lenore knew that Maxwell was never sorry for anything he did and that Gerald was always cleaning up for him.

"I guess the question is," Walker said, moving the meeting along, "what exactly is your boss looking for, Gerald?"

"He wants to see if Nate is a match."

"Because he is a sibling," Connor said.

"Yes."

"Does Byron Maxwell intend to acknowledge Nate as his son then?"

Morris shifted, glanced at Lenore, then back to Walker. "He was hoping that Lenore could convince him to get tested. Say it was a friend's child or something."

Lenore gave a sarcastic laugh. "You must be joking. Maxwell wants my son poked and prodded to save his own child, and he wants me to lie to him to get him to cooperate? You must both be out of your minds." Her voice was deadly calm and even, but the flashing in her eyes warned Morris off. "If there is even a possibility that Nate is tested, the rules of engagement will be mine."

Both men looked at her and waited for her to speak.

"I will discuss the matter with Nate and explain to him that his half brother needs a donor. If he wishes to be tested, he can. If he wishes to meet his sperm donor, his sperm donor will meet with him. What Nate negotiates after that point is his own doing. He will not be alone with Maxwell. Connor and/or I will be there, and any meeting, should there be one, will take place here, on a Saturday or Sunday.

"It's less likely they will be seen together here and recognized than in D.C. I do not want Nate or myself, for that matter, to be caught up in a media circus should word get out that Maxwell has a child by a woman other than his wife. Did you get all that, Connor?"

"Yes, I did, Lenore." He played his role perfectly.

"Did I miss anything?"

"For now, I think that should be enough. Should Mr. Maxwell agree to your terms, there might be other things to consider."

"Fine," she said, standing up and glancing at her watch. "I have another commitment. Should Byron agree to the terms I have suggested, call my attorney. I won't mention anything to Nate until Byron agrees," she said to Morris.

Both men were already standing, a testament to country club breeding. She extended her hand to each and walked out.

Lenore then walked into the nearest ladies' room, dashed into a stall, and proceeded to become violently ill. All the ugliness, all the struggles, everything had come flooding back to her when she saw Gerald Morris, more so than when

Maxwell had walked into her house unannounced the week before. Maybe it was because MP was there with her, maybe because of simple shock. But the full reality of the situation had hit her hard today.

Morris had warned her about Byron before she started sleeping with him. Sleeping nothing—they'd never spent the night together—before she started fucking him. In her twenty-year-old mind, it had been romantic, and she had called it making love, but there was no love on Maxwell's part.

He used her, fucked her, and discarded her and her child. Now, because of circumstances she could not control, he was coming back to do it to her again. This time she thought it was uglier than that. It was rape. Though there would be no physical penetration, the emotional fallout would be akin to rape.

As she leaned against the stall door her cell phone started ringing. Lenore thought about not answering, then dug it out of her purse and, looking at caller ID, saw it was MP.

"Hello," she said in a raspy voice and tried to clear her acid-burned throat.

"*Mo chuisle*, where are you? I know Morris left because I saw what he looked like when he gave his name at the desk."

"Ladies' room. I'll be out in a few minutes." Her voice was clogged with tears, and there was no disguising it.

"Are you alone?"

"Yes."

"I'll be right there."

"But –"

The phone went dead.

****

MP quickly talked to the receptionist, who took him to the ladies' room and got one of the other women to stand guard to warn off anyone who might take exception to a man in the women's restroom.

"Lenore, come out of there," he spoke softly.

"What . . ." she opened the stall door and was immediately embraced by him.

The tears flowed. She was consumed by them, scorching rivulets burning tracks down her cheeks, her neck, heading for her heart.

There was a small lounge area at the entrance to the restroom, and MP literally scooped her up and carried her there. Settling her on his lap, taking a white handkerchief from an inside pocket of his jacket, he wiped the tears away, then handed it to her.

"Ohh m-my G-god, Michael Pa-Patrick, I'm soo, soorry I fell apart," she said in a shuddering breath.

"It's okay," he murmured, stroking her back in slow, soothing motions.

"No, no, it's not. I don't lose it or fa-fall apart. I'm n-not some weepy heroine who can't get a grip."

"Never would have confused you with one." He tilted up her chin and smiled at her. "It's okay to be sad and angry. I'm betting your tears are from pent-up anger and frustration and not from sadness, though. You've never, ever struck me as sad."

"You're right. I'm mad as hell —"

"And you're not gonna take it anymore," he quipped the old movie line.

She did her best to smile. "You're absolutely right and I'm not going to shed any more tears over Maxwell."

"That's my lass." He moved in to kiss her.

She quickly covered her mouth. "While I'd like nothing better, you deserve better."

"I don't care, but because you do, I'll wait until you brush your teeth."

"Thank you." She laced her hand through his and rested her head on his shoulder. "I mean, not simply for understanding about . . ." She pointed to the bathroom stalls. "But for being here, for not staying behind when I said I wanted to come alone."

"Not necessary, but you're welcome." He brushed the hair from her face. A face that several hours ago had been alight with the afterglow of loving was now swollen and tear-stained. "I'd like to take out both Maxwell and Morris and throttle them both."

"They'd probably enjoy it."

He grinned at her and raised an eyebrow.

"I think I'm okay to leave. We've commandeered the ladies' room long enough."

"You sure?"

"Yes, and I want to tell you what transpired in the meeting."

"Give me the keys. I'll drive."

CHAPTER SIXTEEN

As Michael Patrick drove, Lenore recounted what had occurred at the meeting.

Romance writer or not, her personal history with men was limited. Based on what MP had seen, he must think she was some kind of wanton siren, but what he'd seen was a blip on the screen. She involuntarily shivered.

"Are you cold, lass?" MP asked, already boosting the heat.

"A little."

"Do you think Maxwell will go for your plan?"

"I'd say there's a ninety-eight percent chance he will. He wants to save his son. As a parent, I empathize, but as Nate's mother, I want to protect him. I've come up with what I think will help minimize the hurt. Still, there's bound to be some, no matter what the plan."

"I can understand that," MP offered, and then they lapsed into silence.

Out of the corner of his eye, he saw her hand tremble and took it. "*A chuisle*, are you sure you're all right?"

"I'm not sure I'm all right, but I'm better. Thank you for coming and picking up the pieces."

"You're welcome, but no thanks are necessary, and you've already thanked me."

"I want you to know I appreciate you and your kindness. Not every man, or woman for that matter, would walk into the middle of someone else's mess."

He squeezed her hand, "I'm not most people, and I don't do anything halfway."

She gave him a weak smile and sat in silence again.

A few moments later, he added, "Contrary to what you may think, I don't get involved easily and have been intimate with only a small number of women." MP ran his thumb over her knuckles.

"Nikko is right about us then; we write romance because we're not getting any."

"Correction. We weren't getting any."

She laughed a real laugh, and it warmed his heart to hear it. "Are we making up for lost time then?"

"You bet, but it was worth the wait."

"Yes, it was." She raised his hand to her lips and kissed it.

"Am I going to get dog germs now?"

She slapped a hand over her mouth. "Oh my God. I am so sorry, I forgot."

"Teasing you, wee one. I would have kissed you before, too."

"Yeah, probably would have gotten more than dog germs," she said, fishing a breath mint out of her purse. "Hand sanitizer?" She followed up, holding a travel-size bottle.

"Nah, I think I'll risk it."

"We need to work on the book when we get back. I'll brush my teeth, make us some lunch, and then we'll get down to business."

"What do you say we work on some of their more intimate moments? Nik said that you were looking to do squirmy love scenes. You never did elaborate on what those are."

He glanced at her. "You have such pretty color in your face, *a chuisle*."

"Don't tease."

"I'm not. I'd like to do some field research on squirmy sex. Especially now that I have a willing partner." He wanted to get her mind off Maxwell and Morris.

She laughed again.

"Tell me about the squirm factor."

"To me, it's when you read a book and it leads you into the hero and heroine's love life to the point where . . . well, for a woman—when she feels wet and needy. I suppose for a man it would cause an erection and make him feel desire or horny, if you prefer something more masculine and twenty-first century."

"Either works for me. You're working for me."

Doing something totally out of character, she disengaged her hand from MP's and ran it lightly over his fly. "I see."

He let out a sigh. "If you want to stay on the road, Lenore my love, I wouldn't do that again."

"No?" She couldn't help herself and touched him, exerting a little gentle pressure this time.

"Talk about squirmy sex," he said grabbing her hand, bringing it to his lips and giving her index finger a little love nip. "Save it for home, *mo chuisle*."

"After I brush my teeth."

"After you brush your teeth."

"I've read that having oral sex right after brushing one's teeth or using mouthwash adds a little extra zip to the act."

"You wish to conduct an experiment to see if it's true?"

"Maybe. Maybe I can even make you squirm."

"No maybe about it."

CHAPTER SEVENTEEN

"My teeth are all nice and clean. I'm going to take a quick shower and wash the rest of the ugliness away," Lenore said, peeking her head out of the master bath and into her bedroom.

"I'll join you," MP said, rising from his reclining position on the bed. Approaching her, he pulled her in for a kiss. "You taste like a winter breeze."

"Mr. Finnegan, are you going to use that line as part of Cass's dialogue?"

"No, Ms. Held. The book has been forgotten." He kissed her again and walked her backward toward the large shower enclosure, one hand on her and one hand opening the shower door.

Lenore stopped and pulled away laughing. "You coming in with your clothes on?"

Startled, he looked down to see he still wore his pants and shirt. "You've made me brain-dead, woman."

She giggled and started to undo the buttons on his shirt. "As long as nothing else is dead."

He playfully swatted her bottom. "Get in the shower and keep warm. I'll be with you in a minute."

Michael Patrick joined her, wrapping his arms around her waist. She kissed him hard and needy, then moved slowly downward, stroking his penis at the same time. He groaned.

"I'm going to see if my minty-fresh breath adds that little extra tingle I read about. Call it field research," she breathed before taking him in her questing mouth.

"Jesus, Mary, and Joseph," he rasped and braced himself against the tile wall.

"Are they here, too?" she asked and then went back to the task at hand.

He gave a husky laugh and tangled his hands in her hair.

She felt him go steely and her own center grow warm and pliant. His breathing told her he was close.

MP attempted to pull her up, but she shook her head and gently bit him. He wisely left her alone.

A hand massaging his scrotum, her movements were hard and fast now, they were contracting toward his body.

Then he came in a hot, thick jet. The force of it surprised her, but she swallowed the salty, musky semen and felt very proud of herself.

His hands gentled in her hair and he pulled her upward to his chest. This time she didn't resist. Mouth millimeters from hers, he said in a raspy voice, eyes dreamy half slits, "I think your theory works, but I'm pretty sure we would have had the same outcome without the winter-breeze breath."

Then his mouth possessively engulfed hers. He kissed her and caressed her breasts until she moaned her pleasure, and then he slid two fingers between her folds and into her body, moving them gently and slowly and then harder and faster as her body dictated.

"Ooh, ooh . . ." she managed in a hitching breath as she came, head tossed back, white neck exposed. He kissed her there, ratcheting up her pleasure a notch.

"Mmm, *mo chuisle*." He held her close as the water cascaded from the shower jets.

"Bed," she finally managed.

"Bed," he agreed.

****

"Omelets?" Lenore asked. They were in the kitchen now and though it was closer to dinner than breakfast, they'd decided on breakfast food.

"Anything you make will be wonderful; it always is."

Smiling she followed up. "Or a German pancake."

"That sounds good, too."

"You're not being helpful, *mo chuisle*," she teased.

"Hmm, maybe I'll feast on you, Ms. Held."

"Dessert, definitely dessert," she promised. "But I'm starved and have to eat if you don't want me to faint dead away."

"All right, what's quicker?"

"Omelets."

"Then omelets it is."

"Ham and cheese?"

"Sounds great, I'll toast the bread."

"Do you cook, MP? I've never asked."

"Enough to keep myself alive."

She laughed. "I for one am grateful for that. You must have a specialty."

"I do, anything that can be taken from the box and put in the microwave, but I'll let you teach me if you want."

"Maybe," she said and held out a small cube of ham for him to nip from her fingers. "But maybe I want you dependent on me for your very existence."

Looking her in the eyes, he said, "I already am."

He kissed her as the eggs bubbled in the pan.

"Wait," she said breathlessly, "the eggs will burn."

"Can't have that."

"No. Do you think you can keep your hands off me until the food is done?"

"I'll go sit on the other side of the bar, put a barrier between us."

"I think that's a good idea." She expertly flipped the egg creation, then poured some OJ and handed it to him, his fingers skimming hers.

"Are you purposely trying to incite me, MP?"

"Of course."

She laughed and went to butter the toast. A moment later, she was sliding his food across the bar.

"You can sit next to me, lass. I promise to eat, especially now that its delicious smell is wafting into my face. You've incited my hunger." He used her word against her and looked up, his eyebrows suggestively arched.

"You're incorrigible." She took the stool next to him.

"Do you miss your son when he's away at college?" he asked, changing the subject.

"No. I enjoy seeing him when he comes home, or I go to see him in Washington. But it's the natural order of things. In a way, his being at school has given me a freedom I never had."

"Ever think of having more children?"

"My shelf life is getting dated. I'm not sure I could even conceive a child, but maybe. I never give absolutes." She looked at him thoughtfully and asked, "Do you want children, Michael Patrick?"

"Maybe. There is something about helping to mold a new life."

"I agree with you there, and if I had a child now, I think I'd be less stressed, not that being a parent would ever be stress-free. But I think it would be different at my advanced age."

"I'm a few years older than you, lass."

"There's that, too. Even if I had another child, I'd be in my sixties when he or she graduated from high school."

"They'd keep you young."

She gave a small chuckle. "I think that's a crock of shit."

"Tell me how you really feel."

"I don't think children keep you young at any age. I think the mere fact that one becomes a parent ages you immediately."

"But you'd think about having children?"

She cocked her head. "Why the sudden interest in whether or not I want more children?"

"I'd like to see you round and ripe with my child," he said simply, looking directly in to her eyes.

She didn't speak.

He watched her squirm.

"Nice shade of pink in your cheeks," he commented.

"Stop." She gave him a light-hearted fist to the shoulder.

"I'd like to practice in case the possibility ever arises."

He pulled her from her stool and kissed her, then sat her on the counter top and stood intimately between her legs. He opened the button-down shirt she was wearing, happy to see there was not a stitch underneath.

"You're beautiful, Lenore."

He rolled her already hard nipples between his thumbs and forefingers. Then inserted his middle finger into her folds, finding her warm and welcoming. He pulled her to the edge of the counter and opened her wider as he lowered his mouth to her hot center.

She moaned, leaning back to brace herself on the granite and shamelessly spread her legs wider. His tongue found her clitoris swollen and in need of attention. His mouth went to work there, and a finger slid into her, stroking her G spot. Impatiently she rocked herself into his touch. The cold granite adding an interesting contrast to his hot mouth and her even hotter body. He felt her start to come, and he removed his finger and mouth. She almost whimpered, and then he was there, filling her. Pumping into her until they were both spent.

"Your specialty is dessert," she said and nipped his ear lobe.

CHAPTER EIGHTEEN

"I think Amanda would be unhappy that Cass was changing her book so much," Lenore commented. She and MP were working in her office the following morning.

The couple in their story were working together to adapt Amanda's book into a screenplay that Cass was to write and produce. Amanda would not let him adapt the book without her participation.

"I'm guessing you're right about that, lass. So what is she going to do? Plead irreconcilable creative differences and walk away?"

"I'd be tempted if it wasn't a book and according to you we need a HEA. I find Cass to be an irascible jackass with an ego that's out of proportion to his abilities in and outside of the bedroom."

"Do you now?"

"Yes."

"I like the way you take on the plight of your character. But I should tell you that Casper is insecure and has a lot on his mind that he's not shared with your Amanda."

"I should tell you that Amanda's about sick of his act."

Their eyes locked, and then they both started to laugh.

"Should we do something about that? There's a lot of sexual and emotional tension building here."

"How do you propose we take care of it, Michael Patrick?"

"I think she should lose it, as you'd say, and start to stalk out of the office, high heels clashing against the hardwood floor —"

"And then?" Lenore licked her lips provocatively, never breaking eye contact.

"And then he goes after her, grabs her, spins her around, and tells her that walking out is not an option. Their eyes lock, and he pulls her to him, kisses her wildly, and backs her against the closed door . . ."

"Maybe we could see how that would . . ."

What she was going to say was lost when he closed the distance between them and kissed her ravenously.

"Then what happens?" she asked breathlessly.

"What would you want to happen, *mo chuisle*?"

"Not me—Amanda. I think she might slap him."

MP moved back a bit.

Lenore laughed, "I'm not going to slap you. I give you my word."

He moved in closer again, "Good, because I heard the wallop you gave Maxwell."

She'd forgotten about that. Didn't want it in her mind now, so she asked, "What would Cass do after she slapped him?"

"He wouldn't let it get that far. He'd intercept her hand mid strike. Then I think he'd restrain her by either pulling her wrists to her side or over her head and continuing on with what he started. He's too aroused at this point to stop unless Amanda tells him to and means it."

"You mean he won't take her by force?"

"No."

"Hmm, maybe you should restrain me, and I'll try and put myself into Amanda's character, and we'll see how it goes."

He gently took her wrists and held them above her head and eased her back on the overstuffed couch, each plundering the other's mouth.

"I want you," she managed.

"Yes," he said almost unintelligibly.

He let her arms go and started to undress her and she him, frantic desperate movements.

The doorbell rang.

"Ignore it," she pleaded. "I'm not expecting anyone. It's probably the UPS man or something."

He didn't need to be told twice and continued on his mission.

Seconds later, the bell rang again, followed by pounding.

"Jesus, I'll get rid of whoever it is," he said.

She let out a sigh as the weight of him left her.

He was buttoning his shirt as he left the office and padded down the stairs. When he looked through the sidelight, he saw it was the guy who met Lenore at her attorney's office. He uttered an oath and opened the door.

"Can I help you?" MP asked.

The man took in MP, and then smirked.

"Sorry if I'm interrupting something. I'm Gerald Morris. I'm looking for Lenore."

"Ms. Held is unavailable at the moment. If you'd care to leave a message or card, I'll make sure she gets it," Michael Patrick said.

"I'm pretty sure she's here, and what I have to say is important and time-sensitive."

"As I said –"

"It's okay, Michael Patrick, I'll talk to him. We'll never have any peace otherwise," Lenore said from the top of the spiral stairway, neatly put together. But it was plainly obvious she'd been recently ravished.

She came down the stairs, and MP stood waiting for her, placing a possessive hand on her back.

"Michael Patrick, this is Gerald Morris," she said by way of introduction.

The two men shook hands, and Lenore ushered Morris into the entryway. When the door was closed, she rounded on him. "I told you to call my attorney. I have never invited either you or your boss to my home, yet both of you think you can show up here. What would Maxwell have to say if I showed up on his doorstep?"

"I should have called first," Morris said, eyes sliding between Lenore and MP.

"You should have called my attorney as you were instructed."

"I wanted to see you again and tell you what Byron had to say."

"I don't want to see you or your boss. You can call my attorney."

"All right, I will, but can I talk to you for a moment . . . alone?" Morris asked, looking pointedly at MP.

She let out a big sigh and turned to MP. "Will you give us a few minutes?"

He nodded and went into the kitchen.

She motioned for Morris to follow her into a small den off the entry.

He moved to close the doors behind them.

"No, leave them open."

He looked at her oddly but left the doors as they were.

"Talk, you wanted to talk. Obviously you stayed somewhere local last night, but I don't know why, and I understand even less why you'd be here when Philadelphia is an hour closer to D.C."

"I had other business in the area last night and thought I'd take a chance and drive out to see you today. I wanted to invite you to lunch with me."

Lenore laughed.

"I see I've disrupted your day."

"You have, as a matter of fact. What is it you wanted to tell me?" she asked with an edge.

"Byron has agreed to your terms. So —"

"You can call my attorney and arrange some possible dates. I will talk to Nate and see if he even wants the meeting and testing or if he wants to tell his father to go to hell. At this point, that would be my preference, selfish as that may sound to you."

"Byron's desperate. If he had other options, he'd use them but he doesn't."

"Isn't he worried his long-ago dalliance could become public? What if Corrine found out?"

"I can't say," Morris said, looking at his hands.

"Right; for all I know, you two could be screwing each other simple. As I recall, you and Byron have a taste for the same women."

He chuckled. "Not the same innocent girl that you were twenty years ago."

"No. Maxwell saw to that in more ways than one, didn't he?" she retorted, but acid was churning in her stomach. Maybe she could make herself throw up on him. She'd had a character do that once, all over a suitor's expensive riding habit.

Morris reached forward and brushed a stray strand of hair away from Lenore's face. When his finger touched her skin, she jumped as if she'd been burned.

"Don't touch me," she hissed through clenched teeth.

"Would you have married me, Lenore, if I had left Maxwell behind all those years ago?"

"I honestly don't know, Gerald. The fact that you told me you wouldn't, didn't make the offer worth my contemplation. I think you should go now."

He looked at her a moment. "I'll call your attorney and make arrangements."

"Do not ever show up here again, Gerald, either you or your boss. I'll get a restraining order. Is that clear?"

"Very." Morris left and closed the door quietly behind him.

As MP was leaving the kitchen to join her, she was making her way to him.

"*Mo chuisle*, are you all right?"

"I'm pissed. Why after all these years are the bottom dwellers rearing their ugly heads?"

"Morris have a thing for you, too?"

"Why do you ask?"

"He looked at me like he wanted to do me bodily harm."

She gave a weak laugh. "I don't know if he did or not. He tried to warn me about Maxwell before I got involved with him and then asked me to marry him when Maxwell treated me like a street corner whore."

"He did?" MP asked surprised.

"Yes, I don't know why. At the time his proposal, if you can call it that, surprised me. Now I don't know if he was trying to clean up one of Byron's messes, if he was being chivalrous, or if he wanted to put one over on Maxwell."

"You mean, like I have your woman and your kid, too?"

"Yes, or maybe he did care for me on some level. I don't know. But I asked him if I agreed to marry him whether he'd leave Maxwell's staff, and he said no. So there was nothing to consider."

"Another fool."

"I'd like to think so."

CHAPTER NINETEEN

The following Wednesday, Lenore and MP were in the kitchen breakfast nook, enjoying crepes with fresh berries. The early morning light cast a warm glow on the table.

"You're spoiling me, *a chuisle*. I like it."

"I seem to like spoiling you too. Makes me feel good."

"You make me feel good."

"Ditto."

Her home phone started ringing.

"It's Nikko," she said looking at caller ID.

"Probably checking in to see if we got any."

"Hello, Nikko," Lenore said with a smile in her voice.

"Hi, Lenore, is MP there by chance? I tried his hotel and he's not answering the phone or his cell."

"Yeah, hold on. MP, Nik is looking for you."

A puzzled expression crossed his face.

Lenore shrugged and handed him the phone. She motioned that she was going to the office. He shook his head and pointed to her seat. Instead of sitting, she poured them each more coffee.

"Have you heard from anyone on the other side of the pond this morning, or afternoon there, now?" Nikko asked.

"No, why?"

"There's a news article in a London gossip rag, *The Sentinel,* do you know it?"

"Hard not to," MP replied with disgust.

"There's a piece you need to read. We need to get on it and do damage control."

"Nik what is it about?"

"I don't want to talk about it, given where you are and who you're with. It's your private business."

"We're beyond that," he said, looking at Lenore.

"All right, LaSandra is mentioned, too, but only as an afterthought or maybe not, I don't know."

"Give me a hint."

"It has to do with a child that was yours, then your sister's and brother-in-law's, then your brother-in-law split, and your sister and son/nephew died in an auto accident. I'm guessing this is the child you went into debt to care for."

"Jesus H. Christ where did that come from? It's true."

"I'm sorry, so very sorry, MP, and I'm sure what's been reported is not the way it happened," Nik said.

"Jesus."

"MP, take a few minutes and read the article, tell Lenore, and then the three of us can have a conference call."

"All right, thanks for the heads-up."

"We need to get out in front of this. If we have to, we'll get legal involved. I have media contacts in London, and the quicker we squash this, the better," Nikko said adamantly.

"I hear you, lass. We'll be in touch."

"What is it?" Lenore asked. "I can tell by your face it's something horrendous."

"Horrendous is too strong a word. I've known horrendous, and I'm pretty sure while it's awful, it's not horrendous. Nikko shot me an e-mail link to *The Sentinel*."

"The British rag that puts any of New York's to shame."

"Yes, there's an article in there about me and according to Nik, you're mentioned or LaSandra is."

"Terrific."

As they ascended the stairs to her office, the warm glow disappeared, she was feeling chilled to the bone, and the hair on the back of her neck was standing up. While she had no clue what the article was about, she thought she knew who could have been behind it. A shiver ran through her.

"Sweetheart, are you cold?" MP asked.

"An American endearment, is that good or bad?" She was trying to make light of the situation.

"Any endearment I call you is good, honey."

"Okay, handsome."

A laugh escaped from deep in his throat as he bent over to ignite the gas fireplace. Then turning, he took her hands, and they sat on the couch in front of the fire.

"I want to tell you everything about my nephew and sister before we read the article. I'm sure the article will portray me as some kind of a monster and –"

"You're anything but a monster. I've known monsters in my time and some of the scariest have been dressed in pinstriped suits and Armani ties."

"Thank you for your vote of confidence."

She shook her head, eyes glistening. "Don't thank me."

He gave her a wink and a weak smile. "I guess we're both guilty of thanking one another for our natural tendencies."

"Don't let anyone know my secret."

"You have my word." He crossed his heart and kissed her lightly.

"Okay, here is the story of my nephew. You already know the ending so —"

"No, wait before you start; I think I know who could have planted or instigated an inflammatory, ugly article."

"I already thought of that and figured you'd make the leap, even though I hoped you wouldn't."

"I'm sorry. Even when I was an intern, Morris was the king of mean. He ran smear campaigns even when they weren't needed. It's as if he's avenging his family somehow. His grandfather, Donald Morris I, had political aspirations, but he was also promiscuous with not only women but men, and even though it wasn't common forty years ago to discuss such things, Morris's grandfather was the topic of much discussion. The Republicans shunned Donald the First.

"Once they were through trashing the grandfather, they moved on to Morris's father, Donald II, who apparently had a bevy of beauties, his all female apparently, but the gossip was devastating to Morris's mother, and she took her own life."

"Tragic."

"Yes, but that does not give Morris license to rape and pillage."

"Why hasn't he gone after Maxwell then?"

"I personally think that Gerald likes to be the puppeteer and pull Maxwell's strings to do his bidding. He's the real power behind the power. Rumor has always been that Maxwell couldn't care less one way or the other about abortion, but that Gerald Morris has an ax to grind with all women, because one of his girlfriends aborted his child."

"Maxwell is a puppet. That's a subject that ninety percent of the population has a strong opinion about. It may even be higher than that."

"I agree."

"Right now, you need to know the story behind my nephew, and we need to call Nikko. We'll deal with Morris and Maxwell later."

"Okay."

"My nephew was biologically my son."

She maintained eye contact, encouraging him to continue.

"Mary, a woman I was casually dating for over a year, became pregnant. When I found out, I asked her to marry me. She told me she wasn't interested in marrying me. She had her eyes set on a bigger catch. At the time, I was a teacher at the local secondary school, not making very much money."

Lenore reached over and took his hand, squeezing it lightly.

"She told me I was good in bed and nice to look at, but she had no wish to become leg-shackled to me. If I'm not mistaken, that's one of your VR terms. She read a number of historical romances and I think that's where she got it."

She smiled slightly.

"We talked about options: abortion, putting the baby up for adoption, my having sole custody. There was no way she wanted to be responsible for the child. About the same time, my sister, Eva, and her husband, Ian, found out they couldn't conceive and badly wanted a child. Eva was several years older than I, was settled, and seemed to have a great marriage. The four of us talked and decided that Eva and Ian would adopt the child and raise it as their own."

"Why didn't Mary have an abortion?"

"Ireland is still a very Catholic country, and abortion is only legal in very specific instances, like when the life of the mother is in danger, and that's subject to strict interpretation. While we could have gone to London for an abortion, she couldn't do it for religious reasons."

"I understand that. While I'm strongly pro-choice, it wasn't my choice. I've never regretted having my son."

"I know you haven't, Lenore, and I never regretted the fact that my son was born either. Eva and Ian adopted the baby and named him Ian Michael."

"After both you and his adoptive father," she offered.

He nodded. "Everything went well for the first eight years until Ian Michael started getting headaches. It took several months of waiting lists, tests, and appointments and then more of the same before he was diagnosed with a cancerous brain tumor the size of a lemon. He was declared terminal, as I said before, and didn't qualify for chemo, radiation, surgery, or a combination of those things under socialized medicine. The only thing he qualified for was hospice." He said this with some bitterness.

"By that time, I'd had some success with my writing and had some money saved. I took him to Sloan-Kettering in New York City. Brought my sister and her husband, too. But the treatments were long and painful and my brother-in-law couldn't take it. He left his family and headed back to Ireland."

"That happens a lot when one parent can't deal with a child's illness."

"Yes, but his departure sent my sister into a tailspin. They had been married over fifteen years, and she didn't know how to live without him. Not only was her child gravely ill, but her spouse had left her and filed for divorce. She started drinking and taking pills to sleep. Eva became an alcoholic and a prescription drug addict."

"I'm sorry, Michael Patrick," she said in a voice barely above a whisper.

"I know you are. I even told Eva she should go back to Ireland and get herself together, try to set things right with Ian. By that point, Ian Michael was starting to show signs of progress. The radiation and chemo were shrinking the tumor, and the doctors were hoping to do surgery soon. Ian was a trouper and no matter how sick he was, he always had a smile for anyone who came in contact with him." MP eyes were welling up now.

"I was able to keep writing while I was in New York, and my books were selling well. But the medical costs kept increasing. I sold my house in Dublin to help pay the bills. My sister and her husband sold theirs as well. My parents died years ago, so it was the two of us."

"It had to be tough on you, being strong for Ian and your sister."

"Yes, and I was starting to become more worried about my sister as the days went by. I was concerned that Eva wouldn't be fit to take care of Ian when he was ready to go home. While Ian got well, my sister got sicker.

"I was Ian's guardian in the event something happened to her. When Ian was released from the hospital, the three of us moved into a house in White Plains that I rented. I thought that once Eva saw Ian was making progress, she'd get her life in order too. She had a child to take care of."

Lenore could see the conflicting emotions warring on his face: anger, frustration, and hope. She soothed a thumb across his knuckles, wanting more than anything to embrace him.

"When Ian finally got the okay to travel back to Ireland, my sister was drunk pretty much 24/7. She had lost weight; her hair was coming out in handfuls as if she was a chemo patient. Eva was destroying herself not only before my eyes but Ian's as well. He was a smart little guy, and he knew his mum was sick."

"Do you have a picture of him?" Lenore asked on impulse.

"I do," he said, digging out his wallet. "This was taken about a month after he got out of the hospital."

"He was beautiful." Truth was, he looked like MP but she couldn't bring herself to say it. She was so moved by the photo, she had to swallow a lump in her throat.

"A real lady killer," he replied ruefully. "All the nurses loved him."

"So did you."

"Goes without saying."

Sadness washed over his face.

"I told Eva I wanted Ian to stay with me for a while when we got back to Dublin. I'd already made arrangements to rent a flat downtown. Of course, she was furious. So I asked her to move in with me until she decided where she was going to live. Eva told me she knew where she and Ian were going to live."

"With Ian senior," Lenore guessed.

"Yes. Eva told me that she had talked to him and that he was thinking about it. But when we all returned, Ian didn't want his wife and son back. Told Eva he couldn't deal with it if Ian Michael had a recurrence of cancer and that he hoped she understood. He even told her to give Ian to me, and then he'd take her back. But she wouldn't do it."

"She should have."

"She should have but she didn't; instead, she was convinced that if Ian senior saw how well his son looked, he'd change his mind. So when I went to the grocery store, she got Ian, put him in the front passenger seat, and proceeded to drive. Eva was intoxicated. Her blood alcohol level was two point four. Ireland's legal limit is point zero eight. She lost control of the car and crashed straight into a concrete barrier. The Garda estimate she was going in excess of ninety miles per hour. They were in a MINI Cooper and didn't stand a chance."

"My God."

"The bodies had to be formally identified by fingerprints. It's the worst thing I ever experienced."

"Yes," she said simply; words were inadequate. Lenore wrapped her arms around him. Tears came, hers and his. It was such a tragic waste of life.

"I need to get a grip here, *mo chuisle*. I'm not finished yet."

"Not finished?" She looked at him with tear-stained eyes.

"Not quite. No one knew that Ian was my son. People knew he was adopted, but everyone assumed it was a private adoption and left it at that. But my former girlfriend came to the funeral home, and Ian senior was out of his mind with grief, having lost Eva forever. The man loved her desperately, and I'm sure he loved Ian Michael in his own way, at least until he got sick. I think he went along with the adoption to make Eva happy, and for eight years it did.

"When he saw me talking to Mary, something came undone in him and Ian started shouting, 'If it wasn't for you and your whore and your fucking bastard, Eva would still be alive. A child conceived in sin is punished. Your fucking bastard killed my wife. You should have let him die like he was supposed to. But no, you have to go to fucking New York City, Mr. Big Man, to save the day. Well, your bastard is dead. You got yours, you fornicating fucking asshole.'"

MP's retelling was so real it was almost as if there were a recording playing in his mind and Ian's poisonous words were spewing forth.

"Then he launched himself at me and tried to strangle me. Several cousins pulled him off. If they hadn't intervened, I'd have been dead, because I hit my head on a marble table on the way down and was knocked unconscious."

"Oh God," she gasped again and took his hands in hers.

"My cousins wanted me to press charges, but I didn't. Thought the man was so grief stricken he'd had a moment of insanity."

"What did your ex do?"

"Fled. Can't say I blame her. Never seen or heard from her again. Mary probably should have stayed away to begin with.

But the Irish are funny about paying their respects to the dead. Being that she carried Ian for nine months, I can see why she came. Accident was all over the newspapers; that's how she knew about it."

Silence settled over them.

"I think we need some air before we read the article," she said, suddenly exhausted.

"I'll go for a walk with you, Lenore, if we can talk."

"Sure—about anything you want to talk about, MP."

He ran a hand down her face and looked into her eyes.

She took his palm and kissed the center of it. "If you're worried about my reaction to what you did, don't be. I think you were incredibly unselfish and believed with all your heart that Ian Michael would thrive in a stable two-parent home."

"You're right, I did."

"You can't change what happened."

"But you kept your son."

"I did."

"You never thought of putting him up for adoption."

"No, I wanted Nate. Maybe even more so because his father didn't."

"Ian Michael's mother didn't want him, and I didn't feel equipped to deal with being a single parent at the time. When Eva found out she and Ian couldn't have children, it almost felt like divine intervention. That the child, my child, was meant to go to my sister and her husband."

"I can see that and I think you made a well reasoned, rational decision as well as a heartfelt one. And if Ian Michael had not gotten ill, chances are it would have stayed that way."

"That's one of the things I love about you, Lenore, you're a thoughtful, compassionate woman."

"Let's go for a walk and then come back and deal with whatever ugliness the rag has spun. Then you can tell me all the other things you love about me." She flashed him a flirty grin, and he gave her a laugh.

CHAPTER TWENTY

"I got a hit on MP Finnegan and LaSandra Lacy on Seeker," Morris told Maxwell in his office on Capitol Hill. Morris routinely, secretly swept his own office for bugs. He could easily have done the senator's as well but figured that would only make his boss more likely to say things he shouldn't.

Seeker was a computer Morris had set up for his covert use. It tracked people he wanted to keep tabs on without any evidence showing up on his home or office computer. Several days ago, he added MP Finnegan to the system.

"What?" Maxwell asked, intrigued.

"Read it." Morris handed him the printout.

"Did you leak this?" Maxwell asked when he finished.

"Are you crazy, Byron? I was going to ask you the same thing, although I don't think you'd have the resources to gather info like this. The point is, you have too much riding on Lenore's cooperation, and we're already on shaky ground. Once she and Finnegan get word, we'll be the only suspects."

"If not the two of us, then who?"

"I don't know. Did anyone follow you to Lenore's?"

"I might be stupid in your eyes, Gerald, but I would have called immediately if someone was following me. I have to admit, once I was out of the Beltway, I didn't pay much attention," the senator commented.

While Morris would like to have berated Maxwell, he didn't, because he hadn't been looking for tails either. Gerald also hadn't shared the fact that he, too, had showed up at Lenore's unannounced and was summarily tossed out on his ass.

"Start paying attention," Morris said mildly.

"Shit." Maxwell slumped into his seat. "They're going to think it's us."

"I already said that, and I haven't heard back from Lenore's attorney confirming the meeting. She might call it off."

"I'll go right to Nathan if she tries to interfere."

"And he'll go right to his mom, who will be pissed and rightfully so."

"But Nate is an adult."

"Lenore is his mother, and they're close. Some senator comes to him confessing he's his father after all this time, and he's not going to call her? Are you delusional, Byron? Before you even meet him, she'll have made sure she's told him the sordid story of his conception and your response to it. My guess is that he'll decide not to see you or, worse, he'll go public, but I can't see that happening. No one wants the media storm this would cause."

Both men sat for a minute, each in his own thoughts.

Morris finally asked, "Corrine?"

"How the fuck would I know? The woman's a beast."

"Tell me how you really feel about your wife, Byron."

"Fuck off."

"Clever and original as always," Morris retorted and continued. "Even if she had you followed to Lenore's, how would she know that MP Finnegan was there?"

Maxwell's eyes blinked nervously.

"Did you Google Finnegan from your home computer?"

The question was met by silence.

"Are you stupid? So maybe it plays this way. Corrine has you followed. Figuring out you went to Lenore's house is not brain surgery. Get an address, do a record search, or her PI does. You Googled Finnegan, because you're useless and jealous. She checks your search history, because she probably does all the time. I bet you never think to clear it. She gives the intel to her henchman and tells them to wreak havoc. She knew Lenore was one of your interns. I'm sure she thinks you slept with her, maybe thinks you're screwing her again. Corrine could be setting you up for a fall, buddy."

"But why now?"

"Why not? You're not such a catch anymore. One son dead. One son terminal. Heck, if divorce is good enough for Tipper and Al, maybe she figures it's good enough for Corrine and Byron. Going after Finnegan could be a warning shot over your bow. Ties in Lenore, but only as an afterthought and only as LaSandra Lacy."

Byron nodded dejectedly.

"You have to admit the two stories have enough similarities to have tabloid legs. If someone gets hold of yours and Lenore's and compares it to Finnegan's, the similarities and contrasts would be good for a series of articles, if someone did it right. Not to mention the traditional press feasting like Henry the Eighth on your sordid life."

Maxwell ran a hand through his hair, pushed out of his chair, and poured a double scotch from the small bar in Morris's office. Downed it and refilled his glass before taking his seat again.

Gerald watched but said nothing about the booze. Instead he resumed. "I venture to guess only bits of that article are true, and Finnegan's agent or attorney or both will be screaming for a front-page retraction above the fold. MP Finnegan's article will no doubt be touchy-feely and gut wrenching. Shit, if his agent, Nikko Martenstein, can manage it, she might be able to get it in *The Sunday Times Book Review*."

"What am I going to do? If this is Corrine, she'll destroy my life, my career; there'll be no run for the White House," Maxwell lamented.

"White House isn't all it's cracked up to be. She takes you down, you write a book, and become a FOX commentator like others have."

Ignoring Morris, Maxwell said, "Let's say it's not you, me, or Corrine. Could it be someone from Lenore's camp?"

"Don't think so. I've kept an eye on her for years and she's been involved with no one who even hits the radar. She's careful with who she brings into her life."

"Seems she likes this Finnegan well enough," Byron spat. "Could they have leaked it themselves, the agency or the publishing house?"

"They're not above doing those things for publicity reasons, but this story is so ugly and inflammatory, I don't see it. This is way over the top."

"I suppose you're right."

"We need to look at this from eye level, Byron." Morris said seriously. "If your story with Lenore hits newsprint, airwaves, and the web, other women will speak out. Tiger Woods and Bill Cosby will be looking like a choir boys."

"Damn it to hell. Maybe we need to start digging in Corrine's garden."

"It's a barren tundra," Morris said with authority. "I'm always digging. It appears, Byron, you're her first, last, and only. Did she come to you a virgin on your wedding night?"

"Jesus."

"Well?"

"Yes. God damn it, yes."

"Thought so—others besides Corrine and Lenore?"

"I don't have to talk about this."

"Fine, don't, but you'd better think about it. This breaks in the news and others will come forward. Maybe Lenore and Corrine will team up to write a book, *Just Another Notch in the Beltway*." Morris started laughing at his own wit.

Byron Maxwell turned and walked from his friend's office.

CHAPTER TWENTY-ONE

Lenore and MP came back from their walk with clearer minds, went to the office, and brought up the article on Lenore's twenty-seven-inch Mac.

"I'm not sure we need to see it in high definition," Lenore said, disgusted, as she took in the article.

It started: "Michael Patrick Finnegan, also known as MP Finnegan, best-selling romance writer, is anything but a real-life romantic hero."

"Don't let it bother you on my account; I have thick skin."

"No one's skin is this thick. It alleges you and Mary were going to seek a back-alley late-term abortion until your sister came to the rescue."

"It's not true. It's okay. Mary should be the one out of her mind. She's not a public figure."

"Maybe you should both sue them for libel and slander."

"Don't want to think about that now. I need to get some information together. Then we need to call Nikko and get this dealt with. I'm sure she's chomping at the bit."

"You're right."

"I thought you guys were calling me right back and that was over three hours ago," Nikko spat into the speakerphone.

"There was a lot to talk about and information to gather," MP responded.

They'd put the phone on the coffee table in front of the couch, so they could sit together.

"I can tell you it's all false," Michael Patrick said and proceeded to tell her the entire story.

"I had no doubt that it was, but we need to combat it."

"I've got all the ammo you need. People. Your people can call my people," he tried to quip. "I've even signed releases for you to get my bank records and names of people at the hospital you can speak with. I've the names of several people who were at the funeral as well."

"Good start," Nikko said simply.

"The bit about the late-term abortion is false. I tracked down my old girlfriend, Mary. She'll make a statement and have her medical records turned over if they'd help. She explained the entire adoption to her doctor and feels confident he would have noted it. You should also know that she is considering a suit against the rag for libel, slander, defamation of character, and anything she can think of."

"What about you?" his agent asked.

"Don't know yet."

"Fair enough."

He spent the next twenty minutes going through the article paragraph by paragraph and gave Nik all the information he could to neutralize it.

"Good stuff—we'll get on this like yesterday."

"Any idea who floated this trash about Michael Patrick? And better yet, how did they know we were collaborating on a book at my 'palatial estate'?" Lenore asked with rueful laughter in her voice.

"A well-placed American source is all we've been able to get. I've been receiving calls all morning. More from Britain and the European Union, a couple of calls from the usual US rags, but that's expected."

MP and Lenore looked at each other, and MP shook his head no. They'd been debating about telling her Lenore's own colorful story but decided against it.

"Do you think we're being followed or, without sounding too dramatic, spied on?" Lenore asked.

"Good question. I don't know," Nik said honestly.

"We're not going out in public much and neither of us even have photos on our jacket covers. While my pseudonym is by no means foolproof, the entire world is not privy to the fact that I'm LaSandra Lacy."

"Either of you have any stalkers or angry exes?"

"What about your gray man?" MP asked Lenore, raising his eyebrows.

"He knows I write for a living but not specifics. He thought you were his replacement, but he'd have no reason to make you as MP Finnegan."

"Who is your gray man?" Nik asked with a trace of humor.

"John Irving."

"Ah, yes. You can tell me that story later."

"Not much to tell."

"Let me get to it," their agent said.

"Call if you need anything," MP offered.

"I will and I'll have you read whatever we plan to put out to make sure it's accurate. I'm looking for a front-page retraction from *The Sentinel*."

MP laughed, "Good luck with that."

"Let me do what I do; in the meantime, go write some squirmy love scenes."

"Will do," they said together.

"Stop it." Nikko said and hung up laughing.

CHAPTER TWENTY-TWO

No names, throwaway phones, voice distortion devices, who would have ever thought? Corrine pondered this as she sat in the remote section of a cement parking garage outside of Nordstrom's in the Crystal City Mall. She started to drag a hand through her hair and stopped when she encountered resistance from the firm hairspray she now used. Last thing she needed was mussed hair when she met friends for lunch later. She was well aware they were already talking about her.

Riiinnng, Riiinnng!

"Damn it," she said to no one as she jumped, startled by the intruding sound.

No pleasantries or preamble, only the robotic voice that she found annoying and unnerving.

"The device is working. Feedback is interesting. I've sent it to you. I think it might be beneficial if you talk to her."

"Why on earth would I do that?" Her robotic voice echoed back at her, making her cringe.

"Safety in numbers, baby, two women scorned. She, too, was an innocent when she met Caligula. He told her the marriage was over. That you hadn't had relations since the first spawn was conceived. Then you turned up pregnant with the spare at the same time he knocked her up."

"I was still married, and she screwed around with my husband."

"She was a twenty-year-old virgin, brilliant but naïve."

"Weren't we all?" She sighed, the sound reverberating back like an eighteen-wheeler on gravel. "I'll think about it."

There was a long pause.

"Are you there?" the mechanical, stilted voice queried.

She murmured something unintelligible.

"I didn't get that."

The phone was already off.

CHAPTER TWENTY-THREE

Friday morning, Lenore was sitting in her office, nursing a cup of tension-tamer tea and a headache. She hadn't felt this level of stress in a long time, if ever. She had been too young and stupid when she tangled with Maxwell the first time to be stressed. Her main concern then had been her unborn child.

The meeting with Maxwell was set for 10:00 Saturday in her attorney's Philadelphia office. Gerald Morris had relayed that all of Lenore's requirements would be met. He'd even been proactive about the article that was printed about MP. He claimed that they were in no way involved, and why would they be since they were trying to obtain help for Maxwell's son through her. While she wanted to believe it was Morris who had orchestrated the article, she had to agree it would have been stupid. But again, if not Maxwell's camp, then who? She'd been asking herself this over and over again. If it was only about MP, that would be one thing, but someone knew they were working together and leaked it. Not many people knew.

She was grateful that Nikko was successful in getting a front-page retraction, complete with a heart-wrenching article about Michael Patrick's fight to save his nephew/son's life.

The rebuttal story was so well written and fleshed-out within such a short time, Lenore wondered if the ugly article wasn't planted by someone as a PR stunt to get this glowing article of MP into the papers. *The New York Times Sunday Book Review* printed the article as well. Questions as to whether MP and LaSandra Lacy were collaborating on a book together were addressed by their agent's response: "I am not in a position to confirm or deny that rumor." Which, of course, would stir up interest in the idea and both of her authors.

Ink was good—dramatic ink was better. Now that MP was "out as a man," it might have a positive impact on the sale of his books, especially in conjunction with the article that showed him as a truly compassionate, unselfish, altruistic person.

The publisher even gave a definitive yes to their collaborative work the Tuesday after the *Times* article.

The scheme worked to his, her, their advantage; in fact, she was beginning to wonder if MP planted it himself. After all, he wasn't overtly distraught about the piece in *The Sentinel*. Maybe she'd ask him. Better yet, why did she think he'd do such a thing? Trust issues on her side, she thought. She'd call Nikko and see if she had come up with anything before confronting MP. Why wouldn't he leak something? He needed the money. He'd said so himself. Author, agents, publishers leaked stuff all the time to boost sales. Why not MP?

"*Mo chuisle*," MP said as he approached her, then reaching out, touched her face with long, sexy fingers that usually made her want to purr when they lingered on her skin.

She unconsciously jumped as if she'd been branded. Angry with herself for the raw emotional reaction, she tried to push the negative thoughts away.

He was looking at her. She saw puzzlement and concern on his face.

"Sorry, I'm distracted. My mind was in some other less hospitable place." She smiled weakly and took his hand, pulling him down next to her. "Between Maxwell and the ugly article on you −"

"Don't worry about me. Nik did a brilliant job with that, so don't let it plague you." Running a thumb over her full bottom lip, he moved in and kissed her lightly.

She didn't return the kiss and didn't meet his eyes.

"Did I do something to upset you, Lenore?" he asked, tipping her face to his.

Meeting his eyes this time, she saw they were cloudy and guarded. "Did you?" she asked before she could stop herself.

"Didn't think so, but tell me what's bothering you. I can't respond unless I know what you're thinking."

Lenore knew the question wasn't one to ask. She silently berated herself. If he had leaked the story, she'd be angry, hurt, and betrayed. If he hadn't, he'd be angry and hurt by her lack of trust in him. She wasn't prepared to deal with the ramifications of either answer.

"Lenore?"

She shook her head. "It's not you, MP. It's me. I need some time to regroup. Would you mind? I need to pack an overnight bag and get my thoughts in order before I meet Nathan at the Omni in a few hours, and I'm in overdrive. My mind is nowhere good."

"I thought I'd drive you down. I don't like the idea of you driving alone."

"You're a sweet man, but I've hired a car. I'll be okay."

"I'm being dismissed, am I, lass?"

"I hadn't thought of it that way. I usually hire a car if I'm going into the city later in the day."

"Smart lady, but did you think to ask or tell me?"

"No, I didn't, MP. I'm used to functioning by myself, taking care of myself, and I've done fine the last two decades." Her annoyance was evident in her voice.

"But you're not by yourself now."

"Michael Patrick, please leave me alone. I function better alone and desperately need to function on all cylinders for the next thirty-six hours."

"Okay, I'll leave you by yourself, Lenore. I'll be at the hotel; call me on my cell if you need me. If I don't hear from you to the contrary, I'll be here Monday at about 10:00, and we can work on the book."

She'd upset him. His calm, formal tone spoke volumes, but she couldn't deal with it, so she nodded her agreement and said, "Thank you. It will be better next week."

He returned the nod and left her office. She heard his light tread on the stairs and then the door closing behind him.

She should have at least kissed him good-bye, Lenore thought darkly. He'd usually have kissed her. But . . . Oh stop, she chided herself. You wanted to be by yourself and so you got your wish—deal with it. With that, she went to her bedroom to pack. MP and what he did or didn't do would have to wait.

****

Michael Patrick got in his rented Toyota Prius and headed toward his hotel. For the life of him, he couldn't figure out what he'd done or, conversely, what he should have done. With any woman it was hard to tell. But Lenore wasn't any woman. He was beginning to fancy her as his.

Maybe that was the problem. He wanted more of her than she was willing to give. That wasn't true, though; she'd told him she enjoyed spoiling him.

That scene in the kitchen made him smile. He could imagine spending lazy mornings with her in the kitchen, more lazy mornings in bed, and then the two of them writing companionably in the large office upstairs on their own projects or collaborated ones. He had imagined there could be more than this one book they shared.

He shook his head as if to clear it. "Think, Finnegan, think," he said to himself while at a stoplight and lightly pounded the steering wheel. He jumped when he accidentally hit the horn. The driver in front of MP flashed him the finger. "Jesus."

More focused now, he thought back to the phone call from Nik. But even then, after he'd poured out the whole incredible tale of his nephew/son, Lenore understood and accepted his motivations and was not repulsed or horrified by them. On the contrary, she thought they were unselfish.

What was it then? Hell if he knew. Well, at least she couldn't walk away. They had a book contract to fulfill, and he knew she took her work very seriously. He'd have time to figure out what had gotten hold of Lenore Held. Maybe it was that she was simply stressed out and needed time to herself.

Pulling into a parking space at the hotel, he suddenly hit the steering wheel again. The horn blared this time, but he didn't care. "Damn it, Lenore," he said, angrily slamming the car door shut as he got out.

*****

Lenore's mind continued to race as she settled into her two-bedroom suite at the Omni. The accommodations were elegant and well appointed, but she didn't pay much attention. She ordered up tea from room service, sighed, and slumped into the Federal-style blue couch. Nathan wasn't expected to join her for several hours, and she knew exactly what she was going to tell him. She'd had the conversation in her mind many times over the years. The unknowns were how her son would react to the news and what questions he might ask. While she was concerned about the conversation, there was nothing to do about it at present.

The more immediate concern was her nagging doubts about MP. She knew she had trust issues with men but . . . "Oh hell," she muttered digging out her cell phone.

"Nik, sorry to bother you, but have you come up with any new information as to who leaked or planted the story on MP?"

"Well, hello to you, Lenore," her agent said with a lilt in her voice. "No, I don't know anything else."

Lenore didn't say anything for a few seconds.

"Why?" Nikko asked.

"I'm going to talk to you as a friend, woman to woman, okay?"

"Is this something I want to hear, giiirrrlfriend?"

"I don't know, but you're the only one I can talk to about it."

"I'm all ears."

"Do you think MP could have orchestrated the release of the *Sentinel* article himself?"

"Why on earth would you think that?" Nikko asked, truly taken aback.

"I don't know, but it's been gnawing at me."

"Why? MP is full of Irish charm but I've always found him to be an honest man, a man of integrity."

"I agree with you, I guess, but he didn't seem that upset, and he had all the information at his fingertips, who to talk to, who to get releases to, even tracking down his old girlfriend."

"You don't trust him."

It was a statement.

"I want to, Nik. But if you didn't leak it, and I didn't leak it" – and Maxwell's camp didn't leak it, a thought she kept to herself – "who did?"

"Addy?"

"I don't think she knows about Michael Patrick's nephew or his financial problems," Lenore said with a trace of impatient humor and raked the hair back from her face.

"Why would he do it?"

"Financial gain? Increase sales of his books? That follow-up article you did was very moving. What woman who reads romance wouldn't like to see what MP writes about sex and love after reading a piece like that? He's admitted he needs money –"

Nik cut her off, a bit exasperated. "While I'm not doubting what you say at all, I don't see it. The story was tabloid trash at its best."

"Okay, and I might even buy it if it didn't mention the bit about LaSandra Lacy and MP Finnegan writing a book. Who knows about that?" she asked, then continued hotly, "You, me, MP, your partner, maybe your staff, and Addy. Who else?"

"I still don't see it, Lenore. I'm sorry."

"Then do me a favor, question your staff and I'll ask Addison," Lenore said aggressively. "I don't want it to be MP, but I have to know it's not."

"Why not ask him, Lenore?" her friend said softly.

"I almost did. Instead I about threw him out of my house."

"Nice move."

"Yeah," she replied in a breath. "I hate myself for not trusting him."

"It's not him, honey. It's you and your relationship with him; if you can't trust him . . ." Nik let the rest trail off.

"I know. The thing is I'm think I'm falling for him."

"Giirrrlfriend, you'd fallen before you fell into bed with him. It's mutual. It's written on both of your faces. I saw it when we had lunch the other day. Can't you let yourself be happy? We've never talked about what made you so independent and self-contained, but I bet it's a story that rivals MP's."

Lenore said nothing. It was too close to the truth.

"I'm right, aren't I?"

"Yes."

"Call MP. Tell him you love him."

"I can't until I know."

"All right, I'll ask my staff Monday. Since it's Friday, everyone bolted for the door."

"Even Hubble?"

"No, he's still here."

"Is he keeping you company?" Lenore asked, lightening her tone.

"As a matter of fact . . ."

"I knew it. He's the one you're warming the sheets with."

Nikko laughed.

"Don't say a word. I think I have my answer."

"Try and relax, Lenore."

Like that's gonna happen, she thought.

****

Nolan Hubble leaned casually on Nikko's doorframe until he got her attention. "You look way too serious for a Friday afternoon, babe." He continued into her office, sitting on the corner of her desk to face her.

She gave him a half-smile and took him in. He was so unlike Howard, who had been short and wiry. Nolan was tall with the build of a runner. His hair and eyes dark as night except for a few gray stands at his temples.

"I was thinking about who could have leaked the article on MP. Lenore Held is a friend and a client and she's very upset over it." Nik said as she absently removed a piece of lint from his perfectly tailored charcoal-gray suit.

"Why, the retraction was brilliant. Sales for both of their books should increase, and their collaboration will be a best seller before it hits the stands."

The way he said it had Nikko Martenstein cocking her head and pushing away from her desk.

"What do you know about this, Nolan?"

"Nothing," he replied, smirking, taking her hand, and kissing it.

"Nothing my ass. You leaked it." She took her hand from his.

His dark eyes bore into her.

"Do you deny it?" She wanted him to. Now she knew how Lenore felt.

"I neither confirm nor deny," Nolan responded. "But the results will be magnificent regardless of where it came from."

"You arrogant son of a bitch. They are both my clients, Hubble; you had no right."

"Hubble, is it now?" He asked eyebrow arched.

"Would you prefer 'fucking prick'?" She was going for caustic now. "Who in the hell do you think you are? You don't even know LaSandra Lacy or MP Finnegan, and except for our partner meetings, you would know nothing of them working together or why. That's privileged information, Hubble."

"I never said I leaked it."

"You never said you didn't, did you? Look me in the eye and tell me you didn't do it."

He couldn't.

"Why? And why so ugly? My God, MP Finnegan is a GD selfless man."

"Calm down, babe. The tabloid probably got a hint of the story and ran with it. They got hold of the ex-brother-in-law, he wanted his fifteen minutes of fame and told a whopper of a tale." Nolan went to her and attempted to take her hands.

She pulled them out of reach. "Don't babe me. I'm not your babe, or are you simply too ignorant to remember my name? It's Mrs. Martenstein."

He shut up.

"Did you think to discuss it with me?"

"I would think you'd be happy regardless how the article got there."

"Happy to cause two important clients, two dear friends, pain? They're working on a book together, have begun to embark on a personal relationship that has a whole more promise than the one we're in, and you say I should be happy?" she raged, her right hand moving in a sweeping motion. "You're a jackass. Is this how you conducted business at your other firm? No wonder you're no longer there."

"I would have thought the outcome was a good surprise."

"What?"

"MP needs money, his books sell, he gets money. LaSandra's linked and inked to him, her sales increase, their yet-to-be-finished book gets press and forces the publisher's hand to make a commitment."

"You should get a black eye and a broken jaw." She needed to call Lenore. Nikko would not tell Hubble that Lenore thought it was MP who leaked the story for financial gain. Poor Lenore. Poor MP.

"Are you done?" he asked.

"With you? Yes."

"You should be thanking the person who leaked this."

"And you have the morals of Bernie Madoff. Get out before I call security and have them come and take you out."

"You can't be serious."

"As serious as the massive coronary I'm wishing on you this moment. Get out." Her deadly calm voice was punctuated by the stapler she casually lifted and lobbed at his head.

"Ha. Direct hit," she trilled as she picked up the tape dispenser.

"Crazy bitch!" Nolan Hubble bellowed as he fled her office holding his bleeding head.

Nikko got up and closed her door, locking it for good measure.

"Howard, what in the fuck did you leave me with?" she asked the air with tears in her eyes.

She needed to call Lenore, and then she needed to track down her attorney and see under what provisions she could break the partnership agreement with Hubble. Since he didn't and wouldn't admit to any wrongdoing, she had a feeling she was screwed.

****

MP was not going to let this rest. He was not prone to the stereotypical bouts of legendary Irish temper, but he was there at the moment. He sat on the edge of the hotel bed and called her cell.

Thirty miles away, Lenore looked at her caller ID.

"Answer it or let it go to voice mail? Suck it up, answer," she asked and answered herself. "Hello, Michael Patrick."

"Ask."

She hesitated.

"Ask. You need to know the answer."

"Did you have anything to do with the article?"

"No, Lenore, I didn't. But the bigger question for me is why did you think I did, or why did you not trust me enough to ask me to give you an honest answer?"

"I don't know. I'm sorry."

"Yes, you do, Lenore," he said with an edge.

"I knew either way I'd lose. You'd be offended or hurt that I asked, or I'd be devastated if you leaked it."

"So pushing me away was a better outcome?" he asked, voice rising.

"No," she replied, tears stinging the back of her eyes.

"You'll trust your body to me but not your heart and mind. I need your trust more than I need your body. Without trust, the other is simply sex, and I'm not willing to make it just sex between the two of us." God, he wished he could see her.

She was silent.

"I know," she finally said.

"Think about whether or not you believe me and whether or not you can trust me. If you can't give me affirmative answers to both, we need to go back to being business associates."

"I can't do this right now," she said in a strangled voice.

"I agree. You have enough on your plate at the moment. I'll see you on Monday. If you need me, call my cell."

"Michael Patrick," she began, but he'd ended the call. "Damn it."

Her phone rang again—Nikko this time.

"Lenore, it wasn't MP," her agent said without preamble.

"I know."

"You asked him?"

"Not exactly."

"He figured out what was bothering you on his own?"

"Yes."

"Was he angry?"

"Yes."

"I'm sorry, Lenore. It was Nolan Hubble."

"My God," she breathed, shocked. "I'm sorry. I would have nev –"

Her agent cut her off, speaking fast and agitated now. "No, I wouldn't have imagined it either, but he did. Oh, he didn't admit it; he was too smart to do that. But rest assured, he did it. Thought I should be happy with the outcome, too. More money for everyone. Great PR for the new book. Fucking jackass."

"Yes he is. I'm sorry, Nikko."

"Me, too. I was starting to enjoy his company. But I have a business to run and Howard's legacy of integrity and hard work to maintain. I'll be talking to my lawyer to see what steps I can take to get rid of him. I own two-thirds of the company since Howard died; that should count for something.

"I'm sorry he did this to you and Michael Patrick. Do you want to call and tell MP or should I? I'll need to have a formal meeting with the two of you about this once I piece it together. Since Hubble won't admit anything directly, and I'm sure he was smart enough to make sure no tracks are left to trace, it will be tough to do anything legally, and *The Sentinel* will never give him up."

"But why? We weren't his clients; we don't even know him well."

"I don't know. Maybe because he could. While I found him amusing and good in bed, he's also very arrogant."

"I think he was trying to impress you."

"With what a fucking asshole he was? Well, he succeeded."

"I'll call Michael Patrick. He deserves an apology," Lenore said, moving back to topic. She knew how upset Nikko had to be right now. "Call me if you need to talk or need anything at all."

"Thanks, you're a good friend, and tell MP I'll be talking to him soon."

"Will do. Go have a double."

"I might."

****

Nikko sat in her office and let the tears flow. She was not easily given to tears, but she let them swamp her. She had been starting to have feelings for Nolan Hubble. Despite his irascible arrogance, he'd made her laugh and made her hot. Now he'd made her cry and that was unforgivable. The only time Howard had made her cry was when he died.

There was a knock on her door. She ignored it.

"Nikko, let me in; we need to talk."

She ignored him and walked to her small refrigerator to get bottled water. She had been thinking champagne and strawberries, but such is life.

"Nik, honey, let me in."

Nolan, asshole, go away, she thought but said nothing.

This time he pounded on the door. "Nik, you're scaring me."

"Yeah?" Wham! Wham! "You should be really fucking frightened now." She'd flung her black suede Ferragamo Fioretta pumps with four-inch heels at the door.

A while later, she called her attorney and left a message, returned some e-mail, and finally left her office to face a long weekend alone. Nikko knew she'd get over it. If she could begin to move on after Howard, she'd get over Nolan Hubble.

****

"Pick up, pick up, pick up," Lenore chanted to herself, willing MP to answer the phone.

"Hello," he panted.

He was breathing hard and it was noisy.

"Where are you?"

"The fitness center up the street from the hotel. I decided to work off some energy."

She couldn't help but smile at the thought that she'd made him so angry he went to blow off steam.

"Stop flattering yourself, Lenore."

She laughed at his mind reading. "You've gotten to know me pretty well in a fairly short time."

"I don't think I know you at all," he said soberly.

"I'm sorry. I already believed you. You ended the call before I could tell you. Then Nikko called and told me Hubble set up the whole mess. She said she'd call you, but I wanted to."

MP was quiet for a minute. He'd moved to an empty stairwell. "I had to get somewhere I could talk. The patrons here get downright hostile when you talk on the phone."

She gave a small laugh. "I know; I have a membership there."

"Why?" he asked, getting back to the topic at hand.

"I don't know. I think he was trying impress her, if you want my opinion, and it backfired."

"That's who she's been sheet-surfing with then?"

"Yes. I feel terrible for her. She was starting to get over Howard and put herself out there again. She's calling her attorney to see what, if anything, she can do about the partnership. But while it was definitely Nolan, he didn't directly admit to doing anything."

"Jackass," MP muttered.

"I agree."

They were silent for a minute.

"I should have asked you if I had questions," Lenore said. "I should have trusted you, and while I didn't think you had anything to do with the newspaper story, there was lingering doubt in the back of my mind. You were so calm about the whole thing, so prepared with the answers to all the ugly accusations, and then the retraction article was so well done in such a short period of time, it seemed like it was written beforehand. You know, like a celebrity obit."

"If I'd been involved, it would have been the death knell for our relationship, but I wasn't involved. I was, in fact, very pissed about the piece, but you had enough to be dealing with. Thinking Maxwell's group planted it, getting the meeting set up with Nate. I didn't want to add anymore to your stress level by losing it."

"You were trying to protect me," she said faintly.

"Yes, *mo chuisle*, or at least not add to your burden."

She was touched. "Will you forgive me?"

"Will you work on trusting me, and ask me before you push me away and shut me out?"

"I'll do my best. I want to trust you. But I don't give trust easily, and I'm pretty independent."

"I've noticed. I forgive you."

"Thank you."

"While you raise my anger to the boiling point quickly, it's hard for me to stay angry with you long. I wish I'd gone with you. I wish you hadn't pushed me away."

"I'll be home late tomorrow afternoon, and I'll do my best to pull you close if you'll let me."

"Your plan has potential, Ms. Held. Now go relax before your son joins you. You'll need your strength."

"I feel better now that I've talked to you."

"You'll be in my thoughts this evening, *a chuisle*."

"I hope you'll be in my dreams, Michael Patrick."

"I'll be in your bed if you keep it up. You're only down the highway."

"I'd like that, but I don't think it's a good idea. I –"

"I understand, Lenore. I was teasing you."

"Michael Patrick?"

"Yes, love."

"I want this to work between us. I'll work at it. Be patient with me, and I'll try not to make you too crazy."

"You've already made me crazy. But I want this to work too, so I'll be patient, and if I can't, I'll be in your face."

"Fair enough. Don't let any hot babes try and pick you up."

"Only hot babe I want is you. Good-bye, Lenore.

CHAPTER TWENTY-FOUR

"Mom!" Nate came through the hotel room door and gave Lenore a hug and kiss. She was lucky her son was always generous with his show of affection and had never gone through the stage of shunning his mother like a lot of children, maybe because it was only the two of them.

"You made good time. No traffic?"

"Only a little on the way out of D.C., but that's to be expected on a Friday."

He tossed his duffle bag and backpack in the second bedroom of the suite and joined her in the sitting area. She was looking out the window at the historical section of Philadelphia, manic butterflies jumping in her stomach.

"Mom?"

She turned. "I know you're eager to hear this, so let's just do it."

"Like Nike," he added with a half-smile.

"Yes. First let me tell you who your father is. I could do a big lead-up and explanation, but what you want to know is simply who."

He nodded, not saying anything, but looking excited and eager.

"Your father is Senator Byron Maxwell from Virginia." She watched for a reaction, any reaction. Nate sat there stunned and speechless.

"Nate, honey, are you okay?" She reached out and touched his arm.

"Umm," he sat for a minute as if gathering words. "Mom, no offense, but the guy's a right of the right asshole."

"You're correct, and I'm sorry, but it's true."

"Okay, okay," he said and got up to pace the room a bit. "Not what I expected. No wonder you kept it a secret for so long."

"Nate, I kept it a secret, because I gave my word to keep it a secret."

"So you've always said. You sure you weren't embarrassed by your bad taste in men?"

It was said so deadpan she didn't know if he was making a joke or serious.

"I was attempting to be funny, Mom." He came back to her and sat down on the couch.

"Ask me any questions you want, Nate. I'll be honest and give you all the answers you want."

"Why does he want to meet me now?"

"You may have read this in the papers; his son, Jack, has malignant myeloma and needs a bone marrow transplant."

"He wants to use me to see if my bone marrow is a match," Nate said ruefully. "If his remaining son wasn't sick, he'd never have made the overture."

"I can't say one way or the other, but you're right, that's why he contacted me." She was pleased that her son didn't have rose-colored glasses and saw what was what. Lenore continued, "I wanted to tell him to go to hell and did in so many words, but thought I'd let you decide what you want to do. I made it clear to his chief of staff, Gerald Morris that the decision was yours to make. If you want to see Maxwell and hear him out, you can. If you don't want to see him and hear what he has to say, there is no meeting."

"He's not looking to make this public, is he?" Nate asked, fear crossing his face.

"No, it would end his marriage, his career, not to mention the turmoil the media would cause in all of our lives," she replied, keeping her answers short and to the point, trying to be the "better person" and not allow her personal animosity to influence her son's decision.

"Thank goodness for that. I don't want anyone knowing I'm related to that man. I know Jack Maxwell is gravely ill, but he's an asshole, too."

"I didn't realize you knew him," she said surprised.

"Yeah," he said, getting up and pacing again. "He went to school at Georgetown before he got sick; he would have graduated with me this year, in fact."

"I didn't know Nate. And Maxwell or Morris didn't mention it."

"Probably hoping I didn't know him. Hoping Jack's behavior wouldn't color my decision to consider a bone marrow transplant or not," Nate said testily.

She wanted to probe but didn't know if she should.

"Why him of all people, Mom?" Her son was angry.

"I was his intern. I was young and stupid in the ways of men and love."

"Did he ever tell you he loved you?"

"Yes."

"You believed him and slept with him."

Again, she thought they'd never slept together, but that wasn't her son's meaning behind the word, and she said, "Yes."

"Jesus, how could you have been so stupid?" He was almost yelling.

Before she could stop herself, she responded abruptly, "I might have been stupid, but I have you. I never regretted having you. Even if you share Maxwell's genetic material, you are my son, not his. You are nothing like your sperm donor." Tears were welling in her eyes—she wasn't sure how they got there. Blinking furiously, she was trying to keep them at bay.

"Oh, Mom, I'm sorry, I didn't mean to . . . I'm sorry." He embraced her and held her for a minute.

She pulled away and looked at Nate.

"I'm sorry, Mom. You're terrific, and I couldn't ask for a better parent. But I figured you'd have hooked up with someone cooler than Byron Maxwell."

She arranged her mouth in what she thought was a smile. "Sorry to disappoint."

"What do you think I should do?" he asked her, calmer now.

"I'm probably not the right person to ask. I'm your mother and want to protect you from anything that could cause you hurt or harm."

"But you've never been crazy overprotective either. Tell me what you think, both sides of the coin. I know you've thought of both sides."

"I've thought of a lot of sides. But it's important that you do what's best for Nathan Held. I know that sounds like a parental copout but . . ."

He nodded, and then asked, "Maxwell paid you off to stay away?"

"Stay away, stay silent. His wife had the money and —"

"If he divorced her to be with you or acknowledged the fact he fathered an illegitimate child, she would have divorced him. Either way he would have been penniless and lost his political career as well."

"Most likely."

"The man was a spineless coward."

"Yes, but I wasn't. I was determined to have you and raise you to the best of my abilities. I think I did a pretty good job, too. I told someone the other day you were my magnum opus, my best work."

"Sappy, Mom, but thanks."

She laughed. "Maxwell's money, most likely his wife's, allowed me to finish grad school and get my writing career off to a solid start. Writing made being a single mother easier for me. I could work anytime, anywhere. If you needed me, I was there. If you were home sick from school, I could be there and not worry about having to take the day off. Even though I didn't plan my life to be what it was, it worked out fine."

"But you never had your own life until I left for college either."

"My choice, not Maxwell's or yours. I wrote and took care of you. It was what I did. Plus, you have a tidy nest egg to give you a solid start in life. Once I didn't need Maxwell's money for rent and food, I invested it for you."

He nodded. She could see he wasn't sure how he felt about Maxwell's money.

"But you could have made millions if you went to the press. Sold your story to the highest bidder," Nate came back.

"Not my style. I would have come off looking like a slut, home wrecker, gold digger, whatever term you prefer. I'm a private person for the most part, and going public was not my thing."

"Did he ever contact you and find out how I was doing? Ask for pictures of me? Anything?"

"No."

"He didn't want to know me."

"I don't know what he wanted."

They sat on the couch in silence for a moment.

Nathan said, "One day at school, someone thought I was Jack Maxwell. I remember I laughed and said, 'Thank goodness I'm not,' and the girl who confused me for him said, 'No, you're eyes are different, beautiful. Jack's are ice-cold.'"

"You do look like Byron, so if you meet him, be prepared

for that. The young woman was right; you don't have cold eyes. Your father does."

They talked a long while. Nate asked her tons of questions, and she answered them as honestly as she could.

Finally, Nate asked, "When do I have to decide if I want to meet him?"

"Meeting is set for ten in Connor Walker's office. The ball's in your court, honey. You're in control; remember that regardless if you go to the meeting or not."

"I'll think about it. Let's have dinner and talk about something else, like your new book project."

"You're on. Where?"

"Ruth's Chris."

"You got it."

****

Lenore and Nate talked about the book at dinner. She even mentioned Michael Patrick and the fact that they were doing more than writing a book. Nate was happy for her. She knew he secretly worried about her being alone as he went on with the next phase of his life. Lenore thought it was sweet.

Then he shocked her by telling her about a young lady he was seeing, Kelly Hyde. He seemed to be smitten and wanted Lenore to meet her. It was only the second time since Nate went to college that he had wanted to introduce her to his girlfriend. She told him to let her know when, and she'd be there. He'd suggested she bring MP, and they could double date. They both shared a good laugh.

By the time dessert arrived, they were back to his father.

"I think I'll meet him," he said, stirring cream into his coffee.

She nodded.

"After I spent the last two years making you crazy. Trying to get you to tell me who he was. I hate to say it, but it's pretty anticlimactic."

"Sorry."

"I still don't get it."

"I was young, honey. He was older and seemed so wise. People did try and warn me away, but I thought I was different. Thought he loved me . . ." She sighed wistfully. "It was the infatuation of a young girl."

"He took advantage of you, Mom, and was old enough to be your father. It's one thing when two coeds go at it and get in trouble, but he knew better. He was a pig."

She smiled at her son's defense of her. "You're a smart kid. I'm lucky to have you."

"We're lucky to have each other," Nathan said, lightly touching his mother's hand.

CHAPTER TWENTY-FIVE

Lenore had arranged for her and Nathan to arrive at the attorney's office at 9:30. She figured that would give Nate time to settle in. He'd agreed that he wanted Lenore to be with him for at least the first part of the meeting.

"They say that you should always bring someone with you to the doctor's when facing potentially bad news. So the other person can take in the information and ask questions. This is kind of one of those times," Nate said.

"I agree, but I'll leave if you want to discuss anything private with him."

"We'll see. I'm not sure I want to discuss anything. And you know the chance of me being a match for the transplant is only about twenty-five percent. I was doing some research, and I'd guess the fact that we're only half-brothers makes the likelihood of a match even lower."

Lenore nodded. She'd been doing her own research on the matter. "I think Maxwell is desperate. It's my understanding that Jack is critically ill."

"Did they check the National Marrow Donor Program?"

"Yes. There are no matches."

"He's grasping at straws."

"Yes. As a parent, I understand wanting to do everything you can to save your child. Plus, if you're a match, the concern over contaminated blood is lessened."

"Come on. They test that blood extremely well. There are strict protocols. Chances are more likely that I have an STD. Don't worry, I don't," he added with a wicked smile.

She gave an exaggerated eye roll.

"You need to remember to have safe sex. You can still get pregnant and/or get a sexually transmitted disease." Nathan was carrying on with chatter as he did when he was nervous, so she played along.

"Thanks, but you are twenty years too late with that advice. Would you like a brother or sister?" she added.

That stopped him. "You're not . . ."

"No, I'm not." She openly laughed at the horrified look on his face.

"Phew," he said with an exaggerated swipe of hand over his brow. "I never thought about siblings. If you met someone and wanted more kids, I don't care. But don't ask me to change diapers or babysit."

"Deal."

"So this thing with you and the guy is pretty serious?"

"It could be. I'm not good with trusting men."

"I guess you can thank the senator for that."

"I suppose. But I'm working on it. MP's had a crazy life too, so I think we're evenly matched in that department. There's an article coming in *The Times Book Review* section tomorrow. Read it. It will make my saga look like a fairy tale."

"Okay," he said, warily raising an eyebrow.

There was a knock on the conference room door. Connor Walker came in to join them.

"I wanted to let you know that both Maxwell and Morris are here. They're using the facilities at the moment."

"Morris wasn't part of the deal," Lenore said hotly.

"That's why I'm here. If you want him to wait in my office, I'll keep him out," Connor Walker said.

"Keep him out," Nate said. "I don't know him, but I don't want him to be part of this."

Walker looked at Lenore. "Keep him out," she agreed.

Several minutes later, Maxwell joined them.

While both father and son were aware of the fact that they looked alike, coming face to face stunned both of them into silence.

"Nathan Held," Nate finally said.

"Byron Maxwell," the senator returned. "Lenore," he continued, acknowledging his son's mother.

She nodded and said nothing.

Maxwell went on, "You look good, Lenore."

Lenore nodded again and thought he looked like shit but didn't say it.

No one spoke.

Lenore thought Maxwell was afraid to speak, so she kicked off the meeting.

"Senator Maxwell, why don't you explain to Nathan why you wanted to meet him."

"I didn't want to meet him. You said he had a right to meet me if I wanted him to be tested to see if he's a suitable match to be a bone marrow donor for Jack."

Strike one and two, Lenore thought.

Nathan looked at his father with a combination of annoyance and hurt.

Maxwell blurted again, "So will you do it?"

"Get tested?"

"Yes."

"I suppose, but not because of you or Jack, but because it's the morally right thing to do."

Maxwell let out a sigh of relief. "Thank you."

Lenore was surprised he had the grace to string those two words together.

"But," Nate said, "if I am a match, before I agree to donate the bone marrow, I want to talk with Jack."

"I don't think that can be done. His condition is precarious, and I'm sure you're aware that your existence has been kept under wraps."

"Of course, and I don't want anyone to know I'm your biological son. Trust me on that, Senator, but I do know your son, even been mistaken for him once."

Maxwell gave a pained look.

"Not to worry, Father. Once the person saw my eyes, she knew she was wrong. I have your former intern's eyes."

Wow, Lenore thought, her son was pissed at both Byron and Jack.

Nate continued, "I have a few things to say to Jack, and if I'm donating part of my body to save his life, I want to make sure it's a life worth saving."

Lenore had no idea what Nate was talking about but could tell that something he knew about his half brother set him off.

"You've met Jack?" Maxwell finally asked.

"Yes."

"I see. I still don't think it's a good idea. You meeting him."

"Don't you trust him to keep his bastard half brother a secret?" Nate asked.

Maxwell's silence was telling.

"I see," Nate said. "If that's the case, maybe you should make other arrangements, because that is my condition for considering the procedure."

Byron's color was bright red.

"I want to make sure your son, Jack, does not plan to live his life the way he did before he got sick."

Lenore's interest was piqued. Maxwell must have known what Nate was referring to, because he didn't ask what Nate was talking about.

"Why don't we see if you're a match and then discuss this further if you are?"

"No problem, Senator Maxwell. I needed to be up front with you about the conditions."

"Did you put him up to this, Lenore?" Maxwell spat at her.

"I don −" Lenore began.

"My mother has no idea what I'm talking about. She didn't even know that Jack attended Georgetown."

Strike three, she thought.

"Sorry, Lenore," the senator offered grudgingly.

Like hell you are, she thought.

"Nate do you have anything you want to ask the senator?" his mother asked when the silence dragged.

"Nope. Nothing I want to know and nothing productive to say."

"Senator Maxwell?" She looked to him now.

"Can't you call me Byron?"

"No. Anything else?"

When he didn't respond, she said, "Give my attorney the information Nate needs to be tested."

"It has to be done ASAP," Maxwell said.

"I understand and will do it in an expedient manner," Nate assured him.

"I'll get the info to Walker."

"If there's nothing else, I think we're done here. Mother? Senator Maxwell?"

When neither spoke, Nate got up, and so did his parents.

Connor Walker met them in the hallway.

"Senator, your chief of staff is in the guest office up the hall on the right."

"Thanks."

"Lenore, Nate, if you'd come to my office for a few minutes, I have some things to discuss while you're here."

"Sure."

Connor closed the door behind them.

"I wanted to give them a minute to leave before you. Morris thinks someone might be following one or both of them." The attorney left mother and son to talk in private.

"Great," Nate said sarcastically. "I'm serious. I don't want anyone to know he's my father. There's no need, and if word gets out that my mother's alter ego had his love child, the media will go wild. And Mom, I'm sorry, but you most likely are not the only young woman he took advantage of."

"No apology needed, honey. I know I'm not."

"Those other women start crawling out of the woodwork and —"

"Do not go there, Nate. I've had nightmares about it."

Fifteen minutes later, mother and son were on their way.

CHAPTER TWENTY-SIX

Corrine detached the media card that was taped under the ATM at the health club. She couldn't believe she'd resorted to this type of behavior. If it weren't for Morris, she wouldn't have to. Maxwell wasn't bright enough to have her followed and investigated, but his chief of staff was.

Once home, she popped the card into her laptop. She waited for it to load.

Pictures, lots of pictures, while they confirmed her suspicions, were useless for her purposes.

They showed Morris and Maxwell going into a Philly office building thirty minutes after Lenore Held and her son entered the same building. She wanted pictures of Maxwell and Held and her son coming and/or going together. While she could infer plenty from them both being in the same spot at the same time, it left room for argument and question.

She cropped one of the photos and zoomed in on Nathan Held's face. The resemblance was unmistakable; even without DNA evidence, Lenore Held's son was Byron's. She had long suspected he was.

Byron and she had fought bitterly and violently over Lenore Held. Corrine was convinced he was having an affair with her, and he vehemently denied it. The memory was still devastating.

"I know you're having sex with your intern, and I'll not be the subject of gossip and pity because you're a cheating pig."

"I'm not fucking Lenore Held, Rin. She has better taste and class than to screw me." Implying that Corrine didn't.

"Bastard," she had spewed and had hauled off and slapped him.

He had grabbed her wrist and held her fast.

"But if I was sleeping with her, no one could blame me. You've denied me since before Carter was born."

He pulled her closer, taking her mouth with a bruising force, pushing his tongue through her unwilling lips while he plunged his hand into her dressing gown, grabbing her breast roughly. He pinched her nipple hard and twisted it.

Corrine tried to push him away, bringing her hands to his shoulders. But she was no match for his strength, anger, or desire.

He wrapped his free hand around her waist and ground his erection into her pelvis.

"I'll take what's mine, Corrine, if you won't offer it. I'm tired of you denying me."

Corrine was panicked as he pushed her down on to the bed. His full weight was on top of her. She couldn't breathe. "Stop," she sobbed. "Please stop."

He didn't. He seemed possessed. Maxwell got a hand between them and ripped off her underwear and then somehow opened his fly. He forcibly parted her knees with his own and violently shoved into her.

The pain rippled through her. He was thrusting into her hard and fast. Each invasion designed to humiliate and punish her. Tears escaped her eyes. She thought the brutal assault would never end.

When he'd spent his semen in her, with a grunt he finally stopped. Then Byron got up and looked at her as if seeing her for the first time. "Sorry," he had said, running a hand over his face, stuffing himself into pants, and leaving the room.

Six weeks later, and much to her distress and dismay, she had found out she was pregnant.

Corrine had prayed that she'd miscarry, even thought of having an abortion but couldn't face the fallout at the time.

Now she had massive guilt over her second son's illness. Because of his traumatic conception, she had never bonded with him, and now he was most likely terminal. Although it appeared that Byron was attempting contact with his illegitimate child in an effort to save Jack's life. Did he deserve praise or was this simply another self-centered act?

She almost didn't care. She was going to destroy her husband, even if she destroyed herself and others along with him. Corrine was not about to see Maxwell as president, and she was not under any circumstances going to be his First Lady. She wanted to be free. Free of him, free of Jack and his illness, free of the overwhelming sadness and anger that now filled her life.

Later that day Corrine went to see Jack. She knew it was simply out of a guilty obligation, but she went anyway.

She quietly entered his private room and saw him dozing. He had looked so much like his father until the cancer got him. Now he looked like a cross between a shriveled child and a dried-up old man—sad, maybe even tragic. She had certainly become the object of pity among her circle of friends and acquaintances. Truth was, she knew lots of people but couldn't think of one true friend. Because of her marital situation, she kept a distance from everyone. She wanted no one to see the cracks and fissures of her life. D.C. high society would have had a field day with her if they'd had an inkling of what her life was like. Yet she was going to expose it all.

She looked back at her son and was about to sneak out when he said, "Yeah, go ahead and leave. Tell the nurses you were here and found me sleeping. You left, because you didn't want to disturb me." He gave a bitter laugh and started to cough uncontrollably.

Corrine went to the bed and held a glass with a straw for him to sip.

Jack feebly wrenched the glass from her hand, threw the straw at her, spotting her silk suit, and drained the contents quickly.

He started to laugh again, as his mother futilely tried to blot water from her jacket.

"Sorry, about that, Corrine. Hope you don't have an important luncheon to attend after spending time with your terminally ill son."

He'd taken to calling both her and Byron by their first names but she didn't care.

Corrine inhaled a deep breath. "Are you okay?"

"As opposed to what? Taking a dirt nap?"

She looked at him and then said, "You may be ill but that does not give you license to be rude."

"Of course it does. It gives me leave to do exactly what I want. Too bad I can't do much. I'd like to be fucking some well-endowed blonde but can't seem to rise to the occasion." Jack started laughing again and the cough came with it.

This time Corrine stood there and watched him cough himself into exhaustion.

"Bitch," Jack spat breathlessly once he stopped coughing.

"Thank you for the compliment. A gift I developed a little late in life. Had I developed it earlier, I think I'd be in a different place today."

"Hell?"

"No, this is hell."

"Look, Corrine, I don't know why you and Byron come here all the time. You don't want to. It's all about appearances."

Tired of the game with her son, she replied, "Yes, it is, so I think I'll sit here for an appropriate time and then leave."

"It has been noticed that you and the senator never visit together. Have you thought about that?"

"We're both busy people. The only thing that matters is that we visit you."

"Right. Come up with any donors or a donor?" Jack asked with a surly edge.

"No, but I think your father may have a bastard out there he's trying to convince."

"Do I have a half brother or half sister?"

"A brother, I believe."

"I'll be damned. Old man was a stallion. Maybe still is."

"Fact is he could be a match."

"Not much more likely than the general population. We only share one parent."

"Thank God," she said under her breath.

"Could you say that again, Corrine? I don't think I heard you."

"It's worth a shot if he can convince the kid," she replied, ignoring his comment. She knew damn well he heard.

"Yeah, right. This guy anyone I know?"

"Don't know. If it's who I think it is, maybe, he goes to Georgetown. Ask your father."

"Perhaps I will. Give us something to talk about at least."

"You do that," Corrine said, absently blotting at a water spot that had spread over the silk, making the material look grease-stained. She sighed with disgust. "I need to leave. I planned to stay longer, but I need to go home and change before my DAR meeting."

"Glad to give you an excuse to leave."

"You flung the straw at me."

"It was an accident," he smirked.

"Right. I'll see you tomorrow or the next day," Corrine said distractedly.

"Don't put yourself out, and don't let the door hit you in the ass on your way out."

CHAPTER TWENTY-SEVEN

"No, no, no," Lenore said vehemently.

They were working in her office late Monday evening. They'd spent most of the day making up.

"Yes, yes, yes," Michael Patrick said with a hint of humor.

"Amanda is not that fickle. She wouldn't look to her agent for solace after a fight with Casper. Sure, she might talk to him as a brother-type friend with no benefits, but she wouldn't fall into his arms."

"Jake Bishop is attracted to her. He's been pushing his feelings for her under every time they surface. But this is the first time he's afraid of truly losing his chance with her forever."

"Ugh, but she's not attracted to Bishop that way. Not now, not ever," she persisted.

"How about this then," he waited until she focused on him. "Bishop kisses your Amanda, and Cass walks in, misunderstands what he sees – rightfully so, I might add – and walks out. He doesn't see Amanda push Jake away and read him the riot act. Amanda doesn't know that Cass saw the kiss."

"I don't like it, but in the spirit of compromise, okay."

He laughed. "You have very strong feelings about all your characters?"

"I do. I've had characters that are fickle or wishy-washy in their hearts, but Amanda Loring is not one of those women."

"I see."

She looked into his dancing blue eyes and had to smile. "You're making fun of me."

"Not at all. I'm intrigued by how your mind works. How you embrace your craft and your characters' plights."

Lenore eyed him suspiciously.

"I mean it."

"Hmmm."

"And I do appreciate your willingness to compromise."

"You're surprised I did."

"Yes and no. Yes, because you told me the first day here you might take over, and no, because you didn't compromise your character's traits, but rather her agent did."

"Exactly, and if I were writing this book alone, Amanda would have sensed Jake's attraction and nipped it soundly in the bud."

"Would she now, lass?"

"You bet."

"Interesting. How about this? Jake makes moves on your Amanda. She soundly rebuffs him, as you say. Jake then tells Cass that he's an ass and if he doesn't get his shit together he's going to lose her."

"It could work, and we could still do that, but I think your original idea works better. It gives more texture and physicality to the scene and conflict to the story."

Pleased, he leaned over and kissed her. "That's high praise coming from LaSandra Lacy."

"Ms. Lacy's life is not one given to compromise. Ms. Held's, on the other hand –"

"Is one of compromise and adaptability," he suggested.

"Yes, when you raise a child, you . . ." She saw a cloud cross his face. "I'm sorry, MP," she said gently and reached for his hand.

"It's all right, *mo chuisle*." Raising their joined hands, he kissed hers. "Once in a while, the grief still hits me at odd times."

She nodded her empathy. She could not possibly understand what it felt like to lose a child in the way MP had.

Clearing his throat, he asked, "So how long is Cass going to be angry with Amanda?"

"Don't know. It's a man thing. Your deal, Mr. Finnegan."

"He's pretty stubborn and insecure when it comes to Amanda."

"Cass is a pain in the ass," Lenore laughed. "Talk about high maintenance."

"Will your lass walk away?"

"Maybe she should. She's been fighting his walls and insecurities. She's getting tired of it."

"He's not worth it?"

"Since we need an HEA, he has to be at some point, but I think I'll let Cass come to her. Tell her that he wants her and that Jake Bishop can't. Or maybe she walks in on Jake and Cass going at it over Bishop kissing her. Your call, MP. I'll play off of whatever you're willing to give me."

"Will you, love?" He smiled and kissed her nose.
"I will, love." She grinned and kissed his mouth.

CHAPTER TWENTY-EIGHT

"Have they had any luck with finding a donor for Jack?" Corrine asked Byron as they sat rigidly at the dining room table, each picking at their respective meals.

"Lots of volunteers. No matches yet, but the National Database will get a number of potential new donors as a result."

Many of the senator's supporters and people with big hearts had come forward to be tested.

"That's good," Corrine said, with meaning. "What are we going to do now? Wait for him to die? Watch him get sicker? What about going with the best match? I know there are potential ramifications, but at this point, how many options are there?"

"He's too weak. If the match isn't almost perfect, chances are he will die."

Corrine took a sip of her wine, not saying anything.

"I'm going to appeal to the student body at Georgetown for help. I've had Morris write a piece for the school newspaper," he said.

Actually, it was Morris's idea to begin with. Good cover story in case Nate was a match, and if he wasn't, possibly potential donors would come forward who could be a match. They were getting desperate. That's why he went to Lenore in the first place.

"He's going to die," Corrine said in a matter-of-fact tone.

"We don't know that, Corrine," Maxwell said, almost kindly.

She didn't respond, merely looked at her once-handsome husband and noted he looked as haggard and tired as she did. She took perverse pleasure in that.

"Have you seen Jack today?" Maxwell asked.

"I did, but he didn't want to see me."

"I'll go by later tonight."

"Suit yourself, but he does not want either of us there. Says we only come because it would look bad if we didn't. I suppose he has a point," she said sadly.

He reached out to touch her arm, and she flinched away. "Please don't," she said.

"I'm sorry," he said, withdrawing his hand. "I wish things were different."

He sounded sincere, but she knew he was a con, and she was not falling for it. "But they're not." She stood abruptly, tossing her napkin on the table, and left.

****

The senator sat and finished his wine, the wine in the bottle, and finally what remained in his wife's glass. Truly foxed, he decided he was in no state to visit his critically ill son.

Maxwell moved to his library and poured himself a double scotch. He slumped into his desk chair, closed his eyes, and slowly sipped from the glass. Jack thinks that no one cares if he lives or dies, Maxwell thought. His son's existence was his doing alone. The old adage, it takes two to tango, did not apply here. When his wife got pregnant with Jack, she was not doing the tango. It was one of the few things in his life he regretted.

CHAPTER TWENTY-NINE

Later in the week, Lenore and MP were taking a break for lunch after a very productive morning of writing. The sunlight flooded her kitchen, making it feel as warm and cozy as the hot chocolate warming on the stove. A delicious smell filled the room.

"In Victorian times, hot chocolate was a luxury for only the ultra-wealthy," Lenore said.

"Shaving Belgium milk chocolate to stir into hot milk over a double boiler is quite a treat in the current age. It's a far cry from the powdered stuff you nuke in the microwave."

"It tastes better."

"You bet it does, *mo chuisle*."

He got up to give her a kiss. "And the homemade whipped cream . . ." – he dipped his finger into the bowl and traced her lips with it, then devoured her mouth – "is better than the hot chocolate."

"Really?"

"Let's be sure."

He repeated the prior exercise but didn't stop at her lips. He drew a line down her neck to the peak of cleavage he could see above the V of her sweater. Using his tongue, he then followed the path he'd made.

Lenore moved closer and molded her hips to his, feeling his desire for her.

"I think we need to turn off the stove and adjoin to a user-friendly surface," he suggested.

"Yes, but now it's my turn to dabble with the whipped cream." She picked up the bowl and led him to the bedroom.

"I'm a willing dabblee."

"Why am I not surprised?"

Her dancing eyes and beautiful smile left him more breathless than thoughts of the white confection.

"What?" She laughed, taking in his look of awe.

"You." He pulled her to him and cupped her bottom. "You are the most incredible woman."

Her eyes continuing to glisten, she said, "You're pretty incredible yourself."

He pulled her even tighter and kissed her possessively. At that moment, he realized he'd never been properly in love before.

Gently he lifted the bottom of her sweater and let it drift to the floor. Her nipples already aroused, he kissed them through the pink silk of her bra. She arched into him, causing him to moan.

"I'm going to make passionate love to you, *a chuisle*."

"Yes, oh yes."

He leaned her onto the bed and slowly undressed her, teasing and tantalizing her along the way.

"My turn," she said when she was totally nude.

"Not yet, I want to enjoy looking at you, arousing you, watching your skin flush as you come."

She blushed.

"A deeper shade of pink than you are now." He ran a finger from the hollow between her breasts to her clitoris. Making lazy circles, he leaned to suckle her breasts. Then his finger continued downward and entered her slick passage; he added two more. Her breathing hitched and her muscles contracted around his fingers. She was close.

"Come for me, Lenore." She did with unselfconscious abandon. MP liked that he had the ability to make her forget herself.

He lay down with her, still fully clothed, while she snuggled into him. Michael Patrick pulled the blanket over her and kissed her forehead, eyes, nose, and finally her lips. "You are the most extraordinary shade of rose," he said, looking into the facets of her eyes.

"I feel like a burning bush."

"That's an interesting visual."

"Maybe we can ignite," she said, straddling him and going to work on his buttons.

****

The insistent ring of the phone startled Lenore awake. Heart pounding, she grabbed it and swiftly left the room so as not to wake MP. Caller ID showed it was Nathan. She took the phone to a small lofted sitting area.

"Hi, honey," she said in an unused voice.

"Did I wake you, Mom?" asked Nate.

"I was dozing."

"Right."

"I was," she said defensively.

"Okay, you were dozing. I wanted to let you know that I went to be tested this afternoon, and I should know if I'm a match within forty-eight hours or so."

"How'd it go?"

"No big deal. But they did both a blood test and cheek swab. They usually do one or the other. I guess they're being extra careful since its Senator Maxwell's kid they're testing for."

"You're most likely right."

"Yeah, but I was wondering if you and your new boyfriend wanted to come and have dinner with Kelly and me this weekend. By then, I figure we'll need to talk about the transplant or we can celebrate the fact that I'm not a match."

"Sure, I'll check with Michael Patrick and see if he's free. But I'll be there for sure. I want to meet the young woman who's made a place in my son's heart."

"Ditto for you, Mom. Except for age and gender." He laughed again. She was glad to see he was in a good mood.

"Hey, we're not that old."

"Nope, you're hot for a mom."

"Stop," she said, laughing. "Aren't you supposed to be embarrassed to have conversations like this with your mother?"

"Why, I like having the hottest Mom on campus."

"Enough," she said, knowing he was teasing her now. "I'll see if I can get reservations at the Ritz Carlton, and we'll make a weekend of it."

"Sounds good, Mom. I gotta go. I'm meeting a study group across campus."

"All right, but, Nate, are you coping okay with all this? It's a lot for anyone."

"So far so good. Not sure how I'll feel if I'm a match, and I'm concerned that this could leak. Plus, I hate not being able to tell Kelly about what I'm doing. It was okay last weekend. I said I was coming home to visit you, but I think she was hurt I didn't invite her to come with me to meet you. Then today I had to sneak off to get the tests done."

"I'm sorry, honey. I'm taking a big chance here, but if you think she's the one, and you can trust her, tell her. No reason Maxwell and his son should come between you and Kelly."

"Thanks, Mom. I'm not sure if I'll tell her or not, but knowing you trust my judgment means a lot to me."

She felt tears sting her eyes. "I do, Nate. Do what you feel is right."

"I will. I'm sorry, I need to get moving."

"Go. I love you."

"I love you, too, Mom. Let me know when you'll be arriving."

Lenore sat for a moment thanking her lucky stars that she had such a great kid. Then she sighed, feeling guilty about what Maxwell was doing to him and what could potentially happen if word got out he was Maxwell's son.

"*A chuisle*," MP said softly.

She turned and offered him a smile. "Come sit with me," she said, patting the seat next to her.

He gave her a warm kiss and joined her on the couch.

"That was Nate. He called to invite us on a double date with him and his girlfriend. It appears he's pretty serious about her."

"How do you feel about that?" asked MP.

"I'm okay with it. I think he's young, but I'm not about to offer advice, seeing as I was already on my way to becoming a parent at his age. Plus, this is only the second girlfriend he's introduced me to, so he doesn't make a habit of falling in and out of love."

"Practical young man."

"Something like that, I suppose."

"Still something bothers you." It was a statement, not a question.

"Yes. Several things actually. If he's a donor match, he should know by the end of the week, and he either wants to celebrate the fact that he's not or discuss the fact that he is. That and he hates not being able to tell Kelly. That's the girlfriend. I told him to do what he feels is best in that regard. If he does, I hope she keeps his confidence."

"He's your son. He'll use good judgment."

"He's in love. When I was his age and in love, I didn't use any judgment. I was totally ruled by my heart and hormones."

MP nodded soberly.

"But enough of this. Are you free this coming weekend to double date with my son and his girl in D.C.? We can stay at the Ritz and make a weekend of it."

"I'll sleep in the car as long as I'm with you," he teased.

She laughed. "I should warn you that my son will be checking you out."

"As it should be. He values his mum." He ran a finger down the side of her face. "He wants to know that I'm worthy of you. Might be that he thinks no one is."

"No, that's not the case. He's been telling me to find someone." She took a step out of her comfort zone and offered, "I asked him the other day if he'd like a sibling, and once he assured himself I wasn't already knocked up, he said he'd be okay with it as long as he didn't have to babysit or change diapers."

MP seemed delighted by her statement. "I'd think he'd be pretty safe from that, at least while he's in law school. But what if he has children? Will you babysit and change their nappies?"

"Most likely I would. But I hope he waits a while. I think I'm too young to be a grandma."

"Not your typical grandmum, away."

"I'd like to wait at least ten years or so for that momentous event."

"But you've given thought to having a baby, I take it?" he asked cautiously.

"I have," she answered.

"It would be a big change for your life."

"Having a child is a big change for anyone's life. But if I had another child, I'd hope that I had a willing partner this time around. Barring anything unforeseen, that would make the experience a little easier." She smiled tentatively.

"If that partner were me, you'd be certain." He gave her a gentle kiss. "As I said before, I'd like to see you carry my child."

She flushed.

"I've fallen in love with you, Lenore." He picked up her hand and kissed the sensitive center.

Tears sprang to her eyes again. "I've fallen for you, too, MP. Not certain when or how but I realized it last week."

"Were you going to tell me?" He smiled, eyes bright, crinkling at the corners.

"I've been on the verge for days. I love you, Michael Patrick. I've never said those words to anyone, not even my son's father."

"And I've never been properly in love before I met you, *mo chuisle*. I love you."

They looked into one another's eyes, wanting to etch this memory into their minds. He pulled her to him and murmured, "My breath, my forever, I'll love you for eternity." Then Michael Patrick kissed her softly, stealing her heart as he did so.

CHAPTER THIRTY

"His condition is not good. If we can't get the transplant done soon, he might not be strong enough to even have it, if we ever find a match." Corrine was on a rant to someone on the phone.

Byron walked by her office and stopped to listen to the conversation. No doubt she was talking to one of her tennis or golf buddies. Doing her best to garner sympathy.

"Yes, Byron has been using his position, and a number of people have been tested, but none of them match, not even close enough to try a transplant. He's appealed to the student body at Georgetown but the response hasn't been what he'd hoped."

That's because most of the campus thinks Jack's a prick, Maxwell thought and continued on to his office. He'd heard enough of his wife's BS, contrived phone conversation. He marveled at the fact that she had never shared their marital discord with anyone. Probably knew if she did, it would be all over Washington.

The results of Nathan Held's test should be in tomorrow afternoon or the next morning.

Byron wanted out from under everything. Maybe he should write a book and become a newscaster like Morris suggested. Shit, if Sarah Palin and Eliot Spitzer could do it, so could he. He laughed to himself.

Maxwell brought up his e-mail. There was one without a subject that contained an attachment. He opened it. It was a picture of Nathan Held. That's all there was. It was sent from zipperdown.com.

"What the hell," he said louder than he intended.

"Problem?" Corrine asked as she passed his office.

"Uh, no. Don't trouble yourself, dear."

Fucking bitch, he thought. But he'd made her into one, or at least their life circumstances had. His father, hers, their lifestyle. Guilt—that was the overriding feeling he had toward his wife—guilt mixed with loathing. Guilt edged out the loathing a notch.

Question was whom did the e-mail photo come from? He'd send it to Morris's Seeker computer and see if he could find out. He would have his address deactivated tomorrow, although Gerald might think it better to leave it active.

But he was certainly going to get a new computer and e-mail address, one that no one knew.

He stared at his son's picture a few moments longer, then closed down his computer.

There was no mistaking them for close family members, if not father and son, though that would be anyone's first guess.

What would life have been like if Lenore had been his wife, and he'd been around to help her raise Nathan? Would they have had more children? Lived happily ever after? He'd often wondered.

He'd loved her. Maybe he still did. Her body attracted him, but her youthful enthusiasm and brains, an odd combination, had captivated him. Truth was, he'd been thinking of leaving Corrine behind and losing her family's money. He had wanted to run away with Lenore and may have until Rin turned up pregnant after the night he took her. That night had changed so many futures. It still was, he thought.

The picture of Nathan showing up on his personal computer was a warning, but from whom? His logical choice was Corrine, followed by Jack, then Morris.

Jack had more money than he did and could easily afford to have a PI follow him. The money came from a trust set up by Jack's maternal grandfather, and when Carter died, the money that was in his trust had reverted to Jack as well.

Everyone thought Byron had financed the abortions for Jack's girlfriends but, in actuality, Jack had paid for them himself. Jack perpetuated the story of Maxwell taking care of it. He had never known of the abortions until after the fact.

It had taken some fancy footwork to keep them undercover. Maxwell even believed his son had impregnated the girls in hopes it would go public and come back to haunt his father. Morris had taken steps to make sure it hadn't, paying one young woman off and getting the other a high-paying job. But Jack had made sure the rumor was out there.

Then there was Morris. While a long shot, Gerald could have sent the photo to yank his chain. More than anything, Morris thrived on the power his position gave him. It was that fact that made him discount Morris. Plus, Morris knew all of his dark secrets and did not need to send photos to taunt him.

Not many people had his personal e-mail, so that limited the list of possibilities as well. No, he'd bet it was Rin or Jack who sent the picture, or someone hired by them.

He'd wait to see what Morris turned up on Seeker tomorrow. Meanwhile, Maxwell got up to pour himself a double scotch.

CHAPTER THIRTY-ONE

Lenore and MP were finishing breakfast the next morning when Lenore observed, "We have a great job, you and I. Most couples couldn't lounge around like this and enjoy breakfast together on a weekday. Not to mention a romp in bed. Other couples hear the alarm and start the race of the day with barely a peck on the cheek and cold cornflakes."

"You're right, lass. I'll never take that freedom for granted. Nor will I miss an opportunity to romp with you." He gave he a wicked smile.

"Do you think the urgency will fade over time?"

"What? Wanting to jump each other's bones?"

"Yes."

"I don't think so. Will there be times when we have to set the urgency aside? Unfortunately, yes," he replied.

"To deal with other more pressing things, say, like breakfast?" Her were eyes alight with mischief.

"Yes, pesky things like sustenance tend to get in the way."

She laughed. "I wish it were never more complicated than that."

"I propose we do an erotic book filled with nothing but food and sex," MP said.

"Under our current pen names or new ones?"

"Since it will be more like an autobiography, new names."

They both laughed and she slid several more pancakes onto his plate.

"Although at the rate we're going with Cass and Amanda's sex life, we might not be able to muster up an erotic novel with or without food."

He raised an eyebrow at her.

"Come on, MP, your Cass is . . . I don't know what he is. But I know what he isn't. He's not a motivated lover. Is he afraid of Amanda? Is she too overtly sexual for him all of a sudden?"

"I don't think Cass thinks she's overtly sexual at all. I think he believes her to be a cold bitch."

"He should try and thaw her out then. She's sending him signals he's not getting."

"She sends him signals, then backs away with anger or hurt."

"I don't think so, MP."

"I do, lass."

"What would you have her do? Show up at his office in nothing but a trench coat and high heels?"

"That's a bit predictable, don't you think?"

"How about commando to a business meeting. Where she looks perfectly demure but places herself where only Cass can see her attributes?"

They laughed again.

"Would Cass know what to do with her, MP?"

"I'd know what to do with you if you pulled a stunt like that," he said, eyes darkening.

"Do tell," she said, popping the last of her breakfast in her mouth.

"I'll do you one better." He took her from the stool and kissed her simple, then turned her to the heavy oak kitchen table and leaned her over it so her back was to him.

Knowing she was commando under the long shirt, he plunged one hand between her legs and used the other to push down his sweatpants and briefs.

She was wet for him, and he was more than ready for her. He entered her from behind hard and fast. She rocked back into him, anchoring her arms on either side of the table for purchase.

Panting, she said, "Please, MP, now."

He didn't argue or slow her down. He was as desperate as she was.

"*A chuisle*," he cried as he began to come, pumping into her harder and faster until all conscious thought was centered on their connected bodies.

Spent, he lay on top of her for a moment. Michael Patrick kissed the side of her face and murmured Irish endearments.

"I don't think Cass could do the scene justice," Lenore finally managed, voice still husky.

"What about your Amanda?"

"I don't give a shit about her at present."

MP let loose a deep rich laugh. "You are irrepressible, lass." He kissed the back of her head and lifted himself off of her. Then he helped her right herself from the table. Turning her, he kissed her soundly and ran his hands under her shirt to touch her breasts.

"While I enjoyed this very much, I missed the rest of you."

A slow smile touched her lips. "The rest of me agrees, but the other part felt marvelous in its own right."

"It did." He nipped her nose.

"And I hate to disrupt the urgency of this creative research, but the cleaning lady will be here any moment, so we should take a shower. In the interest of saving time, I suggest we do it together."

****

For a midwinter's day, it was warm and sunny. Lenore and MP decided to take advantage of the good weather, visit the Mercer Museum in Doylestown, and have lunch at one of the quaint restaurants in town.

"This place is like a hoarder's paradise." Michael Patrick looked up at the ceiling in the museum atrium to see a whaleboat, a stagecoach, and a Conestoga wagon suspended from the ceiling.

"I've often thought the same thing. There are over 30,000 items on display here."

"Amazing," he said, looking about the six-story concrete structure, which was designed to look like a castle.

"You have real castles in the UK," Lenore observed.

"None like this and chock full of stuff."

"You're right, I suppose. Henry Mercer was a historian and archeologist. He built this place in 1916 to showcase his many collections."

MP nodded and took her hand, pulling her farther into the museum.

"It's cold in here, *mo chuisle*. Are you warm enough?"

"Concrete keeps it this way year round."

He turned her to him and pulled up her coat collar, tucking in the flap at her chest.

"Don't fuss." She playfully batted his hands away. "I'm perfectly fine."

He kissed her nose. "Your nose is even cold."

"Stop," she giggled, taking his hand and leading him through the dizzying array of items that encompassed the six-floor structure.

They passed everything from items used in early medicine to tinsmithing and dairying.

"Can't imagine being bled." She shuddered, looking at the display of primitive equipment and basins designed to collect blood.

"I agree with you, love. Seems counter-intuitive. I noticed in several of your books, heroes or heroines extract promises from their significant others to make sure they're not bled when serious illness has be fallen them."

"Yes . . ."

She stopped suddenly and looked behind her.

"What is it?" he asked.

"Nothing, I guess, a feeling that someone is watching."

He turned to look and saw no one. "Place is kind of creepy and cold. It might make a person feel like they're being watched."

"Ghosts," she said in a mock ominous tone.

"You never know, lass. Someone who was bled with one of these instruments of torture could still walk in the land of the undead." He trickled his fingers down the back of her neck.

She squirmed away from him, laughing.

"MP, I'm sure I saw someone, a fleeting glimpse," she said seriously.

He looked again. "Maybe one of the stray schoolchildren hiding from a parent chaperone."

She shrugged and took one more furtive look around.

"Lunch," he suggested.

"An offer I can't refuse."

They walked to the parking lot. She smiled up at the sky, enjoying the sun on her face.

"Wait in the car," MP said quietly.

"Wha –"

"Please," he said softly but with insistence.

She reluctantly took the keys.

****

"What are you doing here, Mr. Irving?" MP asked in a less than friendly fashion.

"I . . . I was taking advantage of the nice day," John Irving stammered nervously, eyes darting. He was sitting in a nondescript gray Ford Taurus with the driver's window rolled down.

Lenore's comment about him being gray seemed to fit.

MP eyed the camera around his neck.

"That's good. I hate to think you were following Lenore."

"Wh . . . Why would you think that?"

"I think you know why," MP said, reaching for the dangling camera.

John Irving hit the window up button but somehow the camera strap got caught, and the camera hung outside the window.

Michael Patrick grabbed it as Irving hit the gas to back up the car. The tension on the strap caused it to break free of Irving's neck, leaving the camera in MP's possession.

Irving slammed the car into drive and headed right for MP. It was clear his intention was to mow him down. MP skillfully avoided injury by launching himself over the three-foot retaining wall that ringed the parking lot.

Tires squealing, Irving sped off.

"My God," Lenore breathed, running up to him. "Are you okay?" She wrapped her arms around him.

He was about to chastise her for not waiting in the car but stopped short when he felt her trembling. "I'm fine, *a chuisle*. I'm fine," MP soothed and kissed the top of her head.

"I was so frightened – not at first, but when he backed up and then tried to run you over." She was crying.

"Shh, love, I'm well, truly." He guided her back to the car.

"Lenore," he said, stopping and turning her to him. "Lenore, sweetheart, stop crying. I'm fine. Look at me." He tilted her chin up to his face. It broke his heart. "See," he said kindly.

She nodded mutely and inhaled a deep breath.

"Better?"

She nodded again.

When they got to the car, he opened the door for her and helped her in. Once inside, he said as lightly as he could, "You did see someone—not a ghost or an apparition, but a gray man. He's stalking you, Lenore."

She laughed weakly. He could see tears threatening to spill from her eyes.

"Should we go home?"

"Yes," she mustered a smile. "Let's go home." She attempted to fasten her seatbelt, but her hands weren't steady, so he took the latch and did it for her.

"Okay?"

"Okay," she said thickly.

He handed her the camera and began to back out of the parking spot.

"Oh my God," she exclaimed, causing him to reflexively slam on the breaks.

He looked at her looking at the camera view screen and saw she was chalk white. He pulled back into the spot and took the device from her still shaking hands.

MP started going through a slide show of the pictures and quickly determined that Lenore was not the only stalkee. There were pictures of her son, of her and Nate, of Morris and Maxwell, and of him and Lenore. But Irving was clearly fixated on Lenore. There were easily a hundred pictures of her.

"*A chuisle*, where did you meet Irving?"

"Barnes and Noble Café. The place was busy. I had a table for two and was by myself with coffee and a brownie. He asked if he could join me. MP, he didn't seem weird or creepy or anything at all. Told me he worked in information technology, had his own company, JIT. Short for, you guessed it, John Irving Technologies." She gave a bitter laugh. "I checked him on Google. He seemed legit and real. He lives in a rented condo a few miles from my house."

"How long did you date him?"

"Eight weeks or so."

"Does that include the time you were hoping he'd disappear?" he asked, putting a little levity in his voice.

"No. That was about another four weeks."

"Determined to see you again. I'd have gotten the hint if a woman gave me the brush-off for four weeks."

She gave him a wry smile.

Before he continued, he asked, "You okay to go?"

"Yes. Sorry for the histrionics, but something came over me when I thought he might hurt you. Even when I knew you were okay. I was swamped with relief and feelings I couldn't control."

"It's alright. I'm flattered you were so worried about me."

"Let's go home," she said

"Yes." He reached over and took her still trembling hand and brought it to his lips.

"Do you want to contact the police?" he finally asked.

"Honestly, if I thought he was stalking me for me, I'd get a restraining order. But the cops would want the photos, and while there are a fair number of me, there are a significant number of Morris, Maxwell, and Nate, not to mention you as well. The photos of Nate, Morris, and Maxwell were taken in Philly.

"Morris told my attorney he thought they were being followed. Maybe I was followed and led Irving to them."

"Smart girl." He squeezed her hand and noted the color was coming back to her face.

"Question is: Is he a professional PI who was hired to get close to me to gather information, or did someone hire a PI who approached JI to obtain information on me or from me?"

"Good questions. Someone in Maxwell's camp?"

"Since they're taking photos of Morris and Maxwell, it's most likely not one of them. Could be Corrine Kennedy Maxwell, his long-suffering wife or raving lunatic bitch, depending on whose side you take."

He could tell the initial shock and fear were wearing off. Her mind was engaged and her emotions in check. "No cops?" he asked.

"I'm going to call my attorney and see what he has to say. If we go to the cops, this will go public. If I go to Connor, he can get to Morris. Morris has resources to check these things out."

"But Lenore, whether you think so or not, Irving is obsessed with you. There are easily a hundred pictures of you taken on different days. He's been watching you."

She let out a big sigh. "I don't have time for this."

"You need to think about it, love. I don't want anything happening to you any more than you want anything happening to me. Fair enough?"

"Yes. But if that's the case, then it's more likely someone approached him after the fact, and he, himself, is not a PI. I guess it's better for my ego, too. I'd hate to think the only reason a gray man would be interested in me was because he was paid to be."

He started to laugh. "It might be he was paid to come on to you and then fell for you. The anger he exhibited at the house was real, Lenore."

"Maybe he was only angry because my no longer dating him put a monkey wrench in his plans."

He glanced at her sideways. "Maybe you should write romantic suspense. You seem to be able to see all the angles."

"Best twist would be if I set up the entire thing."

"Tell me you didn't."

"No, I didn't," she said, almost hostile.

"There now, the color is fully back in your pretty face," MP said.

"You were baiting me?" She gave him a playful shot to the arm.

"Guilty as charged. It's not me either," he added.

"Afraid I'd over think this and decide it was?"

"Even if you did, you'd ask this time, wouldn't you?"

"Fact is there's no reason to think it. Why are you setting out to make me angry?"

"I like you feisty."

She laughed a real, honest-to-goodness laugh, and it warmed him. "I love you, Lenore." He lifted their joined hands and brought hers to his lips.

CHAPTER THIRTY-TWO

"Jesus," MP said as they turned onto Lenore's block.

There were an ambulance and three cop cars in front of her house. She didn't even think Yardley had three cop cars.

"What now?" she asked.

"There's your gray man's car." MP pointed to the gray Ford.

"Oh God, MP, Maria was there alone." She was moving toward both the door and hysteria with equal velocity.

"Hang on." MP grabbed her arm before she could let herself out of the car. "You go charging in like that and you're likely to get yourself shot."

"You have a point," she said, taking a steadying breath to get herself under control. "But let's hurry. I need to make sure Maria is okay."

"Let me come around your side before you get out."

He could see the pulse point in her neck beating way too fast. The only time he wanted to see that was when she was aroused—by him—certainly not from fear and terror.

"Lenore, love, take a deep breath. If Maria needs you, you can't fall apart."

"You're right. I'll keep it together."

He shoved the camera under the seat. "Ready?"

"As I'll ever be."

"If need be, tell them he was following you but nothing more. Someone may have seen the confrontation at the museum and put two and two together," MP said.

"All right," she took his hand as if it were a lifeline.

A cop met them at the door.

"I'm the owner," she took out her wallet to show him her driver's license.

"Appears you've had a home invasion," the officer said.

"Is Maria all right?" she asked as calmly as she could, but her voice trembled.

"Yeah, she's fine. Can't say the same for the perp. She said he was a former boyfriend of yours."

"Is it John Irving? His car's outside."

"Was John Irving. He's dead, ma'am."

She felt MP's arm come around her waist.

"How?" she asked in barely a whisper.

"According to your housekeeper, he demanded to be let in. Said he left something of his in your office and wanted it. She told him to come back, and he pushed his way in, shoving her into the kitchen counter. She told him if he didn't leave, she'd call the police.

"He took exception to that and came after her. A scuffle ensued, and she got her hands on a knife from the butcher block on your counter and stabbed him. Her aim was good. Dead on to the heart," the office said with admiration.

She started shaking ever so slightly. MP's arm tightened around her.

"Can we come in so the lady can sit down?" MP asked.

"Yeah sure, but stay out here. The kitchen is where the altercation took place. Body is still there. Waiting on the ME, and then he'll be taken to the morgue."

"Please, she needs to sit down," MP said again. The cop looked at her and quickly moved out of the way.

"Can I see Maria?"

"Once they're done questioning her."

"Are you sure she's all right?"

"Physically yes. She's understandably upset."

Lenore nodded.

"Do you know what he left here that he wanted so badly?" asked the officer.

"No, he never brought anything here. He was only in my office once."

"Were you still seeing him?"

"No, I haven't dated him in several months."

"Why did you stop dating him?"

"He wasn't my type. No particular reason other than I knew the relationship wasn't going anywhere."

"He wasn't violent or anything? Didn't hit you or assault you in any way?"

"No, but he was following me, us, this morning."

Lenore explained what happened in at the museum, leaving out the part about the camera.

"He tried to run you down?" the officer asked MP.

"Yes, but I jumped over a small retaining wall that surrounded the parking lot, and he took off."

"Did you make a report in Doylestown?" he looked between MP and Lenore.

"No, I wanted to move on," Lenore said. "I figured if he followed me again, I'd get a restraining order."

"Attempted murder is serious."

"I guess we didn't think about it that way," MP said.

The cop looked thoughtful then asked, "How did he take the break-up?"

"I never told him it was over. He came to the house and let himself in. He found MP here and had angry words for me. Then stormed out slamming the door. That's when he was in my office, the one and only time."

"He let himself in?"

"Yes, the door was unlocked, and I had the music on pretty loud. He claims he rang the bell and that I didn't hear it. Tried the door, it was unlocked, so he came in."

"Mind if we look around upstairs?"

"Not at all." She vaguely wondered if she should call Connor or tell them to get a warrant, but for the life of her she couldn't imagine what he was looking for.

"Would you come up with me and go through exactly what happened?"

"Sure," she replied and led him up the stairs. MP followed.

"You stopped seeing Irving in favor of Finnegan?" the cop asked.

"No. Mr. Finnegan and I are working on a project. We recently became involved. I'd stopped dating Mr. Irving about a month before, but he kept calling to ask me out. I should have told him it was over, but I thought he'd get the hint and stop asking."

"Yeah, that should have been a hint. About when was that?"

"Wednesday four, five weeks ago maybe?" She looked at MP for confirmation.

He nodded.

"Take me through it. Where he stood, how he acted . . ."

"Um, Michael Patrick and I were dancing and he'd come up the steps. He yelled something like 'I should have known.' I asked Michael Patrick to give us a few minutes. John was extremely angry. I'd never seen any real emotion out of him before and was surprised."

"Did he scare you?" the cop followed up

"No. The couch was between us, and he was gripping it so tightly his knuckles were white. I said I was sorry and he yelled back something to the effect that I was only sorry that I got caught here with MP. Then 'Love Stinks' came on my computer; that's where the music was playing. I thought it was ironic and went to turn it off. John yelled 'leave it' and left. He closed the front door with such force the sidelights rattled."

"He came in by himself and went out by himself."

"Yes."

"Could he have left or hidden something?"

"Maybe when he came in and we didn't even know he was here, but he left in too big of a hurry."

"You never found anything unusual or something of his he left behind?"

"No, but I don't utilize all the rooms in the house all the time so if he hid something, it could still be hidden but if he left something here in my office, I have no idea what it could be."

"Where was he standing when he was holding onto the couch?"

Lenore thought for a second. "Not quite to the center, a little to the right."

After snapping on some gloves, the officer ran a hand over the top of the couch. Then crouched on the floor and ran his hand under it. He asked for MP's help to pick up the couch. The two men moved it a good three feet. There was nothing on the floor under the piece of furniture, not even a dust bunny.

The cop started taking the cushions off the couch. After rooting around for several minutes, he came up with something that looked like a watch battery.

"What is it?" Lenore asked when he held it up.

"If I'm not mistaken, it's a listening device."

"A bug?" MP and Lenore said together.

The cop gave a small chuckle. "Yes."

"Why would anyone want to bug my office?" She knew, of course, and she felt MP's hand rub her back. He knew, too.

"What are you two working on?"

"We're writing a book together," MP offered.

"What kind of book?"

"A contemporary romance."

The officer raised an eyebrow at MP, then, as if a light bulb went off, asked, "Are you MP Finnegan?"

"Yes," he said with a small smile.

"My wife has read all your books, had me read the article in *The Times* the other week. I'm sorry about your son. I have a boy the same age."

"Thank you," Michael Patrick said softly.

The officer was quiet for a minute.

"Could he have been spying for that tabloid rag? What was it? *The Sentinel?*"

"I suppose anything is possible," she said quietly, MP continuing to move his hand up and down her back, calming her.

"You're LaSandra Lacy?"

"I am. That's my pen name."

"Wife loves your work, too. Can't wait for your new book to come out."

"I'll give you a few books to take home for her," Lenore offered, glad the officer was off on his own train of thought.

"That would be great. Could you sign them?"

"Yes." She gave him what she hoped was a warm, friendly smile. She went to a drawer where she kept a few extra copies of her books and pulled out three.

"You know Irving could have been following you to get pictures for the rag. Exploit your personal relationship. Kind of adds up," the cop again.

"Maybe," MP agreed.

Lenore sighed in relief.

"What's your wife's name?" she asked.

"Janice."

Lenore wrote the inscription and handed it to the officer.

Janice: Thanks for being a loyal reader. All the best of everything. LaSandra Lacy.

"This is terrific. I'll be a hit tonight."

MP offered the expected chuckle.

"Do you think there are bugs anywhere else in my house?" Lenore asked.

"We'll have a sweep done. Also check and see if we can figure out where the device was transmitting. Sometimes it's to a recorder placed outside a building so the perp can come and retrieve tapes and put in new ones. More often these days they're programmed to a computer. Range depends on the sophistication of the bug."

Both MP and Lenore nodded.

"Can I see Maria now? She won't have any legal problems because of this, will she?" Lenore followed up.

"It looks like self-defense to me, especially since we found the bug."

Thank God, she thought.

"I'll see if they're done with her."

They were, and Maria was more angry than shaken. She promised Lenore she'd be back at the normal time next week. The women embraced and Maria went home to tell her family the harrowing tale.

The crime scene people were finishing up in the kitchen and office.

"Got a place to stay tonight?" the cop asked. "We won't be done here for a while and can't check for bugs until tomorrow."

"We can stay at a hotel," MP said and gave the cops his cell number. Lenore did the same. Then went to pack a small overnight bag.

****

Lenore and MP decided to check out of his hotel and limit talking in the car to the innocuous. Lenore had suggested one or both places could be bugged, and while JI was dead, there could be someone else out there listening.

Once checked into their room at the Hyatt Princeton, Lenore flopped down on the bed and sighed.

"Now what?" she asked.

MP plopped down next to her and pulled her close to him.

She rested her head on his chest and burrowed in closer. He offered comfort, warmth, a feeling of safety. Every time he touched her didn't have to lead to sex. But if she kept thinking about it, it would.

"You said you wanted to call Connor Walker."

"Yes, but he's a lawyer, and I have to be careful as to what I say. Keeping the photos could be considered obstruction of justice or something. But I don't want to go right to Morris either. I certainly don't trust him and Maxwell."

"I can see why. Call Walker and let him know about what happened at the house, the fact that there was a bug, and that JI was following you before his demise."

"I can't believe he's dead. That he attacked Maria. He was such a passionless person, right down to his gray car."

"I thought the same thing when I saw the car. But maybe that's how he did what he did. Under the radar, nonthreatening, never calling attention to himself."

"You're right. A person in his position wouldn't want the spotlight on him. I always thought it was because he was a computer nerd."

MP laced his hand through hers as it lay on his chest.

"I can't believe it," she said again. "And I'm ashamed to say this, but I don't care that he's dead, other than it involved my housekeeper and my house."

"You don't have to mourn for a man who was obviously up to no good and may have sought to do you harm, Lenore."

Reluctantly she sat up. "I need to call Connor, and I need to call Nathan."

Lenore told Walker the entire story, except for the pictures.

"How do you know this isn't someone from a crazy tabloid trying to get dirt on you and Finnegan?"

"Because I do."

"What are you not telling me?"

"You're a lawyer."

"Damn it, Lenore," Connor said with unusual ferocity. It made her jump. "Your personal safety may be in question; Nate's, too, for that matter. I don't give a rat's ass about Morris and the senator, but there's that potential as well. What are you not telling me?" he all but demanded this time.

"Listen closely. Morris thinks they were followed from D.C. They were, or I was followed from my house and from the hotel to your office, leading someone to them."

"You know this?"

"Yes."

"Okay, before I forget: Is your son photogenic?" asked Walker pointedly.

"Yes."

"I'll need a few good shots for the employee newsletter. We're featuring our interns this month."

"Okay, but back to the topic at hand. The cop believes that JI was involved in the *Sentinel* piece. His wife reads both MP and Lacy."

"Lucky break."

"I gave him several autographed books to take home."

"Good thinking."

"On occasion."

He chuckled. "You think I should clue the boys in?"

"Not that I want to, but I think one of them has the resources to deal with it."

"I'll take your word for it."

"Let me know what happens. Call my cell. I'm at the Hyatt in Princeton. But don't tell anyone."

"Wouldn't dream of it."

"Attorney-client privilege."

"Exactly."

Next she called her son and told him a similar tale and concluded, "I wanted you to be aware of what happened here. If you think someone's following you, you might be right."

"Got it, Mom. I'll deal with it. It's not exactly as if I'm hanging out with the Maxwells."

Then she remembered that he should have gotten back his results from the tests he took to see if he was a suitable match for Jack Maxwell's bone marrow transplant and asked him about it.

"I'm not as good a match as the senator hoped I'd be. But I'm the best match so far. I might be his only option. They're going to talk to him and let me know."

"You okay with all this?" Lenore asked, picking up something in his voice.

"Yeah, it's sad that this stuff happens. Jack's a prick, but I'd never wish him ill or dead."

"I know, honey. I'm sorry."

"Mom, it's not your fault." Then changing the subject, he asked, "We still on for Friday?"

"You bet. I'm looking forward to it. We'll talk some more then."

"I love you, Mom. Be careful."

"You too, Nate. I love you." She felt tears stinging her eyes. Where did they come from? Why was she such a watering pot?

MP came up behind her and rubbed her shoulders. "Relax," he whispered in her ear.

She arched into him.

"Your muscles are tight. Lie down. I'll rub your back. Wait." He pulled her sweater over her head.

"That feels heavenly," she purred as he massaged her back and shoulders. "Don't stop."

He kissed her back, then drew his tongue down her spine. She shivered. He continued to taunt and tantalize. Lenore started to turn over. "Stay where you are, lass." MP undid her bra clasp and slipped it off her. Rubbing the imprint the band made around her rib cage, then lower, slowly removing her pants and panties.

"No fair. I'll play, but you need to be undressed, too," Lenore said.

"Hmm," he nuzzled her neck. "Is that a request?"

"At the moment. I could issue something stronger if the need arises," she laughed. "I see it's already arisen." Her voice was laced with amusement as he rubbed against her teasingly.

"Since you asked so nicely, I'll comply with your request."

MP disrobed and rejoined her on the bed, coming up behind her.

"Up on your knees and hold the headboard."

She looked at him suspiciously over her shoulder.

"No, love. Nothing that squirmy," he said, reading her mind.

She laughed and did as he asked.

He moved her hair to the side and kissed her neck, then down her back as he caressed her bottom.

She enjoyed the feel of his lips and tongue on her back. Goose bumps rose on her skin and she gasped as his fingers found their way to her vagina and clitoris.

Reaching back with one hand, she attempted to touch what she wanted, but he would have none of it and put her hand back on the headboard.

"You'll have what you desire very soon."

She could feel him sliding between her buttocks and pushed into him.

MP positioned her hips so he could enter her more fully. "Stay still for a moment," he said.

She did and felt him slide into her slowly. As her muscles tightened around him, drawing him deeper, he groaned with undisguised satisfaction.

When he was fully seated in her, she used the headboard for leverage to push into him. To her surprise, he let her control the pace. His thumb circled her clitoris and aroused her further. As she began the freefall into orgasm, her pace quickened, and her muscles clamped and held him tight. He let out a growl before they both crashed to the bottom.

Michael Patrick helped her stretch out, then lay down and pulled her on top of him.

"Feel better, *a chuisle*?"

"I feel drugged."

"Good. I'd like you addicted."

"To you or the sex?"

"Both, I believe."

"At least you're honest."

"Always."

She sighed. "I suppose I should feel bad about having sex when there's a dead body in my kitchen."

"Why? You didn't make him dead or even wish him thus."

"I guess I'm numb about the entire thing."

"Do you question everything you feel? Don't you ever just go with it?"

"I've been going with and doing it a lot lately."

"Are you bored or complaining?"

"No, if I could block out all the noise and concentrate on what's good, I'd probably be dead from happiness."

"Well now, we can't have that, can we? Guess that's why there's a balance," MP joked.

"You know what I mean."

"I do, love." He kissed her nose.

"I do feel better. Some of the tension has left, and now I'm tired."

"I'll hold you."

She sighed and snuggled into him.

CHAPTER THIRTY-THREE

"What are we going to do, Gerald?" Byron all but whined.

"I've got someone going over to that John Irving's house. Hopefully, we'll beat the local cops. Can't imagine there's too many of them, and if they're processing Lenore's house that should take a while. She's got a big house —"

"How do you know?" Maxwell interrupted.

"Said a palatial estate in the tabloid, so I figured it was big." Morris lied with ease, no telltale stumble or body language to give him away.

Byron looked at him and nodded, "It's big all right. Has a pool and a hot tub in the backyard, too."

"She's done well for herself."

Maxwell snorted.

"Anyway," Morris started again, "I'm hoping they get in and get anything linking you to Lenore out of there."

"It might be too late. That picture I got came from somewhere, and you can't seem to trace it. If it's Corrine, I'm sure she already has copies of everything, probably in triplicate."

"I bet the guy panicked when Finnegan confronted him."

"Yeah, but even I wouldn't have been stupid enough to try and get the bugs out with the housekeeper there, especially when she wouldn't let him in."

"Panic does strange things to people, Byron."

"But Lenore probably wouldn't have even suspected bugs. The Irving guy could have gone over there one day to pretend to apologize or to beg for a second chance and get the bugs then."

"Is that what you would have done?"

"Don't know."

"Anyhow, we owe Lenore big-time. She could have not told us or spilled all to the cops, but she didn't."

"She doesn't want to be linked to me, nor does Nathan. Lenore would do anything to protect that boy."

"Why do you find that odd? Most parents would go to any means to protect their child. Even you're taking the extra step to try and get Jake that bone marrow transplant he needs."

"I suppose."

"Anyhow, that was a lucky break – that and the fact that the cleaning woman killed him. He can't talk to anyone."

"Is that woman legal? Can we get her deported?"

Morris gave him a give-me-a-break look. "She's legal. I checked her out when Lenore hired her four, five years ago."

"Did you check out this John Irving guy?"

"I did, and there was nothing that stood out about him. I'm guessing someone enlisted his help after they figured out he and Lenore were dating."

"Couldn't have lasted long."

"Six, eight weeks I'd guess."

"What about this Finnegan guy?"

"Seems fine. Moral, family man," his friend said, raising an eyebrow at him.

"Something I'm not, you mean."

Morris shrugged.

"So we'll wait and see what our guy comes up with?" Maxwell asked.

"That's all we can do for now, that and hope we get there before the cops."

"All right, I need to go and deal with Jack."

"Is he going to go through with the transplant even though it's not a true match?"

"Don't know. He said he'd think about it. He's worried about graft-versus-host disease. It's a complication that occurs after a stem cell or bone marrow transplant in which the newly transplanted material attacks the recipient's body."

Good Lord, he sounded like he memorized that from a textbook, Morris thought.

"Yes, but only identical twins are near-perfect matches, so no matter who it was, there'd be a risk," Morris said.

"But Nate is further off the perfect spectrum than I'd hoped."

"Expecting a miracle, Byron? Even if Nate was yours and Corrine's, there'd only be a 35 percent chance of a match."

"I thought I was due for one," Maxwell said dejectedly.

Morris wanted to rail and make fun of him, but Maxwell was too pathetic, so he let it go.

"If Jack wants the procedure, you'll let Nathan meet with him?"

"I don't know that I have a choice."

Morris found himself wishing that Jack would go to sleep and never wake up.

****

"*Mo chuisle*, it's your phone." MP gently nudged Lenore awake and handed it to her.

Sleepy and bleary-eyed, she answered. It was Walker.

"I see."

"Well, that's not good."

"I bet," she laughed. "Let me know if anything else develops."

"Oh, and before you hang up, I have news from Nate, too." She told him about the not-quite match that might have to do.

"Will do, thanks."

"Talk about a wake-up call," Lenore said. "Byron already received a picture of Nate, and Morris hasn't been able to trace the origin. E-mail was nothing but a photo."

"To taunt him? To say we know about your other son?" MP asked.

"Most likely. Morris said he'd take care of it, and Connor, I'm sure, didn't want to know how. Nor do I for that matter."

CHAPTER THIRTY-FOUR

The following day, Lenore and MP were finishing room service breakfast when the call from the Yardley PD came.

Lenore looked less than happy as MP watched her. She got off the phone furious.

"That SOB put a bug in the kitchen. It was bad enough that there was one in the office. I told you all about my dealings with Byron in the kitchen and, and, well—we've had some pretty energetic sex there too."

At that he had to laugh. "Yes, and it's a recipe I'd like to whip up again."

Taken by surprise at his response and humor to the situation, she calmed herself a tad. "It was wonderful, wasn't it?" Her eyes were bright at the memory.

He wrapped his arms around her and pulled her to him, kissing her lips lightly. "It was off-the-charts sensational. I'm sure JI or whoever was listening was more than jealous."

"This is ridiculous, MP. What if somebody leaks the audio?"

"I'd be lying if I said I didn't care. But the fact is we're two, single, consenting adults who happen to love one another, and if we want to make love in the kitchen, it's no one's business but ours. Plus, what was done is illegal so if the tapes are leaked and the cops find out who, he or she will be in trouble with the law."

"I'll be mortified."

"You'll get over it. There is nothing wrong with having sex and enjoying yourself."

"Hopefully, it won't leak."

"So only the two rooms were bugged?"

"Yes."

"Well, that's good. Now I can ravish you in any room of the house in private."

"You can." Grinning, she let him kiss her again.

"They found nothing in JI's house. So, either Morris got to it before the cops, or there was nothing there to find. Irving could have had an office or worked in another location."

"Don't think so. I don't see your gray man doing anything over the top."

"But I'd never think he'd bug my house or stalk me either."

"You have a point," he conceded. "But I think someone approached him to do this. I don't think he was hired directly by the person who wanted information. I think there was a third party."

"I know you do. But who wanted the information? Most likely Corrine. I think she's every bit as resourceful as Gerald Morris. But the point is, we can go home."

"I like the sound of that. Is the place still a mess? Do we need to deal with clean-up or anything?"

"Uh, I didn't even ask. We'll have to see when we get there. I should have thought to ask about reporters, too. Shit, what is wrong with me?"

"Not your everyday routine, *mo chuisle*. Cut yourself some slack. We can stay here another night or at least the day and go home in the middle of the night before they come back, if they do."

Her cell was going off. "It's Nik. It must have hit the news somewhere. I'm sure she has news alerts set up on us, or her crazy partner does."

"Don't tell her about Maxwell."

"I'll play it by ear," she said as she engaged the call.

"Are you and MP okay?"

"Nik, we're fine. We weren't even there. My housekeeper was. She killed him."

"Poor woman, but good for her. Some crazy guy demands to get into your house and won't leave? Stabbing him is a good alternative to a gun."

"Um, I suppose."

"I already asked my partner if he hired the asshole. He says no, and I tend to believe him. I can tell when he's lying."

"I think John Irving was stalking me, Nik." She told her agent about him following her at the Mercer Museum.

"Good thing the MF is dead."

"I hate to agree, but I guess so."

"Although why did he insist upon getting into your house if you weren't there?"

The police must not have released all the information. Nikko didn't seem to know about the bugs.

"Don't know," she replied.

"Probably to wait for you to come home. Ambush you and MP or something."

"It's possible. I think he was a wacko. I checked him out but . . ." She let the sentence trail off.

"Yeah, lots of them. One is my partner."

"I'm sorry, Nikko. Is that getting any better?" Nik had found out that there wasn't much she could do about the partnership agreement that Howard and Nolan had entered into, so the office was like the War of the Roses. She had her side and he had his.

"Doll, don't be sorry. Not your fault he turned out to be a prick. I hope Howie comes back to haunt him."

"Me, too," she said sincerely, knowing the chances of that were minimal.

"But if Howard were still around, he would have shown his face before now. So I know that won't happen. I wish he would, though. I miss him," Nikko said.

"I know you do, honey," Lenore said softly.

"Enough of my pity party. Are you okay? I mean, the guy you dated is dead, he was stalking –"

"Honest, I'm fine. It's unsettling, to say the least, on several levels, as you've mentioned, but I'll be all right."

"Finnegan dealing?"

"Yeah, he is. I don't know what I'd do without him." She turned and flashed him one of her brilliant smiles. He returned one in kind, dimples making an appearance.

She turned her back so she wouldn't lose her train of thought.

"At least the news articles didn't mention LaSandra Lacy and MP Finnegan. They did use your name, Lenore Held, and it only seems to have hit your local papers, the *Bucks County Courier Time* and the *Philly Inquirer*, probably on the local news, too."

"Could be worse, I suppose. We had to leave my house overnight and didn't even think to look for it on the news. It was a crazy day yesterday."

"I'm sure. I'll let you go."

"Thanks for checking on us."

"We are not national news, only Bucks County and Philly," she told MP.

"Good, we should be able to go home. If we see news people camped out, we'll keep going."

"Sounds like a plan. I miss being home."

"I know you do, lass."

She went to him and wrapped her arms around his neck. "I love you, Michael Patrick Finnegan."

He grinned. Her spontaneous declaration pleased him.

"I love you, too, Lenore Held."

She lifted her head for a kiss.

****

"Lenore, let me go in first and see what's what," MP said as they began to enter the kitchen through the garage entrance.

"Sweetheart, I'll be fine. I'm a mom and have seen and done all kinds of gross and ugly. I'll hold it together."

"I have no doubt." He liked that she called him sweetheart. She didn't use many endearments, but when she did, he saved them up, each a cherished memory.

The house smelled medicinal and lemony. While she didn't care for the odor, the kitchen was not trashed nor the dark tile floor stained or damaged.

"It could have been so much worse, MP. He could have killed Maria or held her hostage and waited for us to come home and –"

He knew where she was going and cut her off. "I know, *a chuisle*, but he didn't. With that imagination and brain of yours, you'll have us scared out of our wits in no time," he teased.

"You're right. I want to work on the book," she said. "Normalcy."

"Whatever the lady would like."

"That will have to wait for later."

He raised an eyebrow at her and grinned, a sinful grin that had mischief step-dancing in his eyes.

They settled in her office with hot chocolate, a plate of cookies, and a great deal of creative energy.

"As soon as the meeting's over, lass, he's going to lock the door and take her hard and fast," Michael Patrick said.

"She's counting on it," Lenore said, delighted.

Wicked woman had on black stockings and a garter belt but no underwear and she made sure he knew it. The secret was for him and only him. He had to avert his eyes from her or lose his train of thought. They were working on staging and lighting and needed to get it right.

She was able to carry on as if she weren't bare assed, her pretty lower lips blowing him kisses every time she crossed and uncrossed her legs. In fact, the vixen seemed unruffled by his furtive glances between those legs. But he'd bet she was wet and eager for him, and if she wasn't, she would be.

Meeting finally over, he ushered everyone out, closed the door, and locked it, then leaned against it as casually as he could and looked her up and down. On the surface she was every bit the proper workingwoman: knee-length skirt, black thigh highs, jacket and shell to match, a tasteful rope of pearls around her neck. Cool, elegant, professional – that's the picture Amanda projected to the world. "Perception is reality," as she always said.

He pushed off the door, his eyes now fastened on hers.

She turned then and looked out his window, appearing to take in the city.

Cass came up behind her, moved her hair to one side, and then nuzzled her neck. She arched into him. "You're something, Amanda."

"What might that something be?" she asked huskily.

"Right now you're a devil in a Talbot's suit."

She laughed.

One of his hands snaked between her legs from behind and to her inner core, plunging two fingers into her. She jerked at the suddenness of it.

"You're wet for me."

"More often than you know," she murmured.

"We'll have to discuss that in detail later."

She ground her hips into his thrusting fingers.

"Put your hands on the windows. Palms open and flat."

She did as he asked. Maybe for the first time ever, since they met.

He let her feel his arousal through his pants and her skirt, but it was unmistakable. She made some unintelligible sound. He liked that.

"Widen your stance for me."

She did.

He added another finger to the other two.

"Ahh, ahh," she breathed.

He took his fingers away.

"No, not yet," he informed her.

She didn't speak, didn't beg, kept her legs spread apart, and her hands flat on the window.

His hand came around the front of her now and teased her clit.

"You teased me all through that meeting, Ms. Loring, and now it's payback time."

She moaned as he stroked her. Her inner thighs wet.

He kissed her ear and ran his tongue around the curve of it, then nipped her ear lobe, causing her to jump involuntarily. Still she said nothing.

The sound of him unzipping his pants was all but deafening in the otherwise silent room.

He noted her breathing was erratic and shallow.

"Spread those lovely legs as far as you can," Cass directed.

She did.

He hitched her skirt above her waist. Her bottom was round and near perfection. He wanted to see if she had freckles there, too, but that would wait for another time.

One of his hands opened her to him, and he entered her slowly.

"Please."

"Since you asked so nicely." He pushed the whole of him into her.

"Yes," she sighed.

He felt her muscles contract around his cock, drawing him deeper. Cass thrust into her hard and fast, kissing the pulse beating frantically in her neck as if it were trying to break free.

"Yes." She almost cried it this time.

Amanda was now meeting him thrust for thrust, no longer able to hold herself still. She heard his breath as ragged as hers.

"Come with me, Cass. I don't want to go alone."

He groaned as her muscles spasmed and clamped around him, milking him for all he was worth. Condom, he thought in the dim recesses of his mind. He'd deal with the consequences later. He couldn't stop now.

"Casper," she called out, as he grunted, groaned, and growled his own release, until finally he whispered, "Amanda."

He leaned into her, both of them breathing hard. He brought his hands up to cover hers on the window and then gently brought them down.

Cass kissed her cheek. This was more than games and sex. What this was, he didn't want to think about yet. But he knew she felt it, too. He could see it in her deeds and hear it in her voice.

He brought their joined hands together and encircled her waist. Finally, he turned her around to face him and there were tears in her eyes.

"Sweetheart," he almost whispered, "Are you okay?"

She smiled and nodded.

He drew her to him and then picked her up. He never dreamed she'd be like this, soft and emotional, under that hard-as-nails attitude. Cass kissed her forehead and carried her to the couch.

He laid her down gently and brushed stray strands of golden fire from her delicate face.

"I want to make love to you. The only thing I want left on your body is the strand of pearls."

She watched as he began to undress her.

"It's great," Lenore breathed when he finished reading the passage. "I like it a lot."

"Squirmy? Edgy?" he teased.

"Yes. But I like the sentimentality in it. You can feel the dynamics of the relationship shift."

"You can, can't you?"

She nodded. Lenore knew she was flushed.

He tucked her hair behind an ear and kissed her.

"In need of that release you told me about?"

"Yes."

"Me, too."

He began removing clothes, and so did she. Pressing her back on the couch, he took every inch of her and made it his. *My breath.*

"Sounds like the audio track to a porn movie," the senator spat. Morris's men had gotten to Irving's condominium before the police and had retrieved his laptop.

"Jealous?" Morris asked.

"Hell, yeah," his frat brother answered honestly.

Both men laughed.

Morris turned off the "sound track" to *Great Sex in the Kitchen*, as he'd come to think of the clip. He didn't need Maxwell any more distracted than he was.

"The bigger concern is the tape where she confesses her relationship with you to Finnegan. Wouldn't have happened if you'd not gone there."

"How do you know? She obviously cares for the man."

"She'd never told her own son—your son—she wouldn't have told him if you hadn't barged into her house. You required an explanation, and he asked her point blank if you were her kid's father. Woman doesn't lie."

Maxwell was silent.

Morris continued. "Moving right along, we know Irving was stalking both Lenore and us. He was fixated on Lenore."

"Ya think," Maxwell drawled sarcastically.

"The man is dead, and that's a good thing for Lenore, because no matter who hired him for the job, he had it bad for her. There are about 500 photos of her from multiple days over a number of weeks. Over a hundred since Saturday alone."

"Creepy," Byron conceded.

"Anyhow, we still haven't figured out who hired him. My team is still working on it, and maybe they'll find something, but whoever it is, is well-hidden."

"It's got to be Rin."

"Maybe. Or maybe someone Rin put up to it or fed information to her."

"Could be Jack, too."

They'd been covering the same ground over and over again.

"I think we need to do something preemptive. I want you to tell Corrine that I think someone is following us and see what kind of reaction you get."

"What if I read her reaction wrong? What if she doesn't give me any?"

"Do you want me to do it, for God's sake?" his staffer said, exasperated.

"Yeah, I'd prefer that."

"All right. I'll tell her we're concerned for her safety. I'll do it tonight while you're at that rubber chicken dinner for the Literacy Foundation."

"Okay," Maxwell said pouring himself a double scotch.

****

"That was Walker. Message was cryptic, but my best guess is that Morris's people got whatever JI had in his condo—audio and photos," Lenore said and felt herself color. "Thank goodness there was no video."

"If questioned, I could say it wasn't you. I'll say it was Addy."

She started laughing, mirth collecting in her eyes. "That would make her decade."

"Yeah. But I do like that she's been working from home."

Lenore had asked Addy to work from home while she and MP were finishing the book. She was too much of a distraction flitting about. Of course, Lenore was not so blunt when she told her.

"It's worked well for her, too. Her mom is staying with her while she recuperates from hip surgery."

"I don't want her back full-time, Lenore. I like her, but I like my time with you alone much better."

"We'll see once this mess shakes out. I'm worried for her safety at the moment."

He nodded his agreement.

"Maybe I'll have her come in one or two days a week, and the remainder she can work at home."

"A compromise."

"Yes, and if you're keeping score, I think that's number two."

"Not keeping score, simply teasing you, wee one."

"Hmm." Lenore eyed him suspiciously.

"Really, Ms. Held."

"Anyway, appears JI was stalking me along with everything he was doing. But he's dead, so that's a nonissue."

"For you, but I'm going to keep tight rein on you. Make sure someone else doesn't take an unhealthy interest in you."

"If anyone has or does, it will most likely be Corrine Kennedy Maxwell."

She clicked and clacked on her laptop and brought up a photo of the woman and turned it for MP to see.

"You see this woman hanging around, duck and cover. I'm certain if given the least provocation, she will shoot to kill."

"You're serious."

"As a heart attack," she said earnestly.

He took a good long look at the senator's wife. "She was a beauty once."

"Yes, I think that's how she and Maxwell got together—looks, a mutual admiration society."

"Bit harsh, aren't you, Lenore?"

"I might be," she said candidly. "I've not walked in her shoes nor had a husband who was, and probably still is, a serial cheater. Nor, thank God, a son who's died and one who's terminally ill. You're right, MP, I apologize. I am being harsh."

"*A chuisle*, I didn't mean to upset you."

"No, you didn't. I never looked at it from 100 yards out. I would never trade my life for hers."

MP studied her for a second and then pulled her onto his lap and held her. She burrowed in close to him enjoying the sensation.

"I think I'll go make dinner," she finally said.

"Anything I can to do to help?"

"Sit on the other side of the counter."

*****

Gerald Morris rang the bell at the Maxwell homestead. While large and pricey, it was cold. It was not a home in the way Lenore's was. He needed to get a grip, too. His mind was wandering way too often to Lenore Held, and that boat had definitely sailed.

The housekeeper answered the door, asked him to wait in the parlor, and said Mrs. Maxwell would join him shortly. How many people used the word parlor anymore? Not many, he ventured. He walked around and looked at posed family photos of plastic people and objets d'art.

He turned to face her as he heard approaching steps. Morris offered neither hand nor cheek. He had learned long ago that Corrine was not one to coddle with social niceties. She looked like shit, he thought. Easily ten years older than she was. Her body was in impeccable shape for a fifty plus woman, but her face needed a major cosmetic overhaul. Life had not been kind to her.

"Corrine," he said simply and inclined his head.

"Gerald," she returned, sat on the couch, and motioned for him to sit in the chair across from her.

He did so, pulling up his pant legs to save the creases.

"To what do I owe a house call?"

"Byron and I spoke before he went to his dinner function and he thought it best –"

"We both know my husband doesn't think, can't, he's simply not capable. What is it you want to tell me?"

"I wanted to let you know that I believe someone has been following Byron and/or possibly myself."

She smiled and raised an eyebrow that almost announced game on. "Could it be someone's disgruntled husband or significant other? I understand that he has had a number of dangerous liaisons over the years, and perhaps someone is not willing to share."

"Don't believe so, and with the tragic events in Arizona recently, I wanted to make sure you are aware of a potential threat."

A little color was in her cheeks now, a glint of challenge in her eyes. "Bad things happen everywhere, Gerald. Why, I read this morning in the *Philadelphia Inquirer* that one of Byron's former interns suffered a home invasion in an exclusive Bucks County community. The cleaning lady fought him off. Killed him with a knife."

Gerald did his best to keep his face bland. "That's too bad."

"Article didn't say she had been his intern, but I remember the name well, Lenore Held. I wonder, did she never marry or simply keep her maiden name? So many women do that now. I wish I had."

She was good, he thought. She should have been the one running for office.

"There have been so many interns over the years, I don't recall the name."

"Don't you, Gerald? I'd have thought she'd made a lasting impression on all of us. But as you say, so many interns, so little time." She gave a well practiced, demure laugh.

Morris rose straightening his creases. "I thought I'd give you the heads-up. Be careful, Corrine. As you say, bad things happen everywhere."

She took the measure of him. He could see that she wondered if he was making a comment or issuing a threat.

"Don't worry about me, Gerald. I can take care of myself."

"Yes, so I'm told," he said, raising both eyebrows provocatively.

Home run, he thought, as her face flashed red.

"Good night, Corrine," he said and walked to the door, not waiting for or expecting a response.

****

Lenore and MP were eating dinner at the kitchen table instead of the bar. She'd made a quick chicken stir-fry.

"You know all this sex and writing about sex is addling my gray matter," she said, impatient with herself.

"Couldn't it be the stalker, the bugs, or let's not forget the crazy Maxwell clan and the brains of the operation, Morris? Nah, let's blame it on the one thing pleasurable going on right now."

"Hey," she touched his hand. "I was kidding. Kind of like those Catholic wives tales that if you masturbate, you'll get hairy palms, go blind, or something equally as crazy. Too much great sex kills brain cells."

"Sorry, I overreacted."

She was silent for a minute, wondering if she had missed something, and then continued. "We talked about my affair with Byron in this room, and even if the audio was illegally made, it could still be damaging if leaked and don't say it's Addy's voice on the tape," she warned.

"You need to start making a plan as to what you're going to do when it comes out," he said seriously.

"You think it's going to?"

"I do, and I'd hate like hell to see you blindsided. Your pen name will probably be blown, too."

"I've been thinking about it as well. If it breaks, I'm going to have no comment and let Connor deal with it. I'll give him a prepared statement he can read. We'll make sure we have plenty of food and hole up until the news dies down."

"That's fine. It's a plan. But what about Nate? He's got classes, and it might not be that easy for him to hole up in his apartment and hold a sign to the window with 'No Comment' written on it."

"You're right," she said thoughtfully.

"You could be preemptive and release the information yourself – not you directly, but through Walker."

She looked as if she were going to be sick. "I could never do that."

He persisted. "You could have Walker talk about the bone marrow transplant and say that after all these years, Maxwell approached –"

"No," she cut him off with the word as well as an emphatic shake of the head. "Why are you doing this?"

"I'm worried about everything that's going on, *a chuisle*. I'm worried sick about your safety. If Corrine is out to get you, she's not going to do it herself; she'll hire someone."

"Why wouldn't she go after her cheating husband?"

"Maybe she'll go after everyone."

"My God. Nate. What if she goes after Nate?" Tears and a mother's panic welled in her eyes.

"*A chuisle*, calm down." He held her tight. "I'm not saying this to distress you, I'm saying this, because I'm worried for you and for Nate."

"You should be worried for yourself, too. JI tried to kill you yesterday." She held him closer, seeing the scene again in 3-D.

"I don't think I should be seen in Washington. I'll hire a car and have Nate and Kelly driven up if he's amenable to it."

Her cell rang before he could speak.

"Shit, it's Walker. This can't be good."

She engaged the call and listened to her attorney. She got up, pacing the kitchen. Eventually she stood still and leaned against the counter.

"Jesus. What a nightmare," she said, dragging her free hand through her hair.

When she closed the phone, her hands were shaking again. She took a step and actually faltered.

MP didn't even hesitate, picked her up, and carried her to bed. Propping her up on pillows he said, "I'll be right back."

Three minutes later, he returned with hot chocolate. "It's real milk and real chocolate. Not from the double boiler but from the microwave. I promise it's good."

She looked wary.

"I didn't poison it, Lenore."

She smiled, shaking her head. "It's not the hot chocolate."

"Then what?"

"I know on top of everything else this is going to sound crazy," she started.

"What is it?" His face was full of concern.

"See, I don't act like this. I'm not a watering pot, I don't swoon, I—could be pregnant. We have been less than diligent about using condoms." Tears were now rolling down her cheeks. "Oh God I'm sorry." She covered her face with her hands.

"For what, love? Not because you're crying or because you might be with my child." His hand automatically went to her womb. "I don't want you sorry for either one."

"But —"

"But nothing. If you're pregnant, we'll get married right away. It was going to happen anyway. I didn't want to ask you for fear of scaring you off. Special license, isn't that what you call it in your books when a couple need to get married fast?"

"Yes, but do you want a leg shackle and a baby all at once?"

"Yes, and even if you're not with child, I want you as my wife."

Tears flowed. He handed her his white handkerchief.

"Do you carry these for me?"

"I bought new ones for you, but I've always carried them."

"Quaint habit," she said, taking a deep breath.

He handed her the hot chocolate, and after she took a few sips, he said, "While I'd rather be snuggled with you here in bed and contemplating baby names, what did your legal man have to say?"

"It's what started this entire crazy jag. Corrine is the one who's behind this," she said and went on to explain.

"Jesus," he said, taking her hand.

"Mary and Joseph, we need them, too," she teased.

"And everyone else we can rally. The woman's got brass ones."

"Yes. Connor thinks your idea might have merit, especially if we can get Maxwell to unite with us. Even if we don't make a preemptive statement, we should develop a plan that the major players buy into and stick to once word is out. We also need to clue in Nikko in case, as you pointed out, my pen name is outed."

"I agree."

"But I'm not doing anything unless Nate is on board."

"I understand." He rubbed the top of her hand, trying to soothe away all the chaos.

"I know we need to tell Nikko about this, so she can have time to spin. But I don't want to meet anywhere near Hubble. He might have her office bugged for all we know."

"Then ask her to come here, and we'll double up on two New York trips."

"Okay."

He got up from the bed.

"Where are you going?" she asked, missing his warmth already.

"To the drugstore."

"For . . ."

"A pregnancy test."

"It might be too soon."

"Then it will be here when the time is right."

"If it will make you happy."

"If you're pregnant, I will be over the moon."

She laughed, thinking of the use of moon in her book titles. Well, this was yet and still another full moon moment.

Lenore tried to feel upset about possibly being pregnant but couldn't. If she was, the child was meant to be. MP would make a wonderful father, maybe a husband, too. For some reason, marriage had never entered her mind. She'd thought they'd live together, but that was apparently never his intent.

She had been emotional and borderline hypoglycemic when she was carrying Nate. Lenore was also exhausted the first trimester. She touched her flat stomach. "If there's someone in there, hello," she whispered and smiled to herself.

CHAPTER THIRTY-SIX

Lenore awoke the next morning to see MP watching her. "I'm going to feel incredibly bad if I'm not pregnant."

"We'll keep practicing then, and if we're meant to have a child it will happen. If not, we'll wait and be grandparents to your Nate's children, spoil them rotten, and send them home."

She laughed. "I hate to ask, but what's the scoop on the test?"

"You knew I'd read the box."

"Dah, of course."

"They recommend at least fourteen days after ovulation but certainly no less than seven."

"My period is due in three days. Can you wait?"

"No, I bought two tests," he said, handing her one.

"All right."

"You urinate on the stick, and if there are two lines you're pregnant, and if there's only one, you're not."

"Got it," she said, taking the box with her into the bathroom and closing the door. She was almost surprised he didn't follow. She read the directions herself anyway, peed on the stick, and set it on the counter. The results would appear in five minutes or not.

She washed her hands, combed her hair, and brushed her teeth. If she was not pregnant, then she was turning into a loon.

"We still have three minutes to wait," she said. "I hope I don't disappoint you. I feel bad that I said anything."

"I won't be disappointed." He kissed her to make his point.

She snuggled back down in the covers and rolled into the warm spot he'd left.

Lenore had fallen back asleep immediately and was woken by MP jumping on the bed and kissing her breathless. He was beyond over the moon. "There are two lines, *mo chuisle*, look." He showed her the test stick, she smiled, and her eyes misted. His happiness was so genuine that she couldn't help but revel in it.

"I'll be here every step of the way, Lenore. I told you I don't do anything halfway."

"Apparently not," she teased. "Pretty quick, too, I might add."

His delight and joy were infectious, and she let him sweep her away with them.

"I love you, Lenore."

She kissed him sweetly and welcomed him into her arms, her body, and her heart.

****

"What are you doing?" MP asked when he saw Lenore making two carafes of coffee.

"One regular and one decaf."

"Decaf for you, I take it."

"I'll wean myself off the caffeine. If I go cold turkey, I'll get headaches."

"I'll go caffeine-free with you," MP said.

"You don't have to. I'm not convinced that caffeine in moderation is bad for anyone. In fact, a number of studies show it's actually good for you. But on the off chance it's bad for the baby, I won't be drinking it for long."

"No reason for you to be making two pots of coffee. In a few weeks, we'll both be caffeine-free."

"Okay. Are you going to gain weight with me, too?"

"Maybe."

"I should warn you, I was borderline hypoglycemic with Nate, and I need to have OJ and crackers or some other kind of carbs handy in case I get light-headed and woozy like I did last night. But don't be freaked. It's what made me think I might be pregnant."

"Anything else I need to know? I want to know everything."

"The tears, they maybe here for a while. Don't take them personally."

He laughed. "Raging hormones."

"Raging hormones got me into this predicament. Pregnancy hormones make me cry." She was laughing with him.

He wrapped his arms around her and tugged her in for a kiss.

"Omelets will burn. Let me go." She batted his arm lightly with the spatula to be released.

"Yes, ma'am."

"Please don't ma'am me. I hate that. Makes me feel old. I like *bitch* better."

"Those hormones make you feisty, too?"

"No, I always have that tendency."

"Do you now?"

He playfully grabbed for her.

"Other side of the counter. Go now."

He patted her bottom before he did.

"When do Nate and his young lady arrive?" Michael Patrick asked, taking his assigned stool.

"Kelly. About 6:00. I can't wait to meet her."

"So you've said."

"Michael Patrick, you're not worried about meeting Nate are you?"

"Of course I am, love. Like I said the other day, I want him to think that I'm worthy of his mother's love and attention," MP said sincerely.

"He'll like you. I think his only criterion for the significant other in my life is that he treat me kindly and with respect."

"I should leave bruises only where he can't see them then," he teased.

"Exactly. But let's not tell him or anyone about the baby yet. I want to make sure that everything is all right. It's so early, I don't want to jinx us. Plus, it's nice having the baby as our secret for a little while longer."

He smiled. "Never took you for superstitious, Ms. Held, but I do like the idea of keeping the baby to ourselves for a bit. Although I'm so ecstatic I could burst."

"I can tell. I'm amazed and shocked myself, but I'm going with your euphoria."

"Lenore, I want to get married."

"Are you sure? I'm okay with living together," she said as she slid an omelet and hash browns across the bar to him.

"You don't want to get married?"

She saw disappointment on his face.

"You'll gladly have my child, but you don't want me?"

Not disappointment, but upset and hurt, both were clearly visible now.

She came around the counter, set her plate next to his, then insinuated herself between his legs and looked directly into his eyes.

"I want this baby's father a great deal. That's why the baby is here." She placed his hand on her stomach and left hers on top of it. "But I don't want you to feel you have to marry me because of the baby. We've only known each other for four months and become intimate in the last several weeks." Tears were threatening. "Damn it." She swiped angrily at them. "Point I'm trying to make is I'm okay with waiting to get married. I love you but don't need a piece of paper to make me secure in that love."

He took his thumb and brushed the tears that looked like raindrops from her lashes.

"*Mo chuisle*, I meant what I said yesterday, baby or no, I want you to be my wife. I love you. Knew I did as soon as I shook your hand and looked into those incredible eyes of yours. At that moment, I knew you were meant to be mine."

He put a hand in his pocket and pulled out a ring. Her eyes went from his face to the ring and back. It was a spiraled circle of diamonds and opals.

"But when −"

"Did I get the ring?"

"Yes."

"I had a cousin send it to me shortly after I met you. I wanted to be sure I had it when the moment came."

She looked dumbfounded.

"It was my grandmother's, then my mother's, and I'm hoping you'll consent to being its next owner." He held it poised to slip on her finger.

"But I'm independent to a fault, I take charge, don't often compromise −"

"Do you love me?" he asked, cutting her off.

"You know I do, but −"

"It's enough. Lenore, will you be my wife?"

His eyes locked on hers, and they looked at one another for a long minute. He was still holding her hand and the ring.

"I," she faltered, "yes." She expelled a big breath with the word. "Yes, I'll marry you."

They were still caught in each other's gaze as his slid the ring home. Then pulling her close, he gave her a gentle, savoring kiss designed to seal the deal and capture her heart all over again.

The kiss ended as slowly as it began. They looked at one

another again, and then he looked at the ring on her hand and said, "It's more beautiful there than I imagined."

Lenore peered down at it then. It sparkled like a newly minted Waterford chandelier. "It is beautiful," she agreed. "The fit is perfect."

"I know. I traced the inside of one of your rings and took it to the jeweler to size so it would be perfect the moment you put it on."

"That was taking a chance."

"No, it wasn't. If it wasn't going to be you wearing this ring, it would have been no one."

"Are you for real?" she asked, smiling tearily at him.

"You bet, as a heart attack, like you say."

"I believe you and maybe more important, I trust you with my heart."

He hugged her close. "That means the world to me."

"I know." More tears rolled down her face. He took out his white handkerchief and wiped them away. She smiled at him and laughed. "Happy tears."

He sat her on a stool. "I'll nuke your omelet. I don't want my bride passing out on me."

"You'll be handy to have around."

"I plan to be."

He poured two wine glasses of orange juice and handed her one. "To us."

"To us," she echoed, and they tapped their glasses together. Then he kissed her and got her breakfast from the microwave.

"When do you want to get married?"

"I don't know, MP. When the craziness dies down?"

"We have no idea when that will be, and I'd like you to be mine before the baby makes his or her presence known."

"You mean before I get a baby bump?"

"Yes."

"Traditional, are you, Mr. Finnegan? Your writings don't support that."

"Bohemian, flower child Ms. Held. Your writings don't support that."

She laughed at him, at them.

"We can go to a JP, I suppose. Do you have dual citizenship?"

"I do, lass, so I'm not marrying you for a green card."

She laughed again. "No, if you didn't, I wasn't sure if that would be a complication or not. Now it's not even a consideration."

"Sure and it's one less thing for you to worry about."

She looked at the ring. "It's lovely. Thank you."

"No, *a chuisle*, thank you for honoring me by consenting to wear my ring."

"Don't make me cry, Michael Patrick," she warned. "Can we think about the wedding for a day or two? I shouldn't blossom that fast," she teased, ballooning out her shirt.

"Not too long, though."

"I promise, and we can even tell Nate and Kelly," she said.

"You sure?"

"I'm sure."

That earned her a smile and a kiss.

"Can we work for a while?" she asked once the dishes were loaded in the dishwasher.

"Of course, the baby will need a college fund."

They settled in her office with the two carafes of coffee.

Lenore booted up the computer and asked, "So does Cass get Amanda pregnant with their unprotected sex? I noted the no-condom conundrum, but that didn't stop him. I meant to ask where you were going with that before you took care of my need for release."

He was watching her. "You're so lovely when you blush."

She felt her face flushing even more. "Must be the hormones."

"No, darling, don't think so. You are one of the few women I know who still blush. It's very endearing and disarming. You could get a man in all kinds of trouble with that."

"Yeah, look at all the trouble you're in, daddy, husband, lover."

They were both laughing.

"Back to Cass and Amanda, Finnegan. What did you have in mind?"

"Don't know for sure. I thought we'd talk about it."

"We could have her not be pregnant and one or both be disappointed. Conversely, she could be knocked up and one of them could be unhappy about it. I'd say Cass, based on his thoughts of dealing with consequences later. Or they be could like us and be happy about it or maybe get there in the end."

"Should we let it play out for a while? Amanda's never been pregnant and wouldn't necessarily read the signs as clearly as you did."

"You mean she'll think she has the flu? I don't want to do the flu. Everyone does that."

"What about your symptoms?"

"Maybe, they're less obvious. But that's weeks away yet, in the book, I mean."

"Yes. I know you want to work on the investigation as to who's sabotaging the production."

"I do . . . but I have something. Amanda is injured, not seriously, although the accident is meant to kill her. Cass insists on taking her to the hospital, and she refuses x-rays. He becomes angry with her, and she blurts out that she's pregnant with equal anger."

"Very good, Ms. Held."

"Okay, now we need to get from here to there," she said excitedly.

CHAPTER THIRTY-SEVEN

"Where did the day go?" Lenore asked rhetorically as she fixed her hair and make-up in the master bathroom.

"We had a great day and got a lot done," MP replied from behind her, kissing the side of her face.

"Yes, we did," she agreed and gave him a fetching smile in the mirror.

"You should have taken a nap," he said.

"Not when I'm on a roll. If the kids weren't coming, I would still be working."

"I don't doubt that."

"I should have made dinner."

"No, we'll go out. It's fine. I called the Yardley Inn, and we're set for 7:30. That will give us time for a drink and a get-acquainted chat. You can fuss with food tomorrow."

"You're right."

"You describe yourself as difficult, but you always concede graciously," he teased.

"I have no problem admitting when something makes sense. Continue to make sense, and I'll continue to be gracious."

"Duly noted," he said, a dimpled grin crossing his face.

She finished dressing and studied her reflection. Her dress, a teal green, long-sleeved silk blend with a scooped neck and belted waist, made her look elegant and brought out the green in her eyes.

"You are a vision, Ms. Held, truly stunning—rich and intricate."

"Thank you, Mr. Finnegan. You look very handsome yourself—every bit the scarlet I said you were."

He was wearing a black cashmere blazer, black turtleneck, and gray wool slacks.

"I love the way your jacket feels," she said, running her hand down his arm.

"And I love the way you feel." He enveloped her in a hug. "You smell fantastic, too."

She giggled, "You are so full of Irish blarney, I'm going to need waders to keep the bullshit off of me."

"Charm, *a chuisle*, there is a difference."

"The line must be a fine one to detect," she laughed as she disengaged.

"I need to make sure towels and toiletries are in order," she said, leaving the bedroom.

"I'll help. Start showing me where things are so I can do my share."

"Okay, but I don't mind. We don't make that much mess."

"I don't mind either. I need to earn my keep."

She showed him where all the towels and linens were kept.

"Are they sharing a room?" Michael Patrick asked.

"Don't know, don't care. They can share or each have their own."

"I suppose that's only fair since we're sleeping together."

"Who says?" she asked.

"Would you prefer to sleep separately while your son is here?"

"I meant who says we're sleeping?" she offered him a naughty grin.

"You are a bad influence on me, lass," he grinned back. "But I think we'll be sleeping at least a bit because this wee one is zapping you." He gently touched her stomach.

"You have a point. They train you early and suck the life right out of you," she laughed. "Let's go down and put our feet up. They should be here soon."

"There's beer and white wine in the refrigerator and red on the counter," she said as they descended the steps. "Cheese is already cubed, crackers need to be put on the platter."

"Are you talking to me or yourself?"

"Mentally checking everything off. It helps if I say it out loud."

"You nervous about the girlfriend?"

"A little."

"*A chuisle*, it will be fine. Plus, she won't be living with you, so even if you hate her guts, you'll only have to deal with her for short periods of time."

"MP!"

"That's better. Color is in your face. I was having you on."

"You're terrible. I'm not sure I like you anymore."

"Nah, you love me."

"I do at that."

He pulled her in for a kiss and the door flew open.

"Have to remember to lock the door," MP whispered and she smiled.

"Caught in the act, Mom," Nate said genially.

"Michael Patrick Finnegan, this is my son, Nathan Held. Nathan, Michael Patrick," Lenore said, ignoring the color rising in her cheeks.

"It's a pleasure to meet you," they said at the same time. Everyone laughed.

The remainder of the introductions were completed.

"It's wonderful to meet you, Ms. Held, and thank you for having me," Kelly Hyde said nervously.

"Please call me Lenore, and I'm pleased to meet you as well."

Kelly was a tall young woman with wavy blond hair, blue eyes, and a shapely, trim figure. Her nose was perfectly proportioned to her face, and she had a bow mouth. If she were a character in one of Lenore's books, she would have described that mouth as made for pouting and kissing.

"Come on in, we'll have a drink before we go to dinner. We're going to the Yardley Inn. I hope you don't mind."

"No that's great, Mom. I'm going to put our stuff upstairs," Nate said, grabbing his and Kelly's overnight bags.

"Kelly, would you like something to drink? Beer, red or white wine, juice, soda, water."

The young woman was nervous. "Um, water would be great."

"Still or sparkling?" Lenore asked.

"Still."

"Lenore, sweetheart, go sit with Kelly; I'll bring in the drinks."

"Thanks, I'll have an OJ."

He smiled at her and winked.

The two women sat in the great room.

"Your home is lovely Lenore. Thank you again for having me."

"I'm delighted you were able to come. While you're here, make yourself comfortable. If you're hungry or thirsty, help yourself. If you need an extra blanket or towel, rummage for one."

"That's very kind."

"Drinks ladies," MP said with a megawatt smile.

He handed out their orders. He himself had a Sam Adams Winter Ale.

"I didn't know what Nate would want," he said.

"He'll find what he wants. He's used to helping himself."

"I heard that," Nate said, bounding into the room holding a Sam Adams as well.

Michael Patrick held up his bottle and said, "May your pockets be heavy—Your heart be light. And may good luck pursue you each morning and night. Cheers."

"Cheers," echoed his companions.

"How's the book coming?" Nate asked as he sat down next to Kelly and wrapped an arm around her shoulder.

"Great," MP said. "Your mother is the most amazing woman."

"She is, isn't she?" Nate winked at his mom.

Two winks in one night, Lenore thought, beaming back at Nathan.

They talked about the book and happenings at Georgetown. Kelly asked MP questions about Ireland.

"I've always wanted to go," she said, "but haven't made it there yet."

"If Lenore and I go for a visit, you and Nate are more than welcome to join us."

"Really?" The girl's eyes got big and excited. "That's very nice of you."

Lenore reached over and took MP's hand, smiling.

"Oh my, that is the most beautiful ring," Kelly said as the light played off the diamonds and opals.

Lenore hadn't even given a thought to the ring this afternoon or how they were going to break the news of their engagement. The ring had fit so perfectly, it was as if it had always been there.

"Nate, I gave your mum the ring. I've asked her to be my wife. I hope you'll approve."

Nathan gave MP, then his mom, an appraising look and asked his mother, "Does he make you happy, Mom?"

Lenore smiled. "Yes, honey he does."

"Do you love her, Michael Patrick?"

"More than anything."

Playing the part of male head of the household, Nate

crossed one leg over the other and said, "Then I give you my blessing, but if you make her unhappy you'll have me to answer to."

"Fair enough," MP said and offered his hand to Nate, who instead clapped him on the back, then went to hug and kiss his mother. Kelly joined in, too.

Lenore smiled at her son and fiancé, tears brimming in her eyes.

MP handed her his handkerchief.

****

"That went extremely well," Michael Patrick said when they finally made it to bed.

"It did," she agreed. "Nate likes you. I told you there was nothing to worry about."

"Ditto for Kelly and you."

"She's a little shy, but I like her."

"It's tough to compete with the three of us. Your son is like his mum, smart and quick-witted." He nipped at her mouth.

"Why thank you. I think that's a compliment."

"It is, lass. Now come closer because it seems like forever since I've held you."

"I was thinking the same thing."

He helped her undress, and she did the same for him.

"Are you tired?"

"Not too tired, if that's what you mean."

"Hmm, I want to hold you for a little while first." He pulled her to him and luxuriated in the feel of her. "I can't ever remember feeling this wonderful, Lenore."

She sighed and snuggled into him. "I kind of like it, too."

"You okay with the baby and the marriage and all? I've invaded your life and your body, too." He gently circled his hand on her belly.

"I'm a little frightened by the idea of a new life, especially all at once. I like order and logic, and this situation defies both. But it's a new chapter, heck, a new book, and I'm eager to see where the plot leads. I want this mess with Maxwell over. I need to find time to talk with Nate, too. I don't get the sense he's told Kelly anything, but I don't want her to think I'm talking about her to Nate and make her uncomfortable."

"You'll figure it out, Lenore. I think they make a fine young couple."

"Me, too. She seems to hang on to his every word."

"Ahh, young love."

"Are you saying I don't hang on to your every word?"

"Don't want you to. But young people are often consumed by one another."

"Excuse me? We're not? I beg to differ."

He laughed. "I think we are the exception to the rule."

"Hmm, I don't know about that. I only know about us."

"Good. I'm the only one I want you to know about."

"Ditto, for you. Now how about we make love before your child turns me into a pumpkin." She kissed him and maneuvered on top of him.

"Sassy, aren't we?"

"Oh, honey you've not seen the half of it."

CHAPTER THIRTY-EIGHT

"Lenore, *a chuisle*, I think your Nate might be up. I don't think his girl is."

"Kelly, his girl—am I your girl?"

"You bet." MP smiled and kissed her.

"Incorrigible," she scoffed and got out of bed, throwing her robe on.

"Kiss me before you go. I'm used to making love with you first thing in the morning."

"Don't start." She kissed him, made her way to the bathroom, and hurriedly brushed her hair and teeth.

"I love you," he whispered as she left the room.

It melted her heart. "I love you, too."

Nate was indeed in the kitchen, making coffee.

"Hey, Mom, good morning."

"Hey, yourself. I thought you'd sleep in."

"I wanted to talk to you and knew you'd be up early to make my favorite breakfast."

"You bet, chocolate, chocolate chip waffles."

"Do you make them for your husband-to-be?" he asked in mock dismay.

"Nope, only for you," she teased back.

"But seriously, Mom, he seems like a nice guy. I'm happy for you."

"He's wonderful. I think I must feel a little like Kelly does when she looks at you."

He looked a little embarrassed. "I love her, Mom."

"I'm happy for you. Both of you."

"She's going to come with me when I go to law school."

"Will she go to grad school or work?"

"She's hoping to teach elementary ed."

"Terrific! She has a wonderful personality to work with children. She seems to be kind and patient and a good listener."

Her son smiled, "You like her then?"

"Yes, very much."

"I'm so glad. It means a lot to me."

She stopped taking ingredients down from the cupboard and turned to hug him. "Honey if she were a troll with four eyes and had the personality of Hannibal Lecter, I wouldn't care as long as she made you happy."

Her son laughed. "Exaggeration?"

"Maybe, a little."

They laughed and he popped several chocolate chips into his mouth.

"Has Jack decided what he's going to do?" Lenore asked.

"No. But I've decided I don't want to meet him."

"Really?" Lenore was genuinely surprised.

"It's a big risk. We look like twins, except for the eyes. I don't want to be linked with the Maxwells. If anyone sees us together, someone will talk."

"Nathan, someone might talk regardless. Conversations were taped in my house. Maxwell has them. Most likely someone else does, too. My kitchen and office were bugged."

"Damn it."

"My sentiments exactly. Maxwell was here talking about you and Jack in my office, and I told Michael Patrick about him in this kitchen. Stupid man should have never come to this house."

"You wouldn't have told MP about my father?"

"I don't know. I don't think so. Not until Byron came here and it became clear who he was did I even feel a need."

"I haven't told Kelly. Maybe I should if you think it will become public. I don't want her stalked by media people and paparazzi."

Lenore nodded her understanding.

He continued. "Part of my decision also rests with the fact that I'm not a very good match. I barely make 'acceptable,' and there is a good chance that my bone marrow will attack its host, in other words, Jack."

"Graft versus host disease," his mother said.

"Yes, and it can lead to death, especially in someone as weak as Jack. It won't even be known how bad it is until about three months after the transplant takes place. Jack will be on medication to suppress his immune system to lessen the chance of GVHD, but it also makes him more susceptible to other illnesses. He could die before he even gets GVHD."

"I know. I did some reading on it, too. But if he wants the transplant, you'll go through with the procedure?"

"Yes, that's another decision I've come to. It's not my call whether he lives or dies. And if he's given a second chance at a relatively normal life and squanders it, that's his own fault."

"And if he hurts others along the way?"

"I'm pretty sure all the chemo has killed his sperm, and if he had it frozen, the only woman he could get pregnant would be fully aware of the fact because it would be in vitro."

There are other ways to hurt people, she thought, but Nate knew that.

"I respect whatever decision you make and will back you up."

"Thanks, Mom. I knew you would."

She poured the batter into the waffle iron.

"Want some coffee?" Nate asked.

"Sure," she said, thinking she'd have to work on her decaffeination plan once they left. "You make good coffee."

"Thanks. Any idea when or who would take this public?" Nate asked casually.

"The *who* is most likely Maxwell's wife or someone hired by her who would leak the news. The *when* is unknown." She told him about Morris's meeting with Corrine.

"What a bitch! Why would she do that to her own son, even if she had no regard for her husband?"

"Not a clue, honey. Nor why now after all these years."

"Jesus."

"I talked with Connor about maybe doing something preemptive if we thought this was going to go public. At least take the wind out of her sails. See if Maxwell would go for it, something to do with the bone marrow transplant. But if Jack doesn't go for the transplant, there's no point, and maybe it will go away."

"You don't believe that, do you?"

"Not really, only because whoever wants the dirt on Maxwell has pulled out all the stops. A man was killed right here in this kitchen."

Nathan looked around the room as if remembering that for the first time. "Kind of macabre as we get ready to eat decadent waffles, don't you think?"

A wry smile crossed her face. "Will that stop you from eating them?"

"I hate to say it, but absolutely not."

"Me either."

She took the waffles out of the iron and put them on his plate.

"Have one with me while the next round cooks."

"An offer I can't refuse."

"But I need to know what you think, Nate. I know you don't like the idea of it getting out that the senator is your father, but if it's going to come out anyway, wouldn't you rather be on the offensive than the defensive."

"Of course, but how can you predict if/when we should do it?"

"I think we'll know a bit better once Jack decides what he's going to do. If he decides no on the transplant, we can hold off on the preemptive statement and have an agreed-upon plan with the senator and Morris as to what we'll all say or not say when it does go public."

"You're right, we need one consistent story and an agreement to stick to it. So, we'll play it by ear, but I'll need to explain it to Kelly."

Lenore nodded and put more waffles on his plate. "Nate, if I could make this go away, I would."

"I know, Mom. It's not your fault. For the life of me, I don't understand why Mrs. Maxwell would want the public scrutiny or humiliation this could bring on her. Not to mention an end to a run for the White House."

"Maybe she wants to ruin her husband. Doesn't want to live in the White House."

"The scorned woman and all that?"

"Yes. She's a wealthy woman in her own right. I've never understood why she stayed with Maxwell all these years," Lenore said.

Michael Patrick joined them after a while. He kissed Lenore and greeted Nate.

"Chocolate, chocolate chip waffles. You've never made these for me," he teased.

"Nope, they're Nate's favorites."

"I thank you for coming, Nate. I can't wait to taste this culinary delight your mother has whipped up."

"How do you stand all the Irish BS, Mom?" Nate asked good-naturedly.

"I only believe that which I want to, and then I call it charm."

"Must be a fine line between the two," Nate shot back.

Both Lenore and MP started laughing.

Kelly joined them shortly after and everyone had their fill of waffles.

"Lenore, you'll have to give me the recipe so I can make them for Nate."

"Sure, except I kind of just do it, but I'll do my best and you can tweak it as you go along."

"It's not an exact recipe?" The young woman looked panicked.

"I'll make it as exact as I can. I'm sure Nate will love it, however you make it."

Lenore made eye contact with her son.

"I'll love whatever you make," Nate said.

Kelly rolled her eyes.

They all laughed.

"MP, maybe you can teach me some of that Irish charm," Nate said.

****

While Nate took Kelly on a tour of Yardley, MP and Lenore settled in her office and picked up where they had left off the day before.

"Cass doesn't want Amanda on the set because he's worried about her safety –"

"And she's worried about his. It's a two-way street, you know . . ."

"He doesn't want to close down the production. He needs the money."

"Not that badly, and she's told him she will give, or lend, him the money if his fragile male ego prefers."

"He thinks he's invincible."

"He's not. Plus, she's told him she suspects Bart, his drunken half brother, who thinks Cass has money he doesn't."

"He's not ready to confront him yet. Cass wants more proof."

"Like Amanda's head on a pike?"

"The attempt on her life will be the catalyst he needs."

"Hmm . . ."

"I hate to interrupt. This collaboration is almost more intimate than the kiss we walked in on yesterday," Nate teased mercilessly from the doorway.

"We're near the end of our book and working toward the climax –"

Everyone started laughing.

"Poor choice of words," MP said, "but we've been arguing about the hero since I named him, and Lenore likes to belittle the shit out of him. Her heroine, thank goodness, has warmed up to him, however."

"What's his name?" Kelly asked, coming into the office, Nate behind her.

Lenore started laughing. "Go ahead, tell them."

MP raised an eyebrow at her. "Casper Grossman."

Kelly tried not to laugh, but Nate let it rip.

"We call him Cass most of the time." Lenore came to MP's rescue.

"I like Cass," Kelly said quickly.

"Casper the friendly ghost," Nate sang.

His mother laughed.

MP mock-scowled at her.

"What the heroine's name?" Kelly asked.

"Amanda Loring."

"I like it. Has a good ring to it," Nate's girlfriend offered.

"Yeah, I think it works," agreed Nate.

"Actually, Cass has grown on me," Lenore said. "I think the readers will be okay with it, too."

"Do you, lass?" MP asked, seemingly pleased.

"Yes, I do. People can't help the names their parents saddle them with."

"Agreed. What doesn't kill you makes you stronger," Nate said with a laugh, and Kelly giggled even though she tried not to.

"All right, how about lunch?" MP asked, wanting to change the subject.

"Sounds like a plan," Nate agreed, always ready to eat.

They all got up to go downstairs.

Lenore wobbled when she got up.

"You okay, Mom?" Nate asked, suddenly by her side to steady her.

"Got up too fast." She laughed it off.

MP glanced at her but gave nothing away.

"You're sure?" he asked before letting her go.

"I promise."

"This happen before, MP?"

"A couple of times, but it's normal for some people who sit in the same position for too long. I can attest to the fact that your mum is healthy. She can outrun me on the mule barge path up the street every day."

"I'll be watching you," Nate warned as he let her go and joined Kelly.

MP came up beside Lenore and followed the kids out of the office.

He wrapped an arm around her and gave her a long look.

"I'm fine," she mouthed.

He looked at her dubiously, and if they hadn't had guests, he'd have carried her to bed, brought her lunch, and made her nap.

"I think I'll take Kelly to New Hope after lunch and get some ice cream. She's never been. You guys want to join us?"

"No, you kids go ahead, enjoy yourselves. I have some bread rising for dinner and some prep work to do —"

"I bet," Nate said, "Like beating MP until he changes the guy's name. Casper Grossman indeed." He laughed again. Lenore and Kelly did their best to hide their mirth.

When they were gone, Michael Patrick looked at her and said, "You're going to take a nap."

"I'm fine. My blood sugar went low."

"Why didn't you say something? Like 'I'm hungry, thirsty, MP, can you get me an OJ?' I'd have gotten the clue even though your son and his girl were in the room."

"Kelly," she offered again. "I'm fine."

"You're going up to nap for a while, if I have to carry you up."

"I'm going, all right?"

He followed her.

"I can get there myself."

"That may be, but if you get light-headed and fall backward, I want to be there to catch you."

"Jesus," she muttered.

"Maybe he'll help, but I'm first on the list."

****

To her surprise, Lenore did nap. Baby was making its presence known. As long as she wasn't puking, she didn't care. She hadn't with Nate, but every pregnancy was different, they claimed. I'll sleep as much I need to; I don't want to be sick, she thought to herself as she rolled over and saw Michael Patrick next to her on the bed with his laptop. Of course, he was watching her.

"Did you watch me the entire time I slept?"

"Not the entire time. I wrote some, edited some, but I like watching you."

He leaned down and kissed her.

She rolled over to look at the clock. "I need to put the bread in."

"I did it a half-hour ago."

"You did?"

"Since there was a recipe on the counter, I looked to see what the oven setting was and once it reached 350, I put the bread in the oven and put on the timer for 90 minutes."

"Thank you."

"You're welcome." He kissed her again and then set aside the computer and snuggled with her. "Do you feel better?"

"MP, I didn't feel bad before. I'm having a baby. I'm not ill."

"I'm still going to see that you take care of yourself and get enough rest."

"We'll put some crackers in the office and some OJ in the small refrigerator up there. I meant to and forgot. But people who get up too fast do get light-headed sometimes, with child or not."

"They do, and you are. I'll not have you falling over or passing out and hurting yourself."

She sighed, exasperated, but let it go. He was concerned and not being a pain in the ass for no reason. In fact, she said, "Thank you."

"For what, *a chuisle*?"

"Being worried about me."

He smiled, "You're welcome."

"I'm still not used to having someone around."

"This is new to both of us, and we'll find our way together, deal?"

"Deal."

She snuggled back into him, and they both must have dozed off. Her cell was ringing from the night table on MP's side of the bed.

Lenore reached over his waking form to get it.

"Hi, honey."

"Are you kidding?" She asked bolting up and swiping the hair out of her face.

"No, we'll come and get you in MP's Prius."

"Yes, right on Main Street. We'll be there in a half-hour to forty minutes. I'll leave my phone on if you need me."

"At this point, you never know."

"I love you, too."

"They parked in the lot behind the police station, of all places, and when they returned to the car, all four tires were slashed," Lenore said in a rush as soon as she closed the phone.

"But they're okay?" MP asked.

"Yes, I think Kelly is shaken up."

"Smart girl." MP said, getting up from the bed.

"The police station is on Main Street. We need to go and get them."

"Of course." He held out his hand to help her off the bed and to make sure she was steady. She took it. "It will be all right, *mo chuisle*." He murmured in her hair as he embraced her for a moment.

"I hope you're right."

CHAPTER THIRTY-NINE

Lenore looked into the visor mirror under the guise of getting an eyelash out of her eye to see if they were being followed out of the police station's parking lot. They weren't.

Nathan and Kelly were in the backseat of MP's Prius looking tired and worn.

Lenore's car was being flat-bedded to the Acura dealer, and the tires would be replaced on Monday.

"I'm sorry, Mom," Nate said.

"Nothing for you to be sorry for. You were even parked behind the police department."

She didn't know if Nate had told Kelly about the Maxwell saga and didn't know how much to say, so she said little.

MP took hold of her left hand. Until he did, she hadn't realized it was trembling.

"Mom, Kelly is the second cousin of Corrine Kennedy Maxwell," Nate said with a bit of an edge.

"I see," she said, gripping MP's hand.

MP glanced in the rear-view mirror and looked at both Nate and Kelly. Nate was colored with anger, and Kelly was white with upset.

MP looked at Lenore. She was paler than Kelly.

"Lenore," he said softly, "are you all right?"

"I'm fine, MP."

He nodded.

No one spoke the rest of the way home.

They pulled into the garage, and MP said to Lenore, "Wait and I'll come around."

"I'll get her, MP," Nate said.

MP opened the door for Kelly, who all but ran into the house.

"Are you okay?" Lenore asked her son, knowing how betrayed he must feel.

"I will be. I'll call a taxi and have her taken to the train station. She'll be in D.C. in a few hours."

"Are you sure, honey?" she asked. Lenore and Nate were alone in the garage.

"Yes, I'm sure. I feel dirty and stupid."

"I understand." She did, too; they weren't empty words.

"I know you do, Mom, and at least I'm not pregnant like you were."

"I don't think she could have faked the way she looked at you."

"She claims she loves me."

"It could be true."

"We've been seeing each other since the beginning of the school year. She set out to trap me, entrap me; I'm not certain what the story is. Funny thing is she knew who my father was before I did. Before I did! Her bitch of a cousin told her she was fairly certain I was Maxwell's son."

"Was Corrine paying her?"

"Her tuition. Apparently, Miss Hyde's father lost a lot of money in the economic downturn—her words, not mine—so her cousin worked a deal with her. Kelly was to extract info from me, except I had none. There is some justice in that. The bitch was paying for nothing."

"Kelly fell in love with you, though." Her voice was soft and quiet.

"I fell in love with her. I'm not certain what Kelly's in. I'd have taken it better if she had told me about this before I told her about what was going on. If she loved me, why didn't she tell me?"

"Maybe she didn't feel it was her place to tell you. Or she hoped it would go away."

"If she loved me, she would have come clean."

"Maybe she was afraid of your reaction or of Corrine's."

"Why are you making excuses for her, Mom? You hardly know her."

"I don't know. Perhaps because I know she means a great deal to you –"

"Meant. I need to get her a taxi out of here. I want her on the next train to Washington."

"I'd feel better if she took my car service. I'll pay them to make sure she gets on the train. It will be safer."

"Whatever you want, Mom."

They went into the kitchen, and MP handed her a glass of juice. She took several sips, then called the car service and finished the rest in one gulp. She wished it were a double anything.

"You don't think she bugged the house, do you?" Lenore asked MP.

"Sweetheart, I don't know what to say right now."

"I'll ask her myself."

MP followed her up the stairs. She didn't even bother to harp at him. Once he saw her safely up, he went to the office.

Lenore knocked on Kelly's door.

"Come in," a thready voice called.

The girl looked much younger than she was at the moment. Her eyes were red and swollen, and her face was tear-stained and blotchy.

"I'm sorry, Ms. Held."

"It's not my forgiveness you need; it's Nate's. I can't tell you he'll ever give it. He feels very hurt and betrayed."

"I . . . I know." The tears started anew.

"Did you tell your cousin you were coming to my house?"

She nodded her head yes.

"Kelly, I'm going to ask you something, and I expect you to give me an honest answer, because if you don't and I find out to the contrary, I will press criminal charges against you."

The girl looked panicked now. Good, maybe she would get the truth out of her. "Did you put any bugs, recorders, listening devices, video recorders, or anything else in my home?"

"No, I swear to you I didn't. I wouldn't even know how to."

"I don't think it's that difficult. Last chance—Kelly, are you telling me the truth?"

"Yes," the girl said, maintaining eye contact.

****

Nate found Michael Patrick in his mother's office.

"Hey," MP said when he walked in.

Nate nodded. "I'm going to ask you this one time, MP, and if you lie to me, I swear I'll rip your heart out."

MP gave him his full attention. The young man was obviously concerned about something. "I believe I'm a man of integrity, ask anything, and I'll answer you honestly. If I don't know the answer, I'll tell you I don't know."

"You are not in any way tied up with this Maxwell mess, are you?"

"No, I'm not, Nathan."

"I want to believe you, but after Kelly, I don't know who or what to believe."

"I can understand that."

"My mother loves you, and for years it's been the two of us, only the two of us. You hurt her, and I will make your life a living hell."

"I don't plan on doing that. I love your mother, too, more than I've ever loved anyone or anything. I'll love her until I draw my dying breath. There you have it. I can't imagine my life without her."

"That's how I felt about Kelly until a few hours ago."

"I'm sorry about that, Nate. I think the lass cares for you."

The young man shook his head no.

MP wasn't going to argue with him. Nate was entitled to his own feelings and thoughts.

"When is the wedding?" Nate asked, suddenly changing the subject.

"Whenever your mum wants it. I'd like it if you'd be my best man. Don't know many people around here, and I'd be honored if you'd do it."

"Sure," Nate said as a ghost of a smile crossed his face. "Don't let me down, MP. More important, don't let her down."

"You have my word."

"That will have to do, I suppose."

With that, Nate left the room. Michael Patrick had to admire the young man for his gumption and balls in the face of his own upset. MP believed that Nate would have beaten him to a bloody pulp if he had been at all involved with any of the Maxwells.

****

The doorbell rang. It was the driver. Lenore talked to him for a moment and then went up to get Kelly.

"Good luck," Lenore said to her as she left.

"I'm sorry," Kelly said.

MP came up behind her as she watched the car depart. "Come on, you'll get chilled," he said, turning her from the door, closing and locking it behind them.

"Stop fussing." She managed a smile for him. "Let's go have dinner. The lingering bread smell is making me hungry."

Nate had already found the bread, had it sliced, and was buttering himself a piece. "Great bread, Mom," Nate said with his mouth full.

She laughed a bit and said, "I'm glad you like it."

"What's for dinner?"

"Chicken breasts with artichoke hearts and wild rice."

"Excellent. I'll eat Kelly's share," he said with faux humor.

"There's plenty. You can take home the leftovers and eat them during the week."

"What did you talk to her about, Mom?"

"Nothing. I had a question to ask her —"

"Which was?"

"Did she bug the house with any of the usual or unusual devices, because if I found out she did, I'd have criminal charges brought against her. That was not an idle threat either."

"Man, I didn't even think of that."

"Kelly told me that she did not. How we will test that, I'm not sure. Can't get the police back without raising lots of questions we don't want to answer."

"I'll call a friend," Nate said. "He graduated last year and is working on some of that stuff for the Feds. It might take a few days, but it's worth seeing if she's as much of a bitch as her cousin."

Lenore said nothing. She had no idea where their relationship would shake out and didn't want to be on record as being in either the pro or con Kelly camp.

MP squeezed her hand gently and let it go.

"That would be great. Plus, I think Corrine knows all there is to know. So I'm not sure what benefit there would be to bugging the house again."

"Unless she wants to know what you're thinking about this going public."

"Which we discussed this morning so if the kitchen was bugged, we're already fucked," Lenore offered.

"Succinct and to the point, very good, Mom."

MP laughed and started to set the table.

"Let's talk about the wedding," Nathan said. "MP asked me to be his best man, and I've never been one before, so I have a vested interest."

Lenore beamed at Michael Patrick. He gave her a covert grin.

"It will be good practice before all my friends start getting married."

"We haven't decided on when or where," Lenore said.

"MP said it was your call."

"I know, but I haven't had time to think about it. It will be small. I'll probably ask Nikko to be my attendant." She would have asked Kelly, but that was out of the question now.

"She's pretty hot, but a little too experienced for me," Nate said.

"Well done, Nate. Not too old, too experienced, a very nuanced line. I may use it in a book someday," MP said.

Lenore gently slapped the back of his head. "Hey, I resemble that remark."

"Ah, don't say anything that would embarrass me, guys," her son said.

"And what might that be?" MP asked.

"I like my women experienced or more experienced than I am. They can teach me a thing or two."

"Or three or four," MP added playfully.

"Enough," Lenore said, putting the food on the table.

"Don't wait too long," Nate said.

"Why does it matter?"

"We need something positive to focus on, and a wedding would be just the thing. I'm happy for you, Mom, MP."

"Thanks," they replied.

"Jesh."

****

"It was sweet of you to ask Nate to be your best man," Lenore said when she and MP retired to their bedroom.

"I knew it would make you happy, and I don't know many people here. I might have asked Nolan because I figured you'd ask Nikko, but he turned out to be a shit. After your son read me the riot act this afternoon, I thought it fitting."

"Riot act?"

He told her about Nate's discussion with him after Kelly's confession. "I think after gray man and Kelly, he needed to be straight in his own mind that I wasn't a plant too."

"I'm sorry he came after you."

"It's okay," MP said. "Besides, I thought it was a very prudent thing to do, and it shows how much he cares for you. Most men his age would have been wallowing over Kelly's betrayal, but he wanted to make sure I wasn't a traitorous bastard too."

"That entire thing is sad. He told me this morning he loved her. I know he's hurting. I think she is, too. I don't know the entire situation, so I can't pass judgment on her."

"I notice you played that cool when he called her a bitch."

She nodded sadly and crawled into bed.

"I love you lots and lots, Michael Patrick."

"That goes double for me."

CHAPTER FORTY

"How did your visit with Lenore Held and her kept man go?" Corrine asked Kelly when she visited her the following day.

"I don't think he's her kept man," Kelly answered coolly and didn't offer that Lenore and MP were engaged. "They're both very nice people."

Corrine lifted an eyebrow at Kelly and asked, "So what happened there this weekend?"

"I broke up with Nate."

"You what?"

"I broke up with him. He, his mother, and her friend are all very nice, very decent people, and I can't deal with your treachery anymore." Kelly dug into her pocket and placed four bugs on the table. "I didn't set them. You'll need to find someone else to do your dirty work. I'd guess the guy who ended up dead in her kitchen was yours, too. Am I right Corrine?"

"I won't continue to pay for your final semester of college."

"It's already been paid, Corrine. I checked, and if you make a big issue out of this or cause me problems, I'll spill your story. I could get hundreds of thousands of dollars if I blew the lid off this thing. The only reasons I'm not are my feelings for Nathan and the fact that I genuinely like his mom."

"You ungrateful little –"

"Takes one to know one, cuz."

"Get out. Get out. I never want to see you again."

"The feeling is mutual."

Kelly left her cousin's home at a dead run and didn't stop until she hit the taxi stand. Her hands were shaking, and she didn't know what to do or where to go. How had her life become such a mess? Maybe Corrine would have her killed. Her father had warned her about his cousin, but she hadn't listened. She still needed the courage to go to Nate's apartment and get her things. She didn't know if she could do that, but all her school stuff was there, so she didn't have a choice.

****

"I'll call Connor and Nikko. Set up a meeting so we can decide what to do. I bet Connor can even track down someone to see if the house is bugged," Lenore said after Nate left.

"Yes, then you can have Nate call off his buddy."

MP noticed that she functioned better when she was doing and engaged. She didn't handle inactivity well, didn't relax well. He'd need to change that.

"You're always watching me," she said.

"Because you are a fascinating creature."

"Creature, that's about how I feel today."

"Do you need something?"

"No, I meant emotionally, not physically. Sweetheart, I'm fine. I'm not going to mess with this baby. If I don't feel right, I'll let you know. I promise."

"Okay." He gave her a sheepish smile.

She knew this baby meant everything to him, to her, too, for that matter, but especially since he had lost Ian Michael. Lenore rubbed her stomach and sent a silent "I love you" to her child.

"You need to set up a doctor's appointment and make sure everything is okay."

"I will. Tomorrow. They're not open on Sunday. Feel free to remind me if I forget."

He laughed. "See, you know me pretty well."

"Getting there."

She called Nate's cell and told him to hold off on contacting his friend. Then she called Connor and explained the entire Kelly installment in the miniseries.

"Never a dull moment at your house, is there, Lenore?"

"No, there isn't. I have concerns that if this young woman is desperate for money, she'll go to a tabloid and spill the story."

"I'd agree that's a possibility."

"I also need someone to check my house and see if she bugged it. She claims no, but I can't take her word. Do you know someone who can do that for me?"

"I know someone who knows someone," Walker offered.

"Close enough; let me know when they can get here."

"I'll do that right now."

"We need to arrange a meeting with Nikko. Can't do it in her office because of Nolan. Can you come here for a meeting once the house is deemed bug-free? Nikko hates to go into

Philly." She noticed her hands were shaking.

"Sure, billable hours are a good thing," he joked.

"For some of us," Lenore teased right back. "Let me know when the exterminator can come."

"Will do."

She got off the phone, and MP handed her a glass of orange juice.

"I think I'll get some grape juice, too," she said.

"A little variety might be good."

"I can pretend it's red wine."

"Antioxidants like red wine."

"Good." She held up her glass to him, and he laughed.

She sat in one of the kitchen chairs and finished her juice. "I need a nap," she said honestly. She'd slept terribly the night before.

"Okay, let's do it."

"You don't need to nap with me, MP."

"I'll stay with you. I'll write or something. I like to be where you are. Keeps you out of trouble."

****

"Wha, wha, what . . ." Kelly stammered.

"Am I doing here?" Nate supplied as he met her at the door and took the key dangling from her hand.

"Uh . . ."

"I left my mom's house early. So if your cousin hoped to have me followed, I foiled her clandestine plan. Although what information she hoped to gain by following me to my apartment, I'll never know."

Kelly looked at her feet. "I'm sorry."

"I don't care. I've packed your things." Nate deposited six thirty-gallon trash bags outside his apartment door. He didn't plan on letting her in. "I think that should be it," he said, handing over her laptop bag and backpack.

"I'm –"

"Sorry, I know we've covered that ground. Good-bye and good luck." Nate closed the door in her face and prayed he'd never see her again.

A lot had changed in the last twenty-four hours. Twenty-four hours ago, he had loved Kelly desperately. Now he desperately hoped never to see her again.

He knew he'd move on. His mother had after his father. In fact, his mother was getting married to a man who seemed to love and adore her. Not usually a word he'd assign to a male emotion, but it worked where MP was concerned.

His mother was happy if reserved. She didn't trust easily, especially men. That would be something she and Michael Patrick would work out.

Both his mother and MP had gone out of their way to be kind to Kelly, and then she had turned out to be a treacherous bitch. Enough—he had homework to do.

****

At about 7:00 p.m., Connor Walker's contact's contact came to sweep for bugs and other devices.

"I'm happy to report the place is bug-free. No audio or video devices," the man said.

"And I'm happy to hear it," Lenore said with MP standing beside her, rubbing a hand down her back.

"Here's my card in case you need my services again."

"Thanks, but I know you'll understand when I say I hope I don't."

"I do," the guy laughed good-naturedly and took his leave.

"At least Kelly told you the truth," MP offered as he embraced her.

"That's something. I told Nate I'd let him know what we came up with."

"I'm sure he's had a shitty afternoon."

"No doubt," she said as she disengaged from MP and auto-dialed the phone.

"We are pest free. No critter's listening or watching," she said as her son answered.

"Good," Nate sighed.

"You doing all right?" his mother asked.

"I'll get there." He explained what had transpired since he'd gotten home.

"Ah, Nate, I wish there was something I could do."

"But there's not, Mom."

"I know, but if you need me, I'm here 24/7."

"Believe it or not, that helps."

"I love you, honey."

"I love you, too, Mom. Go get some rest, and don't worry about me. You looked exhausted this morning."

"I took a nap this afternoon."

"Not surprised. This crap can wear a person out."

"Agreed. You get some rest, too."

She filled Michael Patrick in on the conversation.

"Poor kid," he said and took her back in his arms.

She rested her head on his shoulder. "It's not like when he was small and I could take away his hurts with a kiss or homemade chocolate chip cookies. His troubles are adult-sized now and not so easily managed."

"No, *mo chuisle*, they're not."

"I know it's cold and dark, but do you want to go for a walk?"

"Darling, I'd go anywhere with you, but I don't think it's safe."

"You're right. I'm not used to being prisoner in my own home."

"We can go to your gym and walk the track there."

"No, too many people. I wanted only you, me and the stars."

"A lovely thought. Once this is cleared up I'll take all the moonlight strolls you want."

****

Maxwell was in Morris's office.

He filled his boss in on the latest developments.

"The woman is certifiable," Byron spat.

"Yes."

"Kelly is like a niece to us. I can't believe Corrine used her like that or poisoned her mind against me."

"If you care for the girl and want to keep her from selling her story, you might want to track her down. She was apparently living with your son Nate, and he has, not surprisingly, tossed her out on her ass."

"It keeps getting better and better," Maxwell shook his head in dejected disbelief.

"Lenore suggested we band together and go public with this so we can control the spin or at least come up with an agreed statement and plan to implement once the news does go public."

"I can't believe she'd do that. Can't believe Nate would."

"According to her attorney, they've discussed it at length and feel it's inevitable that word will get out, especially with this Kelly complication. She knew about Nate being your son before he did. Corrine told Kelly she was certain that you fathered a child with Lenore and wanted confirmation."

"Jesus."

"If you and Lenore couch this right, you might be okay. No run for the White House, but no resignation either, and you'd have time to decide whether or not to run for reelection or do something different."

"I'll think about it. Is Nate still willing to be a donor?"

"Yes, and you'll actually like this: Nate no longer wants to see Jack as a condition."

"Why the change of heart?"

Morris explained Nate's rationale to Maxwell.

"Smart kid."

"As I've said, he's like Lenore."

"You do have a thing for her, don't you?" Maxwell asked.

"I find her interesting and compelling. I'm not sure *a thing* is the right terminology."

"She's tied up with that writer. Neither of us stands a chance."

"We're over sixty. Neither of us stood a chance without the writer. Why would she want to saddle herself with an old man?"

"You have a point," Maxwell conceded.

"I think going on the offensive might be the thing to do," Morris said.

"Lenore will appear with me at a press conference?"

"No, her attorney will make a statement."

"Great. I'll be stuck with the media vultures and Corrine."

"Think about the feeding frenzy the vultures will have if Corrine releases the story first. You'll be on the defensive big-time. Even a vast majority of your supporters will be clamoring for your resignation, particularly if she releases the tape of Lenore saying you wanted her to get rid of it."

"I could deny it," Maxwell suggested.

"You don't want Lenore as your enemy."

The senator released a big sigh. "Let me think about it."

Morris grunted.

"Should I tell Jack? Maybe he has a right to know he has a brother and his bone marrow is coming from that brother."

"Your call, but be damned sure you're going public with this, or Jack might once you tell him. He's spiteful and I don't think he cares for you or Corrine."

"Who could blame him?"

"Byron, I'm serious."

"Me too."

CHAPTER FORTY-ONE

The next few days were quiet. Lenore relished the relative normalcy, even though nothing was normal. She'd finished *Moon Over the Garden*, and she and MP were racing toward the end of their book, which was still untitled.

"A penny for your thoughts," MP offered as she lay in his arms, the early morning light streaming over them.

"For you, they're free. I was thinking we need a title for our book."

"Indeed. Any ideas?"

"Not really. A number of the titles I've thought of have been done to death. You?"

"None. I haven't thought about it. I finish a book before I title it."

"It kind of comes to you in the end?"

"I guess. What about you?"

"The only requirement I have is that the word *moon* be in the title."

"Why?" he asked and lifted a brow at her.

"If I told you, I'd have to kill you."

He laughed, "Now you've made me curious. Tell me, love, I can keep a secret."

She told him and he started laughing. "That's brilliant, absolutely brilliant. We'll have to have *moon* in the title of our book, too."

"Not sure it works. We have not described the moon in any of the scenes or mentioned the moon at all. There are plenty of bare moon moments . . ." She broke off as if in thought. "I've got it, I think—*Laid Bare*. Physically, emotionally, and professionally Cass is laid bare. All of his layers are stripped away."

"I like it. I think it works, especially the double entendre. I'm intrigued by the way your mind works. Does it ever turn off?"

"When I sleep."

"Don't think so. Your eyes are always moving under your lids."

"You're watching me entirely too much."

"It's one of my favorite things."

"Remember that when we're old and gray and wrinkled and you're sick of the sight of me."

"Don't imagine I'll grow tired of you. And I like the thought of growing old together. Speaking of which, have you given any thought to the wedding?"

"I have. Let's do it here in the sunroom. If it's nice out, we can throw open the French doors. It will be March in a few weeks."

"Sounds lovely."

"Are there people you want to invite from Ireland? Do they need time to make travel plans?"

"You're all I need."

"What about your cousins?"

"I'll invite them if it's important to you."

"Do. I'd like to meet them."

He smiled at her. "I will then."

"There will be Nate, his date if he brings one, Nikko, her date if she brings one, Addy –"

"And her date if she brings one," MP quipped.

"Exactly. Connor and his wife, Meryl, and I think that's it. We can keep it small and low-key."

"Whatever you want."

"I still need to rustle up someone to marry us, too."

"Maybe Walker knows someone," MP said.

"Good idea. I'll ask him."

"How about I bring us some coffee and bagels?"

"Breakfast in bed?"

"Not the kind of breakfast you make but a breakfast of sorts. I'll even make regular and decaf coffee."

"An offer I can't refuse," she said and snuggled down into the blankets.

She'd been to the doctor's the prior day, and she confirmed that Lenore was indeed pregnant. The baby would arrive around Thanksgiving.

Lenore placed her hands on her stomach and made gentle circles.

Speaking softly, she said, "Good morning, little one. Although there is no doubt in my mind that your father will call you 'wee one' or 'lad' or 'lass,' depending on what you turn out to be. We're so excited you're going to be part of our family. Daddy can't wait to hold you and neither can I. But don't make an early appearance. I want you fully cooked when you come into this crazy world."

****

MP had come up and heard Lenore talking. He thought she was on the phone, but she was talking to their unborn child as if he or she were there. It caused a lump in his throat. If there was any lingering doubt that Lenore wanted this child as much as he did, it vanished in that instant.

He didn't want to startle or embarrass her so he said conversationally, "Breakfast is served, me lady."

"I was telling this little one how happy we are."

"Happy doesn't begin to cover it," he said and leaned in for a kiss as he settled the tray on her lap.

They ate for a few moments in comfortable silence.

"We have Walker and Nikko coming for lunch and our powwow this afternoon."

"I remember," he said, a little irritated.

"I wasn't implying you didn't. I wanted to suggest we strategize before they get here." Then she looked at him, "MP, I don't mean to sound like a nag."

"No, I'm sorry, Lenore. I got defensive because it had totally slipped my mind. I didn't mean to imply you were a nag. You're fairly wonderful to live with. I'm sorry," he said again.

"Accepted. I don't want to be a stereotypical wife."

"*A chuisle*, you could never be a stereotypical anything. Now eat. I don't want you dropping on me."

"I won't drop on you, and the doctor told you it was normal."

"Yes, and she did put my mind at ease, but –"

"I'm eating, sweetheart. See?"

He smiled at her. He was the one being a nag.

****

"It smells terrific in here, girlfriend," Nikko boomed as she entered the kitchen.

Lenore momentarily panicked, thinking she'd lost an hour somewhere.

"I'm early. I wanted some girl time. So, if MP's around, toss him out," Nik said dramatically.

"He's working upstairs. If he comes down, I'll banish him."

Nikko was flitting about the kitchen, taking lids off everything and tasting as she went along.

"This chicken Marsala is to die for and the risotto is yummy."

"Don't open the oven," Lenore almost yelled. "It's a pumpkin pecan cheesecake, and it has to rest in a closed oven for an hour after it's done."

Undeterred, her friend turned on the oven light and peered in. "Looks wonderful."

Nikko, turning to the refrigerator, checked out the salad and other veggies.

Lenore watched her agent flying around like the Energizer bunny.

"To what do I owe your frenetic mood?" Lenore finally asked.

"Nolan Hubble is leaving."

"That's terrific. Do you have someone to replace him?"

"Working on it. I'd like to hire two people."

"That's exciting," Lenore said, reaching to help her friend off with her coat.

"No, wait."

Lenore almost jumped back.

"Sorry," Nik said. "I'm excited."

"If I didn't know better, I'd say you were on speed."

"High on life."

Lenore raised an eyebrow and laughed. "Who are you, and what have you done with my friend?"

Nikko shimmied out of her coat. Lenore studied her from head to toe and came back to Nik's face.

"You're pregnant," Lenore gasped.

Nikko, beaming, pulled back her suit jacket and pushed the fabric of her skirt tightly over her barely discernable baby bump. "Yes! After all these years. Howard and I never conceived. Thought one or both of us were faulty."

Lenore was thinking of fertility doctors and treatments but wasn't going there. Nik had never shared any of this with her when Howard was alive. Instead, she poured herself and Nik an OJ and motioned for her to sit at the table.

"The baby is Hubble's?"

"Yes, that's the only downside. But I wanted a baby for so long, then thought that it would never happen, but it did."

"Does he know?"

Nikko shook her head no.

"Are you going to tell him?"

"I don't know."

"Honey, I'm over the moon for you, but he'll find out you're pregnant and assume it's his."

"Of course it's his. I don't sleep around."

"Focus, Nikko. I know you don't and so does Nolan Hubble. Any idea how he feels about kids? Does he have any?"

"No to both."

"It's possible he could want a part in your child's life."

"I suppose."

"Sweetie, you need to do more than suppose. You need to tell him before he realizes and confronts you. It might not be pleasant."

"I know. What did you do about Nate's dad?"

"I told him. He was older and married and wanted no part of a baby, wanted me to abort. I refused."

"OMG, that is so awful. I never knew, and you were so young."

"I survived."

"You did better than that, Lenore, you flourished."

Lenore could feel herself blush.

"Don't be embarrassed by your success. You've earned it."

"She has," MP joined them in the kitchen. He bent to kiss his agent's cheek.

"This is girl time, Michael Patrick. So could you please go back upstairs?" Lenore asked.

"Of course." He eyed her warily.

She reached out, squeezed his hand, and gave him a full smile so he'd know he wasn't the topic of conversation.

He leaned down and kissed her again.

"You two are disgusting," Nikko said with mock disdain.

"Why, thank you, Nik," MP grinned as he left the room.

"Things are well with you two?"

"Yes," Lenore said, watching him leave the room.

"You deserve happiness, Lenore. So does MP for that matter."

"Thanks, because I have something to ask you. Will you stand up for me when Michael Patrick and I wed in a few weeks?"

"Yes, of course I will." Nik enveloped her friend in a hug and then looked at Lenore's ring.

"Beautiful, Lenore. It sparkles like your marvelous eyes—the opals do."

"It was MP's grandmother's and mother's."

"Now it's yours. It suits you. He suits you."

They were both tearing up.

"Damn these hormones," Nik said. "I seem to cry at the drop of a hat." She looked at Lenore all teared up as well and at the two glasses of orange juice. "Oh my God, you too?"

Lenore nodded, and Nikko hugged her again.

"When?" Nik asked.

"Thanksgiving."

"Ha, Halloween for me. It seems fitting. I hope I birth a very talented witch."

"Whoever you birth will be very talented," Lenore said. "But back to Hubble. You need to tell him. Are you sure the two of you can't reconcile?"

"How could I trust him?"

Lenore couldn't answer that.

"That's why he's agreed to leave. I won't talk to him about anything but work and then the bare minimum. He wants more. We were good in bed, very compatible there."

"I see," Lenore said, glancing at her friend's stomach.

They both laughed.

"Claims he made a mistake," Nikko continued. "While admitting to nothing, I might add."

Lenore was careful not to influence Nikko. This was a major personal decision for her and her child. She didn't want her professional disdain of the man to impact Nik's choice.

"Only you know how you feel about Nolan. I know he made you happy, or the sex did, while you were seeing him. You need to do what's best for you and the baby. Tell him, then decide. I can tell you're not sure in your own heart what you want from the man."

"You're right. But if nothing else, he's given me the child Howard and I never had. How I wish we'd had children. Fucked like rabbits, but . . . I loved that man deeply." Tears again.

"I know you did. He loved you, too." Lenore held her friend until her emotions evened out.

Getting herself together, Nikko asked, "So when's the wedding?"

"MP wants it before I start showing. He's quite traditional, believe it or not."

"I'm not surprised."

"Two, three weeks at most. It will be a small do here at the house. Nate is going to be MP's best man."

"That's nice. Anything special you want me to wear?"

"Nope, whatever you like. Not sure what I'll wear myself."

"You could wear something sexy—no baby bump for you yet. In fact, you look like you've lost weight."

"Thanks. I think."

"You look fabulous, Lenore. You always do—a natural beauty."

"Please."

"It's true. You have no idea how many men have been interested in you over the years."

"MP caught my interest, my heart, and then my tail," she laughed.

They talked for a little while longer, and when Connor Walker arrived, they all went up to Lenore's office.

"Lenore and Michael Patrick asked that we meet here today so we can outline a media statement if we need one," Connor said, starting the meeting.

Nikko looked from Lenore to MP and back. "What the fuck have the two of you gotten into now?"

The others laughed.

"Lenore, do you want to start at the beginning?" Walker asked.

"All right. Michael Patrick, jump in if I miss something."

"Will do," he said taking her hand.

Lenore told the saga that she'd kept carefully under wraps for so many years. The story finally ended with the Kelly debacle.

"Poor Nathan," Nikko said.

"Yes, but he's getting through it," Lenore said, then continued. "This took longer than I expected it would. Can we brainstorm over lunch?"

"I'm starved," Connor admitted.

"Me too," Nikko said.

"Let's eat," MP chimed in, looked at Lenore, and offered her his hand before she stood up. It was a sweet gesture and she took it.

Lunch was met with an enthusiastic review, and dessert was an even bigger hit.

"So depending upon what Jack Maxwell decides, that will determine what statement Connor releases and when?" Nikko asked.

"Yes. We all thought he'd have made his decision by now but nothing," Lenore said.

"And what if one of these crazies goes to the tabloids? We just experienced that with the *Sentinel* mess. If this Kelly girl needs money, this is one hell of a story."

"We know," MP said. "Maxwell was to head Kelly off and get her some money and a place to live."

"Any word on that, Connor?" Lenore asked.

"Not yet."

"Let us know when you hear," MP said.

"I'm speaking from experience, and the sooner we get out there and hit this head-on, the better," Nikko said, all vulnerability gone. She was in pit bull mode. "I know Lenore doesn't want to appear with Maxwell, but it might be better if you and that fuck-up made a statement together, honey."

"I don't think I could, Nik," Lenore said.

"I don't want her to," MP said.

Nik ignored him. "What about a controlled situation like 'The Today Show'? An interview with Matt Lauer or something? That could work."

"No," MP said with barely controlled anger. "Lenore doesn't need the stress."

"We could pre-tape with the right to have anything we don't like edited out," Nik suggested.

"No," MP said again.

"Okay," Connor said. "This discussion is headed nowhere good, and nothing is going to get resolved today, but there is plenty to think about. I'll check in with Morris and see what's up there. But I agree with Nik. Regardless how it plays out, we need to be prepared to move on this."

"Agreed," MP said. "If you recall, this was my idea in the first place. I simply don't want Lenore out in front of the cameras."

Nodding, Connor got up to go, and Lenore walked him out.

"Thanks for coming," she said.

"Thanks for lunch."

She waved him off.

"I wanted to ask you if you knew a judge who could marry MP and me here at the house two or three Saturdays from now."

"One of my associates is an ordained Methodist minister, if that would work."

"It does and, of course you and Meryl are invited. Nate is best man and Nik is going to stand up for me."

"Are you happy?" Connor asked.

"Except for this Maxwell mess, yes."

"I'm glad. Do you need any legal work done before the wedding?"

Lenore looked at him. "You mean a pre-nup?"

Connor nodded.

"No, but I do need a new will. I'm pregnant, Connor."

She laughed. "You should see the look on your face. 'Shock and awe' doesn't do it justice. But I need to make sure Nate and the baby are taken care of if anything should happen to me. I want Nate's money transferred to him when he graduates in May, the new baby secondary until Nate takes a wife, then it would go to her if something happened to Nate."

Connor nodded. "You've thought about this then?"

"I've thought about a lot of things lately, and a lot's going on. I guess it's payback time for all those years of relative calm. MP says, 'Life is messy.'"

"Yes, sometimes it is, but you'll get through it."

"I have incentive." She touched her stomach.

Connor chuckled. "And here I was envying you that Nate was out of the house and on his way. Meryl and I can't wait until the girls go off to college."

"In seven years, I'll be envying you. But know that this baby is very wanted."

"I have no doubt, and I have no doubt that MP is in love with you either. I can tell by the way he looks at you and how protective he is. Be happy."

"I intend to." She gave him a peck on the cheek and sent him on his way.

Lenore walked into the house to hear MP and Nik going at it.

"I'll not have Lenore exposed to the media and their antics. Everyone will see her face on national television coast to coast, Nikko. She won't even be able to go to the CVS without everyone knowing who she is and judging her for what she did or didn't do twenty plus years ago."

"I see your point but –"

"There is no but, Nik," MP said firmly.

"Time out," Lenore waded into the fray. "No decisions have been made about anything. Let's not do this now."

MP went to her, her hands trembling. "I'm sorry."

"Me, too," Nikko said.

Lenore looked from one to the other.

"Are you okay?" MP asked.

"No, I'm upset and exhausted."

"Go lie down, Lenore, the car will be here in a few minutes," her agent said.

"All right. MP, stay with Nik until the car comes, but don't talk about this business. No one needs any more of it."

"Promise."

She gave him a weak smile. While he didn't escort her up the stairs, he stood at the bottom and made sure she made it safely to the top.

"Is she okay, MP? She told me she's PG, doesn't look it. Looks thinner and sexier than ever; bitch—I hate her."

They both laughed.

"Doctor says she's fine." MP explained the borderline hypoglycemia.

"Explains the trembling hands," Nik said.

"Yes."

Five minutes later, the car came. "Call me if you guys need anything," their agent said as she embraced him.

CHAPTER FORTY-TWO

Maxwell visited Jack in his private hospital room and found him in a foul mood.

"I'm sick of being sick and cooped up in here. Most patients would be home until it was time for them to prepare for the bone marrow transplant. Only reason why I'm still here is because Corrine has money to pay."

"It's to keep you healthy," Byron said with a bored air. They'd been through this before. "What are you going to do about the transplant? Yes or no."

"I'm not going to do it, and I am going to check out of this hell hole. I'll go back to Corrine's, and if she doesn't want me, I'll get an apartment. If I'm still alive, maybe finish school next year."

"Your condition is likely to worsen without the transplant."

"Yeah, I know," Jack said petulantly.

Maxwell said nothing, simply waited to see if his son offered anything else.

"I don't relish the thought of GVHD," Jack said finally. "This supposed match hardly makes the cut. I can't do it."

"You've been through chemo and made it. You'd make it through GVHD."

"Like you'd know that or what it's like to be puking your guts up, for your mouth to be so raw you can't eat or drink, to be so weak you'd rather piss yourself than get out of bed —" Jack's body was suddenly racked with a coughing fit.

Byron offered his son bottled water, which he took and sipped slowly, his coughs subsiding.

"Jack, I know you're scared, and I know you don't care for your mother or myself, but we're all the family any of us have. I'm here for you to lean on if you need me. While I don't always like what you do, you are my son."

"Nice sentiment, but do you love me?"

The question stopped Maxwell cold. Never quick on his feet, the senator wavered.

Jack barked a bitter, harsh laugh and began to cough again. He drank some more water and finally managed, "I was a mistake from the word go. Why is it so important that I live?"

"You're my son, for God's sake, and even though you've acted like a world-class spoiled, rich prick the last several years, I can't let you die without doing everything I can to save you. I'd guess that's a kind of love. I don't know how to effectively express it."

"You sure you don't have more spares out there? Corrine is certain you do. Even thinks you lined up this one who's a potential donor. Is that true?"

Truth or Dare ran through Byron's mind.

His kid laughed again, then cut himself off as he began to cough. "No need to answer. If I have a half sibling, I'd like to meet him, even if he's not a good match."

Byron said nothing.

"I'd even promise not to disclose the fact that he exists. Think of it as my dying wish, Dad. Heck, if there's more than one, invite them all. We could have a reunion of sorts."

He shook his head. Maxwell had gotten a vasectomy before Jack was born. There would be no more offspring from his loins, legitimate or otherwise.

"Don't blame you for not banging the bitch Ice Queen. Can't believe you tussled in the sheets at least four times with that woman. Maybe I wouldn't be here now if the first two weren't duds."

"You don't know what you're talking about."

"And spare me a graphic explanation. My condition is delicate, after all."

Sad thing is, it was. Jack was skin and bones. His eyes were hollow and rimmed in bluish black circles, and his body wore bruises from the lightest touch.

Maxwell changed the subject. "Anyone come to visit besides your mother and me?"

"Nope, haven't even seen Kelly in a while. But I guess she's busy with school."

"I'll tell her you were asking about her when I see her."

"Don't bother. I don't want visitors; plus, I won't be here too much longer."

With his attitude and demeanor, it was a wonder that someone hadn't killed him for sport.

"I have a dinner to attend. I'll come by tomorrow."

"Don't bother. We both know this is a painful exercise for both of us."

"Let me know if you change your mind about the transplant and when you're moving back to the house."

"Back to Corrine's," Jack said pointedly. "But, yeah, I'll do that, Byron."

Maxwell left, listening to the barking laugh of his son that quickly turned into an uncontrollable hack as the door closed behind him.

****

Nikko walked back into her NYC office at about 6:00. She was dead tired and wanted to put her feet up.

She snagged bottled water from the refrigerator, sat in her chair, kicked off her heels, and put her stockinged feet on the desk. Leaning back, she closed her eyes and let out a sigh.

"Long day?"

"Shit," Nikko spat as she sat bolt upright in her chair. "You're an asshole, Hubble."

"Mmm, that's an improvement from the fucking asshole of the last few weeks. I am sorry I startled you."

"Like hell you are."

"Believe what you want," he shrugged.

"I find it's best never to delude myself," she said icily.

He nodded soberly. "I'd say I'm sorry again if I thought it would help."

"It won't." She was weighing what Lenore said in her mind. *You need to tell him, the sooner the better.*

He took her silence as an invitation to come farther into her office. When she didn't stop him, he settled himself in a chair across the desk from her.

She sat up straighter in hers.

"Want to go for dinner?" he asked.

"I want to go to bed."

"I'd like it if that was an invitation, but I suspect it's not."

"You'd be right for a change."

He nodded again.

They sat. A Kimble mantel clock ticking was the only sound.

"I'm pregnant, Nolan," she blurted out of nowhere.

He sat not saying anything.

So much for that, she thought. Son of a bitch didn't even have the balls to be angry.

"I don't expect anything from you. But I thought you should know. I plan to keep the baby. I'm actually quite happy about it." Her voice was even and strong; she held her head high.

"You don't expect anything from me?" he asked incredulously and rose from his chair, approaching her side of the desk.

"No." She turned her chair to face him but did not get up. "I have more than enough resources to take care of the child myself."

"Goes without saying, but you're assuming I don't want to do anything."

"I don't know what you want, Hubble."

"I want you and the baby," he said simply and knelt down before her. "May I?" he asked, moving his hand toward her stomach to touch her.

"Yes," she said, eyes fixed on him.

He parted her jacket and placed a hand on the slightly rounded mound and rubbed gently. "It's hard as a rock," he looked into her face smiling.

Nik nodded uncertainly.

"Our child is right here." He parted her jacket wider and used both hands to smooth her skirt over the baby bump.

"Yes," she said in an uncharacteristic whisper.

He looked into her eyes, then bent his head and kissed her belly.

She watched him, taken with his behavior.

"I'll do everything for this baby and for you."

"We'll make arrangements for you to be part of the baby's life."

"I want to be part of both your lives."

"I don't think so, Hubble. I can't be with someone I can't trust."

"What can I do to prove I'm worthy of you?"

"Worthy is a lofty word. This has to do with trust. If I can't trust you, nothing else matters."

He was circling her belly with caressing fingers, and it felt incredibly good. Suddenly, he lay his head on her lap and put his ear to her stomach. She stopped herself from running her fingers through his hair.

"You can't hear anything," she laughed instead. "At about five months, I'll be able to feel the baby move, and shortly thereafter you'll be able to feel it kick its feet and begin to assert its independence." She was smiling as she spoke.

"When is the baby due?" His hands were back to caressing, and he was looking into her eyes.

"Halloween. A witch for a witch."

"Or a warlock."

"Yes."

"I want to go to your doctor appointments and ultrasounds and birthing classes. I want to be part of this every step of the way."

"Now you're getting ahead of even me," she said lightly.

"Don't think that's possible. I want to touch you." He untucked her silk blouse and unzipped the side zipper of her skirt. She let him.

His hand was hot on her skin. She felt herself respond to his touch. Felt his response as well as it brushed against her leg.

"I love you, Nik, and I'll love this baby. I never thought I'd have a child. This is such a wonderful gift. Thank you." Tears were brimming in his eyes.

It was said with such heartfelt sincerity, she felt the tears spring to her eyes, too. She nodded. "I never thought I'd have a child either. So he or she will be well-loved."

"Yes," he pulled her to him and kissed her long and hard. "I'll work on regaining your trust. I'll do whatever it takes. I was cocky and arrogant . . ."

"Keep going," she said.

He laughed and pulled her to her feet. He slid her skirt down and took in the ripeness of her belly, moving his hands more thoroughly over it now.

"Beautiful," he whispered.

She was being as patient as she could, but soon he was going to make her squirm, as Lenore would say. Sex and chemistry had nothing to do with trust. Neither did love, for that matter.

"I'd like to see all of you if you'd let me."

She wanted it more than anything, but she shook her head no.

He nodded his understanding, kissed her stomach one more time, lingering a little longer than necessary. Then he pulled up her skirt, tucked in her blouse, and finally he zipped the side zipper that was getting a little snug.

"I'll take you shopping for a new wardrobe."

She didn't respond.

"I'm going to see you home."

"That's not necessary."

"It is. It's late and dark and icy. I won't chance you falling."

She was too tired to argue and too emotionally off balance to be totally rid of him. Plus, it was dark and icy.

CHAPTER FORTY-THREE

"I thought you said you loved me."

"Low blow, Mr. Finnegan."

Lenore and MP were working in her office, each propped on the arm of her huge couch, feet touching.

Lenore was typing on the laptop.

"This is work, sweetheart, and while you might lead me astray in bed, you won't here." she said, almost amused.

They'd been arguing over various endings to the book and coming to no good end.

"Should we each write our own ending and see how it goes?" she suggested. "Heck, maybe we could print the book with both endings and let the reader decide."

"Maybe another book. I want to end together on this one."

"The ultimate climax."

"You could say that."

"But is your man Cass going to get over his guilt that his failure to listen to Amanda in the first place almost got her and their unborn child killed?"

"I'd say he'd have to."

"Yeaaah, me too. He wallows in everything."

"Because he takes everything to heart. He believes he should be able to keep your Amanda safe."

"He disarmed his no good half brother and saved all of them. Then got the beam off of her and stopped the bleeding from her head wound."

"He feels it should have never gotten that far."

"You're making me crazy, *mo chuisle*. I think we need a break," she said in a poor imitation of his Irish lilt.

"We do at that," he laughingly agreed. He handed her a small bottle of juice and split a banana with her. While her blood sugar went low often, she could only eat a small amount at a time.

"You are sooo good to me. Thank you."

He leaned over and kissed her tenderly.

"Mmm." She brought her hands up to either side of his face and pulled him closer.

"I like the way you show your appreciation."

Her home phone started ringing.

"Hold that thought," she said as she engaged the call.

MP grinned and left to replenish their OJ and food supply.

****

"Walker says Maxwell intercepted his wife's cousin, found her an apartment, and gave her some pin money. So she should keep quiet. Kelly also said she wouldn't talk about Nate being Maxwell's son, because she loves him," Lenore offered when MP returned, rations in hand.

He was smiling as he put the stash away.

"What?"

"Pin money, does anyone say that anymore?"

She laughed self-consciously, "Probably only my historical romance crowd."

"I like it. It's part of what makes you unique." He gave her a peck on the cheek. "You're quite brilliant, love. Your research and knowledge of the era are astounding."

She smiled at him, eyes bright with pleasure. "You don't find it frivolous?"

"On the contrary. I find it remarkable all the things that remain consistent through the years."

"Yes, there are parallels, but differences too—some important ones. For instance, in my case, as a single mother in Victorian England, I would either have been a kept mistress, well-provided for, or more likely a whore forced to earn her living on the street, ostracized by polite society."

MP looked at her.

"It's true. I'd never have been allowed to become a writer, make a home for Nate and myself, and send him to private school. Nor been allowed to become a proper wife," she teased him.

"I never said anything about you being a proper wife." He snaked an arm around her and gave her a kiss.

She laughed, "But it's true. I'm lucky to have been born in the present day."

"Yes, you are," MP conceded. "But you faced any number of challenges all the same."

"Everyone does. You've had your own. They shape who we are, and I love who you are, Michael Patrick," she said spontaneously.

A brilliant smile lit his vibrant eyes and flashed his dimples.

"I hope the baby has your dimples and smile. You have no idea what that smile does to me."

"Why don't you show me?"

She put her hands on his chest to keep his physicality at bay.

"I have more."

He sighed and sat down on the couch.

"Jack has decided no on the transplant and is moving back in with his parents."

"He's letting nature take its course?"

"Yes, he doesn't want to deal with GVHD."

"I can see that," he said soberly.

"It's sad. According to what Connor was told, Jack's not even well enough for a transplant. Morris thinks the cancer is back and in his lungs, but Jack has had enough and refuses additional testing."

"This entire thing with Nate was some kind of charade?"

"Don't know, MP, maybe. If I wanted to be cynical, I could say it was a campaign stunt to gain Maxwell the sympathy vote or something Corrine cooked up to flush Nate out in the open."

"Politics and self-dealing," Michael Patrick said with disgust. "Does your man think news of Nate will still go public?"

"That's a wild card."

CHAPTER FORTY-FOUR

The next two weeks played out without incident. It was like waiting for the other shoe to drop, Lenore thought as she looked at herself in the mirror.

"You are gorgeous," Nikko said from behind. "No one would ever know you're harboring a minor in there."

Lenore laughed. "You look pretty good yourself."

Nikko was wearing a violet dress suit that hid the existence of her own child.

"Are you sure you're okay with Nolan being here?" Nik asked.

"I'm sure if you're sure."

"I'm not. He won't let me go anywhere alone. He hovers."

"Hmm, I know the feeling," Lenore commented as she put on her lipstick.

"I bet. MP made sure I brought you your juice and crackers."

"He is so excited about the baby and today's wedding, he might need to be tied down."

"Nolan wants to get married."

"What do you want, sweetie?"

"I want to be able to trust him."

"Trust is a hard thing to give. I know. I could have driven Michael Patrick away because I didn't trust him."

"But MP didn't give you cause not to trust him. That was baggage from BM." Nik had taken to calling the senator that because she thought it was hysterical—he's a real shit, she'd said. "Hubble, on the other hand, has given me, all of us actually, cause. Almost resulted in the break-up of you and your soon-to-be husband."

Lenore nodded, looking at her maid of honor in the mirror.

"I don't want to be his advocate. But did he do it to curry favor with you, Nik? Was he insecure with himself and thought if he made a big score, so to speak, he'd earn brownie points? Did his intentions backfire because of a volatile situation he knew almost nothing about?"

"Yeeaah!"

Lenore let out an exasperated sigh. "Think about it. Ask him."

"We have to get downstairs," Nikko said, effectively changing the subject. "You ready?"

"I am."

"You nervous?"

"Nope."

Lenore followed Nikko down her spiral staircase, which was wrapped with a garland of pink roses and baby's breath. She carried a bouquet of white calla lilies, which she had copied from her mother's wedding picture.

Michael Patrick was beaming at her, and she beamed back. Lenore handed Nikko her bouquet and joined him in front of the minister. He took her hands and, kissing her cheek, whispered in her ear, "You've taken my breath away."

"Hey, no cheating," Nate said good-naturedly, causing the handful of guests to laugh.

Lenore was indeed lovely. Her dress was long, comprised of ivory lace, and fit her still-slim figure like a glove. Her hair was down around her shoulders, making her look soft and sexy at the same time.

They exchanged traditional vows, and when the minister announced, "You may kiss your bride," MP took his cue seriously.

Nikko let go with a wolf whistle, and that seemed to bring the couple back to reality.

"You are stunning, Mrs. Finnegan."

"I think I'm stunned, Mr. Finnegan."

They were still holding hands, looking into one another's eyes.

"Let me be the first to congratulate the ecstatic couple," Nate said and embraced his mother and clapped MP on the back. Nikko followed suit, as did everyone else.

For their wedding gift, Nikko had hired a photographer that the agency used to take pictures of the bride and groom.

"That was so thoughtful," Lenore said, embracing her friend as the photographer left.

"I know," Nikko teased. "Now you'll have great photos to put on your book jacket. What better way to kick off your writing duet debut than with a wedding picture."

"Always an angle, Nik," MP teased back.

"I think it's a brilliant idea," Nolan Hubble put in and the other three looked at him like he had landed from outer space.

"I was not serious, Hubble," Nik said with disdain.

MP and Lenore looked at one another, and Nik walked away to talk to Connor Walker and his wife.

"I'm sorry," Hubble said, chagrined. "I can't seem to do or say anything right around her."

MP nodded his agreement, but Lenore said, "Maybe you're trying too hard and not listening closely enough."

"I'm not sure I know what you mean."

"Let it be, *a chuisle*," her new husband said.

"You're forcing yourself into her life, without knowing her true character or nature. Like now with her teasing, maybe even jabbing, us about the pictures. Neither MP nor I have ever put a photo on a jacket cover. Did you know that?"

He shook his head.

"So, while I agree it would be great PR to put our wedding photo out there to help sell the new book, it's not going to happen, and Nik knows that."

He nodded this time.

"Part of our PR is the mystique. MP coming out as Michael Patrick is about as far as we're willing to go. What happened with *The Sentinel* can never happen again. I hope that's understood," Lenore said, not wanting to do this on her wedding day.

Hubble looked at her.

Lenore heaved a sigh. "Listen and learn about Nik and what she does with and for her clients. She's offbeat and so are her authors. If you blunder on as you are, you'll shove her out of your life."

"Thanks for the advice."

"You'd be wise to take it. My wife is a brilliant woman."

"Lovely, too," Hubble added.

"See, you'll get the hang of it."

MP steered Lenore toward the other guests.

"Is he hopeless?" MP asked her.

"Maybe."

****

"What a wonderful day," Lenore said as she sank into her whirlpool bath.

"It was," MP agreed, sliding in behind her.

"I'm sorry your cousins couldn't make it."

"We'll see them when we go to Ireland."

"Hmm." She nestled into her husband and let the jets and warm water relax her body. Not too hot, she had told him. She didn't want to cook the baby.

"You're not going to fall asleep on me, are you? Not on our wedding night."

"Worried about consummating the marriage contract, are you, Finnegan?"

"Done that already, woman, and have the goods to prove it."

She laughed, turning to kiss and straddle him.
"No, I'm not going to fall asleep on you, *mo chuisle*. "In fact, I plan to wear you out." Lifting up a bit, she eased herself down on to his erection. "I've been thinking of this all day," she breathed, moving up and down ever so slowly.

"Me, too." He took her nipple in his mouth and slipped a hand between them to find her clitoris.

She moaned, arching her back and riding him faster, water swirling around them, adding to the sensations.

"Don't stop," he groaned.

She gave him a wanton smile and sped up; her muscles clamped around him as she began to come. "Now, now . . ." she chanted mindlessly as pleasure washed over them.

Lenore collapsed against him, their arms wrapped around one another.

"I love you."

"Forever."

"Forever, Lenore. You're my happily ever after."

CHAPTER FORTY-FIVE

"I smell coffee," Lenore said, propping her head on MP's chest.

"Ignore it. We're newlyweds. Let the houseguests fend for themselves."

She laughed, and he captured her mouth in a kiss and rolled on top of her.

"I plan to start most of my mornings this way, wife."

"As you have been for weeks, husband."

"Complaints?"

"None."

"Requests?"

"More . . ."

"More what . . ." He'd hardly entered her, only the tip of him.

"More of that." He slid in further. "Yes." She was looking into his eyes.

She pulled him deeper.

"More . . ." he said and so it went until they were both sated.

There was increasing clamor downstairs. "I don't want to get up."

"I told you we should have gone to a hotel or sent the guests there."

"You were right. I apologize."

"No need. I plan on keeping you in bed all week—a staymoon."

"A hybrid of the staycation?"

"Yes."

"I like the sound of that, but now I must get up and use the facilities. Your little brat is the cause."

"Go," he laughed, helping her out of bed.

She turned on the shower to warm up, and they shared it before going down to breakfast.

****

"Didn't expect to see you two for a while," Nate said, pouring coffee.

"We've gone decaf," MP said. "I'll make a pot."

"Already done," Nikko said from her perch on the barstool and holding up a carafe.

"Since when did you go caffeine-free, Mom?"

"After the last crazy weekend we had. I thought it was making me jittery because I was drinking it like water. Figured I needed to switch or I'd wear my heart out."

"Ditto for me," MP added. "Plus, no sense making two pots of coffee."

"You must truly love her to give up caffeine," Nolan offered from the other stool.

"I do at that," MP agreed and kissed his wife's cheek, smiling at her.

Nikko gave Hubble a dirty look.

"Hmm," Lenore said, looking at MP who shook his head.

"What does everyone want for breakfast?" the new Mrs. Finnegan asked.

"You know my vote," Nate said.

"I'll go along with Nate," Michael Patrick agreed.

"What are we agreeing to?" their agent asked.

"Chocolate, chocolate chip waffles," Nate answered enthusiastically.

"They are to die for," Nik raved.

"Care to weigh in, Nolan?" Lenore asked.

"I'll go with the group," he said.

"Good answer," Nate said.

"I feel guilty making the new bride do all the work," Nikko said.

"I think the new bride is the only one who knows how to cook, unless Nolan is a cook?" Lenore asked.

"Nope, the microwave is my friend," he said.

"You have something in common with MP then," Lenore said.

"I'm sure that's the only thing," Nik remarked.

Lenore raised an eyebrow that channeled *play nice.*

MP mischievously patted her bottom as he moved past her to get plates, silverware, and napkins. "Let's set the table, guys," he said.

"PW already, Michael Patrick?" Nolan teased.

MP narrowed his eyes at him and said, "Nope. I'm not a jackass who expects someone to wait on him hand and foot because he has a penis."

Nate laughed, taking the plates from his stepfather, and departed for the dining room, MP following behind him with the rest of the items.

"Um, I'll go help them," Nolan said to the two women, looking embarrassed.

Lenore laughed, not being able to help herself. "How is he able to represent clients? He seems to have no filter on his mouth."

"I don't get it," Nikko said. "He's actually very good at his job, and until the thing with MP's son, he was pleasantly annoying and funny. Now he makes me homicidal."

"I can see why." Lenore began to pour batter into the waffle maker. "I still think he's trying too hard. He needs to chill."

"He needs to be lobotomized. I'm sorry, Lenore."

"No need. He's your cross to bear."

"No way, girlfriend."

"I hope it's that easy."

"It won't be but I can dream," Nik said. "He's not leaving the agency now either."

"Things might get better."

"And after the baby is born, I'll be a size two."

"You weren't a size two when you got pregnant."

"Exactly, meaning it's not gonna happen. I was a six btw."

"Noted," Lenore laughed.

"You're a two."

"Hardly." She took the first round of waffles, put them in the warming tray, then poured more batter into the waffle iron.

Lenore's landline started ringing. Looking at caller ID, she glanced at Nikko and said, "It's Connor. It can't be good."

"No."

"Hello, Connor. What crisis befalls us this morning?" she asked, attempting to be light-hearted.

"I'm sorry to intrude on your day," her attorney started.

"It's all right. I know you wouldn't be calling unless it was important."

"The news is out, but your name isn't, yet. How do you want to handle it?"

"How? When?"

"Turn on CNN and call me back. They've been running the story every few minutes."

"Damn it."

"Yes. Call me back."

She numbly hung up the receiver and quickly relayed the pertinent details to Nik as she turned on the TV in the breakfast nook.

"Timing sucks, but it's not surprising," Nikko said, moving to work mode.

Connor was right—they didn't have to wait too long for the story.

"We have breaking news here at the CNN News Center. Senior Senator Byron Maxwell from Virginia dropped a bombshell this morning. Take a listen," the news anchor said by way of introduction.

CNN went to a video of the senator, his wife, and son Jack leaving a D.C. hospital. Jack looked hollow and haggard. His parents looked careworn.

Questions were being yelled at the family. Father and son looked stupefied to see the throng of reporters. Corrine, however, did not.

"The missus looks like she was rode hard and put away wet. I hope I don't look like her in ten years," Nik snarked.

"Shh," Lenore admonished.

Reporters were jockeying for position, trying to get as close as they could to the Maxwells.

Questions were being yelled fast and furious.

"How are you feeling, Jack?"

"Are you in remission?"

"Are you happy to be taking your son home, Senator?"

"Did you find a bone marrow donor?"

Then seemingly louder than everyone else, an MSN reporter called, "Is it true, Senator Maxwell, that you asked your illegitimate son to be tested to see if he was a match for Jack?"

Corrine was doing her best to keep a poker face, but Jack looked at his father slack-jawed and pale. "Why now?" the young man uttered faintly.

Lenore found it hard not to feel sorry for him despite what Nate had told her.

She watched as Maxwell reached for a microphone and spoke in his deep, rich voice that seemed to belie his intelligence level. The crowd fell silent.

"I'm not sure where that information came from. But, nonetheless, it is true. My third son graciously agreed to testing, and while he was a match, it was at the low end of the spectrum. Jack has decided not to attempt a bone marrow transplant at this time. We would ask that you respect our privacy. I have no further comment."

Maxwell handed the microphone back to its owner and ushered his family to a waiting limo.

The reporters went wild, screaming their inquiries fast and furious.

"Who is the mother?"

"Is it true she was an intern?"

"Is it true your love child went to school with Jack at Georgetown?"

To his credit and Lenore's amazement, Maxwell said nothing further.

The anchor was now back on screen asking the same questions. He promised they would be digging for answers and reporting additional information as it developed.

The talking head then went on to draw parallels between Maxwell and Newt Gingrich, John Edwards, Arnold Schwarzenegger, and others.

"It could have been a lot worse," her agent finally said.

"Yes. We need to talk to Connor, and he can get with Gerald Morris, Maxwell's chief of staff, who I'm sure is doing damage control."

Nikko agreed.

"Corrine did it. She set it up, or one of her hired guns did. You could tell by the look on her face," Lenore said.

"Stupid, selfish bitch. Why would she do that to her gravely ill son?" her friend asked.

"Because she is those things. You got it in one, Nikko." MP came up and held Lenore from behind. "We saw it on the TV in the den."

"Oh, my God, Nate —"

"Mom, I'm fine. Relax," he said from behind Michael Patrick.

Nolan trailed not far behind, looking interested but clueless. Obviously no one had filled him in, and Lenore was not of the mind to at the moment.

"Mom, I'm fine. I have good coping skills. But at the moment I'm starved. If we're going to deal with crap, we need fortification."

Lenore gave a nervous laugh and looked from Nate to MP to Nikko. "Plan B?" she asked.

"Yes," they each agreed.

"I'll go call your man, Walker, while you make waffles," MP offered.

"That would be wonderful," Lenore sighed gratefully. "Make sure he talks with Morris."

"Will do." He kissed her cheek and departed to her office.

Lenore poured more batter as Nate snagged some waffles from the warming tray.

"It will be okay," Nate said softly to his mother.

"You're the illegitimate son," Hubble blurted.

"Yes," Nate said simply and put another piece of waffle in his mouth and chewed thoughtfully.

"That is not for publication or discussion," Nikko said firmly. "I hear that you've talked to anyone about this, and I will personally cut off your balls with a pair of dull, rusted scissors, got it?"

He nodded but persisted. "But someone will speculate about the who. I bet someone already knows the details."

"Yes, but not you, Nolan. Got it?" Nik reinforced.

"I said I did," Nolan answered, annoyed.

"Good."

****

"Who's the other woman, Byron?" Jack asked as soon as they were in the limo, being whisked back to the family home.

"I can't tell you. I have a contract with her not to discuss the matter."

"You mean you bought her off," Corrine snickered.

"Do you know who she is? Who they are?" Jack directed the question at his mother.

"Yes, I believe I do. I told you he had spares out there. But it's your father's news to tell."

"Did you arrange for the press, too?" Jack asked.

When Corrine simply smiled, he went off. "Why? You ignorant skank! Why would you want to be humiliated like that? Can't even keep your own husband satisfied. That's what a lot of your so-called friends and acquaintances will say.

"I know you have no regard for me, but doesn't it matter that I'm dying? Were you thinking, 'let's heap on some more stress, pain, and aggro for the terminal boy'? Having you as my undevoted, unloving mother hasn't been enough . . ." He was racked with a coughing fit, and Byron quickly twisted off the top of bottled water and handed it to him. Jack sipped slowly.

"Are you going to allow him to talk to me that way?" Corrine asked the senator.

"Sure, I'd like to know the answers to those questions myself. I agree with Jack. That is the most selfish, disgusting thing you've ever done. You wanted to take me down—why do it while Jack is with us? He doesn't need this. Although there is one thing I disagree with Jack on."

Corrine shifted in her seat.

"You're not a skank. That implies someone who has overt sexual experience. Which definitely leaves you out."

Jack choked on his water as he started to roar with laughter.

"V-very g-good, Byron," his son finally wheezed out.

****

"You guys don't trust ole Nolan Hubble, do you?" Nate asked as they settled themselves in the great room after Nikko and Hubble had left.

"No," MP answered for both of them.

"Why?"

"He was responsible for the *Sentinel* story on MP," Lenore said.

"Great. So he is a loose cannon and doesn't just play one at social functions."

"I'm not sure that's his normal state. I think he's trying too hard to impress Nikko, and it backfires every time he opens his mouth," Lenore said.

"Yeah, he's missing the boat there," Nate laughed and MP agreed.

"Please, let's not talk about him." Lenore could still get distressed by the upset the article had caused her and MP. She was trying to get beyond it, but it wasn't easy.

MP took her hand and gently squeezed it.

Nate got the hint and said, "So for the moment we're saying nothing. Plan B was shut up and see what transpires, correct?"

"Unless you want to, Nate," Lenore said softly.

"No, I don't. But Corrine has told someone who we are. I get the sense the reporters know too. Maybe they don't have enough verification to go public with our IDs, but you could tell they know something. Asking if the mother was an intern, if the son went to school with Jack."

"Yes, and if it goes public, a member of Connor's firm will read a statement confirming facts. The fact it was agreed to between Maxwell and me to keep a private matter private and that you were tested to be a donor and Jack decided against the transplant."

"Which is already out there," Nate commented.

"Yes."

"When the news breaks, I'll need a place to stay. Neither my roommate nor the others in the apartment complex need the press hanging around."

"Connor's firm has a corporate apartment right in Georgetown. I think it's closer to campus than your own apartment is. I'll ask him if you can use it."

"Brilliant, Mom. I like the idea."

"Thanks," she smiled at him. "Will your profs be understanding if you need to hide out for a few days and miss classes?"

"Yeah, I think so, especially once it comes out who my father is. They'll probably give me bereavement time."

"Indeed," MP snorted.

"I'm sorry, Nate," Lenore said for what seemed the millionth time.

"I'm coping," Nate said with a grin. "In all fairness, he did okay this morning."

"I agree with you," MP said.

"Let's see what CNN has to say," Nate said and turned on the TV.

"Too funny," Lenore said when she discovered that they had psychologists on talking about what compelled seemingly successful men to stray from their wives.

"At least that means they haven't uncovered you yet, *mo chuisle.*"

"But they think they've uncovered the flaw in these successful men. They feel they can do anything and there are no consequences. I could have told them that," Lenore laughed. "Either they believe they won't get caught or someone takes care of the mess."

"Like Morris, you mean?"

"Yes, Maxwell's major domo. He couldn't get his shoes on the right feet without him."

"But you had a relationship with him, Mom."

"Yes, but it took me a while to see that side of it. I think he was losing his luster even before he was so ugly to me."

"But you would have married him, if he had left his wife for you?" Nate asked.

"Probably," she said with a shrug. "If I'm honest with myself, I think a part of me thought he would. I was wrong."

"Sorry, Mom."

"Don't be, honey. I think we turned out better for it. Plus, I might not have found MP." She smiled brightly at her new spouse.

"You guys are embarrassing," Nate teased.

"Nik called us disgusting the other day," MP said.

"I was trying to be nice. Nik doesn't know how."

They all started laughing, and the doorbell rang.

Lenore glanced at her watch. "Oh, my goodness, it's the car service."

"I'm packed and ready to go, Mom. You need to stop worrying about me. You did a good job raising me. Believe it or not, I'm fairly competent. MP, make her stop worrying about me so much."

"See, Lenore, he is a smart man. He didn't say make her stop worrying, but rather stop worrying so much. Nate knows you'll always worry at some level."

"I love you guys."

****

Maxwell paced his best friend's home office and ran a hand through his hair.

"Byron, if it helps, I think you did a remarkable job this morning with the press. Masterful even. Lenore and her camp say the same thing, and that includes your son Nathan," Morris said.

The senator nodded. "I feel awful for Jack. His mother's behavior, more than the news of a half sibling, knocked him for a loop. For God's sake, he's dying, Gerald."

"I know. I'm sorry."

"He's in his old room at the moment, but we're having the study turned into a temporary hospital room so when the time comes, we can have hospice care at the house."

Morris was struck by the lucidness of his friend's speech. Maxwell was a strong orator when coached on what to say, but he hadn't been coached that morning and not at the moment either.

"I think that's a good idea."

"He wants nothing to do with Corrine. Feels betrayed by her behavior. Wants to know why she couldn't wait until he was dead to dredge all this up. He thinks she's trying to punish him for being born."

"Is she? Corrine never took to that boy."

"No, it's me she's trying to punish. After all, I got her pregnant."

"Takes two for that to happen."

"In theory anyway," Maxwell said and puffed out his cheeks.

Morris looked at him oddly but let it go.

"Fucking press is all over; Jack's friends can't even come and visit. Kelly's afraid to set foot in the house because of Corrine." He sighed. "It's a mess. I had to run the gauntlet to get out of the driveway. But we need to deal with this head-on. Should I resign?"

"Not if you don't want to. Plus, what you said this morning is true. There is a legal contract that you and Lenore entered into saying you'd both keep silent about this. Both of you have. If details get out, it will not be from Lenore."

"Nor I then. It happened almost twenty-two years ago. You're right. If Newt can run for president with his track record, I'm not going to resign."

"I see no reason for you to. Bigger issue is Corrine. What's her agenda?"

"I asked her not to continue this campaign against me until after Jack dies, in deference to him, not me. Not sure she can even call back what she started. But the doctors say Jack has four to eight weeks left. She's waited thirty years; she can wait a few more weeks."

"Did you have any impact?"

"I don't know. I hate to ask the woman to do or not do something, because she usually does the opposite to spite me."

"Your father didn't do you any favors when he found that one."

CHAPTER FORTY-SIX

"Mom, thanks for coming. You too, MP," Nate said as he ushered them into Connor Walker's firm's corporate apartment, two weeks after their wedding.

"You're welcome, but no thanks are needed, Nate. Family does for family."

Lenore squeezed MP's hand in acknowledgment of his kind words, and he returned the gesture.

"Place is great," Lenore observed as she walked farther into the apartment, taking in the classic elegance of the neutral decor.

"What time is your visit with Jack Maxwell?"

Corrine Maxwell had told Jack who his half brother was in an attempt to make amends for the surprise press conference she'd arranged. Jack, in turn, asked his father to set up a meeting.

"Three o'clock. I know it will be uncomfortable for you, Mom, but Corrine won't be there."

"I don't care. I'd be there for you regardless."

"Since it's been a couple of weeks and nothing has leaked about us, I'm afraid that Corrine might pull something," Nate said.

"Nothing that woman does would shock me."

"Agreed. Maxwell said he asked her not to pull any more shit while Jack was alive. He only has weeks to live. Apparently, Jack won't even look at Corrine, he's so hurt and angry. Can't say I blame him. But enough of this depressing talk. Let's get you settled. The second bedroom is larger; take that one," Nate said, already picking up a small suitcase and walking toward it.

****

The Maxwell house was silent and smelled medicinal.

"I appreciate your coming," Byron said to Nate but was looking at Lenore. "This will mean a lot to him."

"Byron," MP held his hand out to the senator, even though Maxwell seemed to ignore him.

"MP," said the other man, having no choice but to shake his hand.

They did the rounds with Morris as well, except he bent to kiss Lenore's cheek. "Congratulations on your marriage. I wish you every happiness," he said to Lenore.

"Thank you. We are very happy," she said, reaching for MP's hand.

"Where's Jack?" Nate asked, seeming impatient to get the meeting underway.

"Right through here. We've turned the study into a bedroom for now," Maxwell said.

Nate looked at his father. "For now?"

"Yes, we'll turn it back to a study once Jack dies."

Nate gave him a 'you don't get it' look.

"This will mean a lot to Jack; he's been asking to meet you since his mother told him of your existence," Maxwell said.

Nathan nodded his head and walked to the closed door.

He had already told Lenore and MP that he would talk to his brother alone. This would most likely be his first and last contact with Jack Maxwell, and if Jack had something he wanted to get off his chest or something he wanted to share before he died, Nate would listen.

****

"While the boys talk, we can wait sit in the parlor." Maxwell motioned to a large room with double doors.

"Corrine is out?" Lenore asked, wanting to make sure she was not going to pop out of the woodwork.

"Yes, a charity function. You understand."

She nodded and seated herself on a long davenport. MP sat next to her and took her hand. It was cold and clammy.

"Would you like something to drink?"

"I'll have a glass of orange juice, if you have it," Lenore said.

"Vitamin C," Morris said simply.

"Yes, to keep my immune system up," she said simply.

"MP?" Maxwell asked.

"I'll have the same."

There was OJ in the bar, most likely for screwdrivers.

"How is Jack doing?" Lenore asked with compassion.

"Getting weaker by the day. The doctors give him two weeks."

"I am sorry, Senator," she said gently.

"Thanks."

They all sipped their drinks in silence for a long moment.

Letting MP's hand go, Lenore stood and asked, "Where is the ladies' room?"

The men stood with her, and Maxwell told her where it was.

****

Nate stood in front of the closed door taking in the room. There was a hospital bed and every conceivable piece of medical equipment he could think of. Jack was hooked to an IV for nutrition, pain medication, or a combination of the two, Nate didn't know.

"Jack," he said quietly.

His half brother fluttered his eyes and struggle to focus on him.

"I'm Nathan Held." He didn't offer his hand, as Jack looked too frail to shake it.

"Thanks for seeing me. I've wanted to meet you since my mother told me I had a half brother."

Not one to be a hypocrite, Nate simply nodded.

"Too bad you weren't a better match; I might have gone for the transplant."

"I was all set to do it," Nate said honestly and went to sit by the bed.

"I know. I couldn't face it. Even if I lived through the transplant, there was a good chance I'd develop GVHD. I couldn't deal with that after the chemo. I hated being sick all the time. It wasn't worth it to me, and as Byron and Corrine said, I'm an adult and able to make my own decisions."

He nodded his understanding.

"You're the lucky one, you know," Jack said without bitterness.

"Yes, on any number of levels."

"I'm glad you recognize that. Our father is an ignorant, manipulated puppet, and my mother is a cold bitch. Your mother, on the other hand, seems to be remarkably normal."

"My mother is a wonderful woman. The only thing I can fault her for is sleeping with our sperm donor," Nate offered with a wry smile.

His half brother started to laugh. "See, you don't even know him well, and you have the same sentiment. I bet he tries to get close to you after I'm gone."

"Don't be too sure about that. I've given him no encouragement, and he seems put off by me."

"You're smart. You intimidate him. But he'll have no one but Morris, and maybe not even him, once I'm gone. Things with him and Corrine have been bad since the beginning, and I'm sure she'll be filing for divorce once I'm dead."

"I guess the senator will be a lonely man."

"He's not that bad. Just clueless and easily led."

Nate nodded again.

"I know you think I'm a shit and don't like the things that I've done."

"It doesn't matter what I like or don't like, Jack; we all live by our own moral compass."

"Moral compass," Jack laughed and coughed. "I guess my family's directional arrows are both bent and twisted." He laughed harder and started coughing more. Nate held a glass of liquid with a straw for him to drink from.

"Protein drink," Jack croaked out. "Hate it."

"You want water?" Nate saw some on the counter.

Still coughing, Jack nodded his head.

Nate took the top off the water and handed it to him. Jack took several small swallows. "Thanks."

"You need anything else?"

"No, this is fine. They won't tell me, but I think the cancer has metastasized in my lungs."

"I'm sorry," Nate said.

"It doesn't matter. Few weeks, it will be over. By this time next week, I'll be in a coma and on so much morphine, I won't feel a goddamn thing." Jack looked at his half brother and continued. "Don't look so horrorstruck, bro—" Then he started coughing and couldn't catch his breath.

Not sure what to do, Nate flew to the door. "He can't stop coughing. I don't think he can breathe."

MP was the one to respond. He walked quickly into the room. "Gun!" Michael Patrick yelled suddenly in warning, tackling Nathan to the ground. A shot resonated through the room.

"Are you all right, Nate?" MP asked.

"I . . . I think so, had the wind knocked out of me."

"Stay down," MP said forcefully.

Lenore heard the shot as she left the restroom. Her heart started to race as she ran toward the front of the house. "My God," she cried. "What's happening?"

"Lenore. Stop." Morris said while grabbing her by the waist and pulling her into the parlor.

"My husband and son are in there. Let me go."

"Until we get a handle on what's going on in there, I'm not letting you go anywhere. Your husband and son will thank me."

****

Jack's shot had missed his bastard half brother. He couldn't do anything right. But there was one more thing he planned to do, and he'd damn well do it to perfection. Jack Maxwell put the barrel of his revolver in his mouth and pulled the trigger.

****

It was several moments before Michael Patrick lifted himself off Nate. He peered cautiously over the couch and saw Jack's macabre face and dead eyes staring open and wide.

Nate got off the floor and saw blood, a lot of blood. He took inventory of himself, not his blood. He looked quickly to MP; there was blood all over the left side of his body. He seemed oblivious to it.

"Michel Patrick, you've been hit," Nate said as calmly as he could.

MP looked down at his side, touched his fingers to it and brought them to his face to see. He was starting to waver, and Nate went to him. "So I have," he said simply and slid, boneless, into his stepson's arms.

Nate had already hit auto-dial for 911 on his cell and quickly gave them the address, explaining there was a shooting at Senator Maxwell's home. He figured they'd get there faster that way.

Then he hastily grabbed a blanket from Jack's hospital bed and pressed it to MP's wound to staunch the bleeding.

Lenore burst into the room with Morris and Maxwell behind her.

"Michael Patrick," she breathed and knelt down by her husband's side, taking his hand and asking Nate, "Are you okay?"

"Yes, but I would have been dead if MP hadn't pushed me out of the way." Tears ran unashamedly down his face. "Jack . . ."

"I know, I saw," Lenore said in a hushed voice.

Leaning down, she kissed her husband's chalk-white face. "I love you, Michael Patrick Finnegan." Her voice was soft but steady. She was determined to keep herself together for him.

His blue eyes opened for a moment and showed the depth of his feelings for her. He weakly squeezed her hand, and then reached to touch where their child grew before his hand slipped to the floor.

Biting back a sob, Lenore frantically felt his neck for a pulse. It was there but weak.

She could hear the sirens outside the house.

EMTs raced in and took over from Nate, who been applying as much pressure as he could to the wound.

"Will he make it?" Lenore asked, terror for him plain to see in her eyes.

"He's lost a lot of blood. We need to get him to a hospital stat," the EMT barked with cool professional efficiency, while he and his partner worked on MP to ready him for the ambulance.

"Lenore," Maxwell said gently and reached for her. She startled at his touch.

"I'll see to her," Nate said dismissively.

****

The ride to the hospital was harrowing. They'd lost MP's pulse twice. When he arrived in the ER, a trauma team immediately whisked him away. Lenore now paced a private waiting room alone.

Nate arrived a short time later, almost breathless from his haste to get to her. "How is he?"

She shook her head. "I don't know; they took him away immediately, but it's not good, Nate." Tears ran down her face freely now. Her son embraced her.

"He's strong and healthy," he said with confidence that didn't register on his face.

Lenore thought he looked incredibly young at that moment, like a scared boy and not a man. She embraced him harder. "He's lost a lot of blood. The wound is bad, and we don't know what kind of internal injuries there are."

"I'll go down in a while and donate some blood. I'm a universal donor."

She gave a teary smile and touched her son's face. He was kind and compassionate, and she was proud of him. Lenore said a silent prayer of thanks that he was all right. She'd been praying for her husband and for Jack Maxwell's soul as well.

"He saved my life, Mom. If he hadn't seen the gun, I'm fairly certain I'd be dead."

She compressed her lips together to keep the sobs from escaping.

Nate guided her to a couch and embraced her. "Cry all you want. Get it out of your system. You'll need to be strong for MP. You've always been there for me; let me be here for you now."

His words made her weep all the harder.

As the hours stretched on, Lenore felt more and more helpless. She absently walked the waiting room.

"Mom, you've logged miles. Please sit down. You're going to wear yourself out."

Noticing she was feeling like hell, she sat and asked, "Can you hunt me down some OJ and a bagel or something?"

"Of course."

He returned with not only what she requested but a bag full of other foodstuffs as well.

"I thought we might be here for a while," he said while his mother checked out the bag.

"More like a siege," she laughed softly. Then, because he needed to know, Lenore said softly, "Nate, MP and I are expecting a baby."

A slow, amused smile lit his face. "You can't seem to get this safe-sex thing nailed down, can you, Mom?"

In spite of everything, she laughed. "No one knows yet. But in light of everything, you need to."

His face sobered, and he hugged her. "Michael Patrick has even more reason to get well."

"Yes, he does."

"As I said before, as long as there are no dirty diapers to go along with brotherhood, I'm good. And I promise to teach him or her every trick I know."

She smiled.

"When?"

"Thanksgiving. Today it seems appropriate. I hope we'll have much to be thankful for. I already have you and if MP makes it . . ." There was a hitch in her voice.

"He'll make it, Mom. He's got you, a new baby, a great stepson . . ." He gave her a grin.

Lenore swallowed her tears and took a deep breath.

Two hours later, the trauma surgeon came to talk to them.

"Mrs. Finnegan?"

"Yes, doctor. How is my husband?" Her heart was pounding almost painfully.

"There was extensive damage to his stomach, kidney, and tip of his liver. The next forty-eight hours will be critical. If we get over that hurdle, chances are good he'll make it."

"When can I see him?"

"He'll be in ICU once he's out of recovery. Your husband was conscious for a few minutes before surgery. He made me promise to tell you he loved you and that you are to take care of yourself and the child you're carrying." The doctor looked at her as if her husband was delirious when he spoke.

"He wasn't delusional; baby's not due until Thanksgiving."

The surgeon smiled. "Congratulations."

Once the doctor left, Lenore said, "Nate, honey, why don't you go and get some rest."

"Not until I see MP and know you're settled. I'd prefer to take you back to the apartment, too, but I know you won't go."

"You're right. Maybe once I know he's doing better."

"Sit, Mom."

She sat.

"What happened back at Maxwell's house?" She hadn't felt either one of them was up to talking about it earlier.

"I'm not sure." Nate expelled a big breath, then told her what transpired.

"I thank God you were in the restroom when it happened. It could have been you and not MP who was shot."

Tears were in both of their eyes.

CHAPTER FORTY-SEVEN

Corrine entered the study and took in her son's grotesque form. Both Morris and Maxwell had tried to stop her, but she insisted.

The cops would only let her go so far. The room was a crime scene, after all. Maxwell went and stood next to her. She didn't bother to acknowledge his presence.

"There's nothing else to see, Corrine. It's over," Maxwell said in a quiet voice. He moved to take her arm, and she wrenched it away from his reach. Turning, she left the room and ascended the stairs with cold, clear eyes.

"You're wife's a tough one."

Maxwell made some grunt that passed for assent.

"There's a note, Senator," one of the officers said kindly.

It was evidence and already bagged and tagged. As the cops said, the room was a crime scene.

Byron took it by the corner of the bag and both he and Morris read it.

It was written in a big messy scrawl of half printing and half cursive lettering.

Hey, Corrine and Senator:

At least I can say I went out with a bang. LOL

Corrine, are you happy now? No more Nathan Held and you didn't even have to kill him. You always wanted him dead. Will you love me in death for ending his existence? Probably not, I don't think you're capable of the emotion, mother dearest.

Senator, how does it feel to have no heirs only airs? Dead, everyone one of us. But I think Nate was the best of the lot. Was it because he wasn't Corrine's, or because he was conceived from love, or because Lenore Held raised him? No one will ever know.

Tell Lenore I apologize for taking her son, but it was something I needed to do.

Over and out.

Jack James Maxwell

PS: I'll want a closed casket. LOL!!!

"He didn't even wound Nathan Held, let alone kill him. It remains to be seen if MP Finnegan will make it," Morris said darkly. "While I support a lot of things, murder isn't one of them."

Maxwell sighed. "I guess he figured he had nothing to lose."

"I don't think he had much to begin with, Byron."

The senator nodded.

"Where did he get the gun? Looks like a Colt .357 Magnum."

"Corrine's father's collection. It's missing from the gun safe. He inherited them. He had the key to the safe. Carter never liked guns, but Jack was fascinated by them. He must have taken it out when he got home last week."

"Great," Morris said with a disgusted tone. "You might want to talk to an attorney about anything criminal that could come back to bite you and your wife. Off the top of my head, I'm not thinking of anything, but I'm not a criminal attorney."

"I can't see how. He was an adult, the guns were his —"

"I already said I didn't know, but it wouldn't hurt to check. You might want to keep your wife on a tight leash, too. Who knows what she's capable of?"

"Right now I'm going to call the hospital and check on MP Finnegan. He saved my son's life. I'm not sure I would have taken a bullet for Nate."

"I'm sure you wouldn't have. As I'm sure Finnegan never stopped to think about taking a bullet instead of Nate. Rather his goal was to keep him safe for Lenore. He's a man with balls and integrity."

FORTY-EIGHT

There was a chair bed in MP's room, and Lenore had not left him for more than a few moments at a time and then only to tend to her most basic needs.

Nate had brought her a change of clothes and her and MP's laptops so she'd have something to do while sitting there for so many hours.

She went into a file he had entitled "Wee One." It was a diary for their unborn child. Lenore, carving a connection to MP, began to read it. She discovered that he wrote to the baby when she slept and he kept watch on the bed.

Wee one:
Last night your mum told me you might be swimming around in her womb, and this morning we found out that she was right. Your mum is one smart lady, and you'd do well to remember that if you ever try and pull anything over on her . . .

Baby mine:
You're making your mum so tired. Go easy on her. You and I were a major surprise in her life, and now we've totally taken over . . .

Little One:
Your mum was talking to you this morning, and it was the most beautiful thing to hear and see. She tenderly circled her hands around where you're nesting and told you how much you are wanted and loved. She took my breath away . . .

Lenore read through all the entries, tears stinging her eyes and burning the back of her throat. She decided to pick up where MP left off and started typing.

Hearing MP stir a little while later, she went to his bed. They were only sixteen hours through the first forty-eight. She looked at all his monitors. They seemed to be registering okay, at least based on what she knew: blood pressure 118/83; pulse 68; sinus rhythm on the EKG.

"Michael Patrick, *mo chuisle*," she said, taking his hand and kissing him lightly.

He squeezed her hand.

"Thank you for saving Nathan for me. I don't know what I would have done if I'd lost him."

Tears were spilling down her face. He'd turned his head to look at her, eyes barely open. He must have seen the tears as he gallantly tried to offer her the corner of his bed sheet.

"No handkerchief today?" she asked, understanding what he was trying to do. Yanking several tissues from the box, she dried her eyes. "I love you. The surgeon relayed your message to me and to the nursing staff. They've been taking good care of us. Lots of juice and carbs."

He reached out a hand. She stood close to the bed, afraid if she sat on it she'd set off the alarms on the machines or jar him.

Lenore gently took his hand and placed it on her belly.

"Our baby is snuggled and safe." There was no one about so she lifted her shirt and put his hand on her skin.

She saw the flicker of a smile. "Soon I'll be sporting maternity wear and granny panties," she said lightly. "You need to rest and get better. I'm right here if you need me." She sat back down but he wanted her hand. She let him hold it, needing the connection as much as he did.

Nate came in the early evening; Lenore didn't want him to miss classes.

"Mom, take a break. I'll sit with MP. Go take a shower, comb your hair, and brush your teeth."

She laughed. "I'm not that bad."

"No, but you'll feel better. Plus, MP would expect me to take you to task for not taking care of yourself."

"Everyone's been very kind here."

"Good, they should be. You're easy to be kind to. Now go." He pecked her cheek.

Reluctantly she went.

****

Nathan walked to the bed and looked at MP. A wave of emotions swamped him: thanks, grief, relief, fear.

"I sent your wife to take care of herself. Figured you'd want me to look after her while you're recovering."

MP gave the barest nod. While not Nate's natural inclination, he stepped to the bed to take his stepfather's hand. "Thanks for knocking me out of the way. I'm sorry you were hit." He received a weak squeeze in return. "Rest. Mom will be back shortly, I'm certain."

****

Lenore was startled awake by alarms going off and people running into the room.

"Get him to OR stat," the surgeon on call ordered as he ran beside Michael Patrick's high-tech bed.

She didn't even have time to gasp out a question but knew whatever was going on was sudden and life-threatening.

Staff was doing what they needed to do to save her husband. Lenore willed herself to stay calm and out of their way. Her hands shook uncontrollably, this time out of sheer terror at the thought of losing him so soon after she'd found him, after they'd found each other.

Lenore took a deep breath and sipped some orange juice. Noting the OJ still had ice in it, she couldn't have been dozing all that long. Whatever threatened MP had developed very quickly.

She called Nate to let him know that MP had been rushed back to surgery. Despite her telling him to stay home, he was coming.

"Mrs. Finnegan," an ICU nurse said softly.

Lenore looked up, waiting for news.

"Your husband's bleeding internally. His blood pressure dropped drastically. The surgeon is trying to locate the bleed and stop it."

She nodded numbly, knowing the nurse would only evade or vaguely answer questions. Instead she said, "Please let me know when you hear something. I'll be in the ICU lounge." She couldn't bear MP's empty room.

"He's strong and healthy, Mrs. Finnegan. Those are both on his side."

"Yes," Lenore said turning as she heard feet approaching, hoping it was Nate. But it was Byron Maxwell. He'd called the hospital several times to check on MP's condition. She never dreamed he'd show up here with all the press around.

"How is he?" Maxwell asked, attempting to embrace her.

Stepping out of his reach, she replied, "In surgery."

"Why?"

"I don't wish to discuss my husband's condition with you, Senator. Please leave us alone. There is no reason for you to have any contact with us."

"I was concerned. Finnegan saved our son's life."

"My son. And I'm more grateful than you'll ever know. But now he's fighting for his own life."

He didn't say anything but tried to embrace her again.

"Please don't touch me," Lenore started.

"Leave her alone," Nate snarled, coming through the door.

"I, I was trying to help," Maxwell stammered.

"Then go donate blood, or go pray in the chapel for his recovery. But leave my mother alone."

Maxwell looked at his son for a long moment. "We should get to know each other," he said.

"I know all I want to know about you, Senator, and if I wasn't good enough to know for the last twenty-one years, I'm not good enough to know now." He saw that his mother was pale and needed to sit down. "Please go," he said softly to Maxwell, "if not for my sake, then for my mother's. She's got enough to deal with without you being here."

"Lenore," Maxwell said, ignoring Nate, "if you leave here, be careful; there are press everywhere. The murder/suicide note was leaked." Maxwell gave her a copy of several articles he'd printed from the Internet. "Your names are out there now."

"Damn it to hell," Nate spat. "Thank goodness I wore sunglasses and a stocking cap to sneak in."

Lenore listed.

"Sit down before you fall down." Nate guided her to a couch.

"Please go, Senator. Have the press film you giving blood. I'm sure Morris would agree it'd be a great PR stunt. Senator Byron Maxwell gives blood in honor of the man who saved his bastard's life—details at six and eleven."

"Lenore . . ." Maxwell said.

"Nate's right. Please go. There's nothing you can do here.

I'll have my attorney release a statement. I won't comment to the press myself. I'm going to do my level best not to have any contact with them."

"I'm sorry this happened."

Feeling wary of the man's presence, she said, "I'm sure you are, but I want to be left alone with my son for a few minutes." And to say several prayers for my husband's recovery, she thought.

"Perhaps I'll go donate blood," the senator finally said.

"Good idea," Nate said, turning himself and his mother away from the man.

"How is he?" Nate finally asked when Maxwell departed.

"Not good." She explained what little she knew.

"He'll get through this."

She took a big gulping breath.

Nate held her as she cried.

"Thank you," she managed when Nate gave her a white handkerchief.

"Noticed MP always had one ready, so I figured I'd get with the program."

She gave him a watery smile.

Then Nate continued, "I saw the news before I came over. I didn't want to get into it with Maxwell here, so I pretended not to know, but I called Walker and asked him to release the most bare-bones statement. I hope that was okay. I hadn't planned on talking to you about this until Michael Patrick was out of the woods, but my sperm donor took that option away."

"It's okay. Thanks for getting in touch with Connor. I told him you might be the one to call him, depending on what was happening with MP."

They settled in for the long wait.

Then, like déjà vu the surgeon came to see her three hours later.

"We stopped the bleeding. It was in his stomach. He's stable at the moment, but the same rules apply, forty-eight hours. You need to leave here and get some rest, Mrs. Finnegan. Someone will call you if anything develops."

"I've been resting. Doing nothing but –"

"You need to go and sleep in a real bed and eat real food," the surgeon cut her off. "Take her to get some rest," the doctor said looking at Nate.

"I need to see him," Lenore said.

"He'll be back in his room shortly."

"Thank you, doctor."

When the man left, Nate said, "You're going back to the apartment to sleep after you see him, Mom."

She started to speak.

"No arguments. I'll take you there, then come back to the hospital. Then I'll come and get you in the morning. I promise I'll call if there's an emergency, but you're going to sleep in a real bed and eat real food as the doctor said."

CHAPTER FORTY-NINE

And sleep she did, for almost twelve hours. Lenore panicked when she rolled over and saw that it was after eight o'clock in the morning. Then she calmed herself. No news was good news. Nothing had happened while she slumbered. Nate would have called.

Lenore looked around the bedroom for the first time. It was done in earth tones like the rest of the apartment and was gender-neutral but expensively appointed with heavy oak furniture. The bed had been a cozy nest of down bedding in off-white and provided a welcome change from the hospital chair bed.

After showering and dressing, she entered the kitchen to find Nate waiting.

"MP's fine," he said immediately.

"Thank God."

"Yes, and the surgeons who put him back together. Eat breakfast, and I'll take you back. Hospital is swarming with press."

"Ugh. Did Connor make the statement?"

"Yes, it's on all the news outlets. You can bring it up on the Internet. No pictures of us yet, but I'd guess it's only a matter of time. Your cover as LaSandra Lacy will probably be blown too. There have also been at least ten additional women who have come forward saying that they, too, had an affair with Maxwell while they were interns."

Lenore gave a nervous laugh and booted up the computer on the countertop. She didn't have to search to find it. It was right there on CNN's home page.

Headline read: SILENCE BROKEN in big bold capital letters.

Lenore hit *play*, and Connor Walker appeared on the screen. He looked professionally competent and attractive on screen. Funny she'd never given any thought to the way he looked before.

He went through the basics of who he was and whom he represented, then gave a prepared statement.

"Senator Byron Maxwell and Lenore Held had a personal relationship when she was his intern approximately twenty-two years ago . . ." He gave only the facts and concluded, "All parties have asked for privacy. No questions will be taken and no further comments will be made." Walker left the stage as questions were fired at him.

Lenore sighed, "I think he did a nice job. The facts and nothing but the facts."

"Yes. He was going to come and see you, but I told him no," Nate said. "Figured someone might follow him to the apartment or hospital. Press knows someone was taken by ambulance to the hospital from Maxwell's house. They don't know who for certain. Speculation is you, me, an unknown male." Nate shrugged.

"Assuming all the main players close ranks and keep quiet, they can conjecture all they want, as long as they leave us alone. At some point, they will move on to another story."

"Agreed. But there's always Corrine and Ms. Hyde."

"Corrine is a wild card, but I don't think Kelly will say anything."

"She's called several times trying to confirm it's not me in ICU. I've not called her back. Let her think what she wants."

"Your call, sweetheart," Lenore said softly as she ate toast and drank decaf tea.

"I'm kind of like Nik and her ambivalence about Hubble. It doesn't matter how I feel; if I can't trust Kelly, what else is there? You don't agree?"

"Not getting involved with your love life or Nikko's. I will say that trust is one important component of any long-term relationship."

"Along with mutual respect, love, and sexual compatibility," Nate added.

"Yes," she replied and looked at him sideways. "You read my books." It was a statement, not a question.

"Guilty as charged. It was the easiest way to understand a smart chick's mind."

Lenore threw back her head and laughed. "I'm flattered. But even brainy women make poor choices in men. IQ numbers have nothing to do with emotions of the heart."

"You're a case in point. Look at my father."

"Yes." She sobered, immediately in the present again.

"Sorry," her son said. He'd meant the comment as a tease, not a jab.

She shook her head. "We need to get moving."

"Make sure you wear your sunglasses and the cape with the hood," he instructed.

"All right."

"MP will heal. We'll all get through this. Maybe I should have disregarded Jack's request to meet me, but –"

"Nathan, stop." Lenore put her hand on top of his. "You did the right thing. Don't blame yourself. No one had any idea Jack was a murder-suicide candidate."

"Like the saying goes, no good deed goes unpunished."

"You're too young to be that cynical, honey."

"I'm not. But seeing MP in that hospital bed fighting for his life makes me angry."

"Me, too. Let's go. I'm eager to see him. We've spent almost every day together since we started working on the book, even before we were involved."

"Best friends and lovers."

"Yes."

CHAPTER FIFTY

Lenore entered the hospital room and found MP resting, his color better than the day before. All machines seemed to be doing what they needed to do. But as it had yesterday, she knew everything could change in a split second.

She kissed his forehead and took his hand, gratified to feel its warmth in hers.

"I love you," she said softly in his ear, and he smiled. Not his full dimpled one but a smile nonetheless.

"I've kept up your diary to the baby," she continued. "You have such a tender heart, Michael Patrick, and I expect to share many wonderful years and events with you."

He stroked a thumb over her fingers, seeming much stronger and more alert today. She said a silent prayer of thanks.

"I'm going to sit and work on the laptop. You sleep."

He squeezed her hand once before he let it go and drifted off.

Getting comfortable in the chair bed, Lenore brought up their manuscript. The ending still wasn't quite right, and she figured she'd work on it some more. MP might feel left out, but they had time to revamp it together once he was better. They were well ahead of deadline, and based on present circumstances, that was a good thing.

After several hours of edits and re-edits, she thought she might have it.

Cass was eager to get back to Amanda. Because she refused a CT scan, the doctors insisted she stay in the hospital overnight for observation.

When he entered her room, Cass saw she was asleep with the bed slightly raised. She looked tiny and helpless with the large bandage covering most of her head. The ER doctor told him it had taken thirty stitches to close the head wound. Her eyes and face were more black and blue than her normal creamy complexion.

Amanda's eyes fluttered as he neared the bed. They were slits really. She reached out her hand to him.

Pleased, Cass took it and sat next to the bed.

"Hey," she croaked, doing her best to smile.

"Hey yourself. How are you feeling?"

"Like a beam hit me in the head," she teased wryly, her voice hoarse.

Cass held a glass of water with a straw for her to sip.

"Thanks. That's better." She cleared her throat and ran a hand down the side of his face and studied him intently. "I'll heal, Cass. That hard head I've been accused of having came in handy. More important, the baby, our baby, is fine." She placed his hand on her stomach.

"Amanda, you were almost killed. You warned me about Bart and I didn't listen."

"No one knew he was trying to murder me. Plus, you tried to keep me off the set, and I refused to stay away. You didn't even know I was there until after the collapse. Then you took care of me, us." She smiled and put her hand on top of his. "This is not your fault."

"I should have listened . . ."

"I should have too. If you insist on playing this blame game, then it's a fifty-fifty thing. Let go of the guilt, Cass, please." Her blue eyes—what he could see of them—were watery. "Please," she said again. "I love you."

Cass looked at her, really looked at her, and a slow grin crossed his face. "You love me?"

"Is that so hard to believe?"

"Yes, no." He ran a hand through his hair, trying to regain his bearing. He got up and sat on the edge of the bed facing her and took both of her hands in his. "I love you, too, sweetheart. I want a life with you and our child. I love you, Amanda. Marry me."

"I'll marry you."

Tears of joy in his eyes, he gently leaned in to kiss her, sealing the bargain.

"Lenore," MP said, his voice no more than a whisper.

Quickly, she set the computer aside and went to him. "What is it? Do you need something? Should I get someone?"

"No. You," he managed.

"Shh," she put a finger to his lips. "You have me; rest." Lenore gently kissed his lips. She felt unexpected tears welling. Closing her eyes tightly to keep them away, she ran a hand down his face, feeling several days of stubble rough under her fingertips.

"I did some work on the ending of our book."

"Read it, please."

She got the laptop and did as he requested. When she finished what she'd completed so far, he said, "Brilliant. Your Amanda assumed blame when neither one was at fault. It made him see sense —"

She cut him off, not wanting to tire him. "We can polish it when you're better. Rest now."

"*Mo chuisle*, I'm not going anywhere. Read to me."

"From our manuscript?"

"Yes, from the beginning."

"For a little while."

As she began to read, the short history of their time together spilled forth as well. So much of them was there in the book. The story was rich, the characters flawed but redeemable. Like her and MP. Decisions, not always the best, dealt with head-on.

Love had grown from their work together, from their mutual respect for one another's talents and differences, all the pieces coming together to make them a family, not only her, MP, and the new life that grew inside of her but Nate, too. Finally, she stopped reading. MP needed to rest, and she needed juice and crackers.

She heard him shift. "I'm not leaving. I needed a snack."

"You've been taking care of yourself?"

"I promise, I am. Nate made sure of it. I slept twelve hours last night."

"Thank you."

"You're welcome. Now you rest. I miss falling asleep and waking up with you. I want you well and back in my bed."

A dreamy smile crossed his face as he fell back asleep.

CHAPTER FIFTY-ONE

Days passed, and MP got stronger. From the ICU, he went to a step-down unit and was hoping to be discharged soon.

The press was brutal, painting Lenore as a shameless, home-wrecking slut and Byron Maxwell as a serial womanizer. The latter was true. Most likely the press hoped Lenore would speak on her own behalf if they persisted long enough and made the stories ugly enough. The core group, however, stuck to its promise of no comment.

Funny thing was, it didn't hurt their books sales, which were up a whopping twelve percent combined. Scandal sells, as Nikko always maintained.

Lenore's cell vibrated. It was Nathan.

"Mom, turn on the TV in MP's room. Kelly Hyde gave a statement, and it should be playing again soon."

Her heart plummeted. She wasn't sure what to say. "Nate, I'm –"

"It's okay. I think the statement might turn the tables on Corrine. I don't agree with what Kelly did, but it's not damaging to you or Maxwell."

Lenore turned on the news and explained Nate's call to Michael Patrick.

"Should be interesting," he offered, raising an eyebrow, then motioning for her to join him on the bed.

Kelly's statement had already begun, but it didn't appear they missed much.

"I had promised not to say anything about this matter, but I find it difficult to remain silent as two people are vilified in the press for something they did twenty-two years ago. I know all the players in this saga and must say that Ms. Held was younger than I am now when she made the decision to have and raise her child on her own.

"I know the child she raised grew up to be a warm, compassionate man, who possesses a keen intellect and wonderful sense of humor. She did not set out to destroy the senator's marriage but was rather led to believe the marriage was already over. I will say nothing further on that matter, except that things aren't always, as they appear to be.

"As for Senator Maxwell, I have no personal knowledge of his behavior with women outside the bonds of marriage. I can only say he that he has been kind and generous to me.

"Regardless of how one views the behavior of his parents, Senator Maxwell's son is an innocent bystander of events and should be left out of the sordid speculation of the press. The circumstances of his conception were beyond his control.

"I have no further comment. I, like the other players here, will be silent from this point forward."

Kelly walked off the stage, head held high and shoulders back.

MP ran a hand through Lenore's hair. "Do you think Maxwell put her up to that?"

"No, I think she's desperately in love with Nathan. But I'm concerned she put herself out there."

"Let it go, *a chuisle*. You can't do anything about it."

"You're right. But I can't believe that an event that happened so many years ago is still causing ripples."

"Ripples? Since when are you one for understatement?"

They both laughed.

"I can't wait to get out of here," MP grumbled, changing the subject. "I want to be home."

"Soon. Everyone is amazed at how quickly you're progressing. You're a medical miracle."

"Love is a terrific healer." He touched her face.

"Oh, MP, when I thought I'd lost you −"

"Hush. You didn't. I'm not going anywhere for a long while."

"Good. You promised to help me raise this baby."

"I always keep my promises."

He kissed her lightly and pulled her back against his chest.

"Isn't that against hospital regulations?" an amused voice asked.

Both MP and Lenore started.

"Nik, oh my goodness look at you," Lenore said, getting off the bed to embrace her friend.

"Yes, look at me," Nik laughed. "I'm getting round."

"You look great," MP said from the bed.

"And you look like shit. This is better? How bad did you look before?"

Lenore looked at her and made a back off face.

"Sorry, I've been hanging with Nolan too much," Nik said.

"Not to worry. It's just that for a few days, it was truly dire," Lenore said softly.

Nik hugged her friend. "Must have been hell."

"Yes. Did Hubble let you come alone?" Lenore asked quickly, not wanting to relive those first days again.

"No. He's parking, dropped me right at the door. I wanted to come sooner, but Nate didn't want me to."

"He's been very protective, and he was right. Things were crazy for a while."

Nik nodded. "What can I do?"

"Nothing. Make sure the new book gets marketed heavily."

"The media have taken care of that. One thing you might want to think about, since the pictures of you, MP, and Nate are out, is using your wedding pictures. If not on the book jacket, then on your websites and/or Facebook pages."

Lenore and MP exchanged a glance. "We'll think about it," Michael Patrick said.

"Do. Now that all your secrets are out, you may as well capitalize on them. Pre-orders have put the new book on the best-seller list before it even hits the presses," their agent persisted.

"We'll think about it, Nik," MP said again.

This time Lenore flashed her agent a *please don't agitate* glance, and Nik moved on.

"When do you get out?" Nik asked.

"Not a much better topic, Nikko, but we hope soon," Lenore answered.

"I'm getting antsy here," MP added.

"Sit," Lenore said and motioned her friend to an extra chair.

She did.

"How are you feeling? You look great," Lenore said.

"I'm wonderful and feel terrific actually —"

"Doctor says she's perfect. Baby is right on target for an October 31st debut." Nolan Hubble beamed as he walked into the room and sat on the arm of Nik's chair.

Whatever Nolan Hubble was or wasn't, he was definitely excited about the baby he and Nikko had created.

"That's wonderful," Lenore offered, settling back on MP's bed.

The two couples talked about babies and watched Kelly Hyde's statement on the news again.

About a half-hour into the visit, a nurse came to check on Michael Patrick.

Lenore had never seen her before. She began to get up from her husband's bed but stopped, taking a good, long look at her.

The woman's gray, strawberry blonde hair was drawn into a severe ponytail, giving her eyes a pulled expression, but Lenore knew the face. "Hello, Corrine, what can we do for you?"

Nik gasped.

All eyes were on Corrine and the little .22 handgun she was now holding.

"What can you do for me? Haven't you done enough?"

No one spoke. Lenore noticed Nolan maneuver in front of Nikko, who was standing now.

"I'm sorry, Corrine," Lenore said simply and she was, always had been. She suspected that Maxwell had played both women. But he was married when Lenore had sex with him, a willing consort in adultery.

"Sorry? No, I'm the one who's sorry. Sorry I didn't do something about that bastard—your bastard and you—long ago. Kelly even fell under your spell."

"I think it's time you leave, Mrs. Maxwell," MP said.

Lenore had angled herself closer to MP. He was still healing inside and out, and she didn't want him to tear knitting wounds open. If he felt he needed to protect her from Corrine, she knew he'd put himself at risk.

"He loved you. Did you know that?" Corrine asked Lenore.

"I don't think he loved anyone except himself," Lenore said, thinking it was best to side with Corrine on what a lowlife Maxwell was.

Unbeknownst to anyone, MP had pressed the call button when Lenore moved in front of him.

Corrine laughed. "That's a true statement except for you. He loved you. Morris did, too. Did you fuck him as well?"

Lenore felt MP stiffen behind her.

"No. I did not."

A nurse they knew bustled in. "Mr. Finnegan —" she started, then saw Corrine and stopped. "Who are you? You don't work here." The nurse, wasting no time, went directly to the phone on the wall to call security.

"No, I don't think so," Corrine started, then everything happened all at once.

Corrine aimed the gun at the nurse and pulled the trigger. The shot went wide and hit the wall. The nurse screamed and fell to the floor, taking cover, the phone left dangling by its cord.

Then Corrine swung back to Lenore, and as she did Nolan Hubble tackled her to the ground, and Michael Patrick pulled Lenore across his body, out of the bullet's trajectory. Corrine's shot missed its mark as her son's had. This time, no one was wounded.

Seconds later, hospital security and the D.C. cops swarmed the room.

"Are you all right?" MP asked Lenore with concern.

"I'm fine, thanks to you and Nolan." She was flushed and breathing hard.

"You sure?" He placed a protective hand on her abdomen.

"I'm sure." She managed a smile and laced her hand through his. "Are you okay? You didn't pull anything loose?"

"Not a thing, love. Nik, you okay," MP asked as Nolan was still pinning Corrine to the floor.

"Yes, I'm good. Nolan –"

"I'm fine, Nik."

"You should check her for more weapons," Lenore said when the police moved in to take her away. "There's an entire arsenal at her house."

The arresting officer did and found another handgun and a small switchblade in her other pocket.

"My God," Nik exclaimed. "How many people did she plan to kill?"

Lenore said nothing, but her private thought was as many as she could. Somewhere along the way, Corrine Kennedy Maxwell had had a break with sanity.

"He raped me, you know. That's how Jack was conceived. He raped me. I bet he didn't rape you, did he? DID HE? ANSWER ME! YOU OWE ME THAT MUCH!"

Too horrified to speak, Lenore shook her head, tears stinging her eyes.

The cops dragged a cuffed Corrine through the door toward the elevator and started reading her Miranda rights to her.

"I want a lawyer," Corrine said in almost a whisper. The elevator doors opened and, mercifully, she was gone.

The police were all over the tiny room, and MP needed to be moved because it was now a crime scene.

Lenore went to Nolan Hubble and embraced him. "Thank you for saving my life, maybe all our lives. That was a brave, selfless thing for you to do. Someday I'll tell your children what a hero their daddy is and how proud they should be to call you their father."

He looked at her, stunned for a moment, then said with a grin, "Happy to be of service, fair maiden," and gave her a courtly bow.

"Do you think what she said was true?" Nikko asked.

"That she was raped?" Lenore asked.

"Yes."

"If she wasn't, she certainly believes she was. Her rage was real. I don't think you can fake that."

"It's sad," Nik said softly. "If it wasn't for the way she went after you, Lenore, I might almost feel bad for her."

Lenore nodded her head in agreement. "Whatever is going on with her psyche, it's been going on for a long time. She needed help and never got it."

"She'll have nothing but time where she's going. Maybe she'll be helped in prison," Nolan said, draping a protective arm around Nik.

Later, when she and MP were alone, Lenore said, "You're my hero, too. You pulled me out of the way and had the presence of mind to hit the call button."

"Of course I did *mo chuisle*. Did you think I was just a pretty face?"

She laughed at his mock indignation. "No, it's one of the many things I love about you."

"Oh, do tell me about the others."

****

Word of his wife's dramatic arrest came to Senator Byron Maxwell at his Capitol Hill office.

Once he was certain that no one had been injured or killed Maxwell said, "I always knew she was certifiable."

"Indeed," Morris agreed darkly. "In front of a number of witnesses, she accused you of rape, and it has already leaked to the press. I don't care how crazy she is, this is going to cause a shit storm that will make your affair with Lenore Held look like drizzle on a summer day."

"I didn't rape her."

"Did you take her against her will?"

"I was drunk, she was my wife, is my wife, I took her."

"Forcibly?"

"God damn it, I don't know." He remembered the horror-struck look on Corrine's face, in her eyes, the tears on her cheeks.

Morris studied him and shook his head. "Any other women you took by force?"

"No, damn it, no. And I've paid for that night for the last twenty-two years. I was going to leave Corrine, marry Lenore. My career, my father, the money be damned. But then Corrine turned up pregnant and guilt kept me from leaving her."

Morris said nothing.

"Well?" Maxwell demanded.

"Well, what? I have nothing to offer. You created your own hell and will continue to live it. It's too bad you took so many other people with you, especially Corrine and Jack. It's like Kelly said about Nathan; he had no control over his conception—neither did Jack. Both you and your wife wronged the young man. I never realized how badly until now."

"I know," the senator said softly. "I know and I can never say I'm sorry."

"But you can to Nathan Held. I suggest you do that. I also want you to know I will be retiring from public service effective July Fourth, a patriotic day, and that gives you almost three months to replace me."

"You can't be serious." Maxwell was obviously taken aback.

"I am. It's about time I started to enjoy the wealth I've acquired over the years. Travel, sleep when I want, eat when I want, maybe find a lady for companionship."

"Aren't you a little old to have a midlife crisis?" Maxwell inquired.

"You've been in crisis most of your life, Byron. I think it's time to fade into the sunset. It's been a good ride for the most part, but now it's time to cruise."

Maxwell laughed morosely. "You're leaving a sinking ship. Should I resign and be done with it?"

"That's something I can't answer for you, Byron."

****

The following day, Senator Byron Maxwell resigned from public life. His decision was made when he saw his broken wife screaming at her arraignment about how he had raped her. He blamed the Democratic judge for allowing cameras into the courtroom. It was always someone's fault, wasn't it?

But she could rage all she wanted. Even if people believed she was raped, the ten-year statute of limitations was long past. She and the media could make all the accusations they wanted, but he could never be prosecuted. Senator Byron Maxwell would continue to proclaim his innocence.

EPILOGUE

Lenore's dining room table was set for Thanksgiving dinner. She'd prepared a feast, because there was much to be thankful for. Her family and friends were gathering together to celebrate their blessings.

Once the fervor over Corrine Kennedy Maxwell's arrest and Senator Maxwell's resignation had died down, Lenore and Nathan had faded into the woodwork, a significant footnote but a footnote nonetheless, and she was pleased.

Corrine had been charged with a number of offenses; the most significant were two counts of attempted murder. She had plea-bargained and received fifteen years in jail. Lenore figured she'd do ten if she got time off for good behavior. While in the penal institution, she would be receiving psychological counseling at the request of her own attorneys. They claimed she suffered from battered-wife syndrome. Lenore had no idea what she suffered from but was glad she would be getting help.

Byron Maxwell, on the other hand, was free to do as he pleased. Unbeknownst to Maxwell, Jack had left all of his money to him, a tidy nest egg to live off of even after he divorced Corrine. He was said to be writing a book and had received a two-million-dollar advance. Both she and Nathan had been approached with book deals and had turned them down.

Nate was at Yale Law, embracing his studies with zeal. He thought he might want to go to work for the Justice Department after graduation. He'd ignored his father's attempts to have a relationship and had bonded well with his stepfather. Lenore was happy they'd become close. Nate was still conflicted about his feelings for Kelly Hyde, and she refused to wade into the fray on that issue.

Nikko and Nolan were to be married on New Year's Eve. Their son, Dillon James Hubble, had indeed been born on Halloween, much to Nikko's delight. Their relationship had taken a sharp turn for the better after Nolan had subdued Corrine Maxwell. He'd even stopped the crazy, inappropriate social comments, for which both she and MP were grateful. The relationship was still volatile, but it seemed to work for them.

Laid Bare had sold over a million copies and was going to be printed in London at the start of the New Year. They had received a contract to coauthor two additional books with the option for more. Plus, both were still writing their own works. Their wedding picture remained private, displayed on the fireplace mantel in Lenore's office.

Michael Patrick's injuries had healed well, and except for the nasty scar he still bore on his left side, Lenore would never have known that she'd almost lost him.

Lenore was placing a cornucopia centerpiece on the table when her musings of things to be thankful for were interrupted by the thing she was most thankful for.

"There she is, little one. There's your mum," Michael Patrick soothed. "I think she misses you. She's been fed, burped, and changed, and she's still fussy."

Lenore smiled and reached for their daughter. Mia Rose had been born two weeks early but was healthy and usually a very contented baby. The child quieted as soon as she was nestled against her mother.

"I thought she was going to be a daddy's girl."

"Wait until she's old enough to want something. See how quickly she attaches herself to you then.

MP laughed and pulled both his girls gently into his arms. "Thank you for a beautiful daughter."

"Thank you. Half of her is you, too."

"But I had all the fun, and you had all the work."

Lenore laughed now, eyes bright.

"Are you sure you're not overdoing it? You had this wee lass fourteen days ago."

"I'm fine. Don't I look fine?"

"You look fabulous. No one would suspect you just had a child."

"Thank you." She kissed him lightly. "She's asleep; let me put her down. She'll be out for a while."

MP followed Lenore into the nursery, and once Mia was down, both parents gazed lovingly at the little miracle that was their daughter.

"Happy Thanksgiving, *mo chuisle*."

"This is the best Thanksgiving ever."

He kissed her in agreement.

ACKNOWLEDGMENTS

As always, I'd like to thank my closest friends, Gregg, Jane and Karyn, for reading several versions of this work and being my biggest supporters.

Thanks to Nina Alvarez, my first professional contact, in the publishing arena. Her enthusiasm for the story line, characters and dialog, encouraged me to keep refining the work.

My deep appreciation also goes to Marlene Adelstein, who critiqued several versions of the manuscript and always gave me her honest feedback as to what was working and what wasn't.

Finally, many hugs for my daughter Ashley Victoria, who challenged me to write a book when I was "encouraging" her to do her homework. Now finish your own book, challenge back at you. I love you, baby.

ABOUT THE AUTHOR

L.A. Long is an insurance industry executive by day. She lives in Bucks County, Pennsylvania with her family and three cats.

Made in the USA
Charleston, SC
04 January 2017